WINDS of Evil

BOOK ONE OF THE LAODICEA CHRONICLES

WINDS of EVIL

BOOK ONE OF THE LAODICEA CHRONICLES

SHARON K. GILBERT

WHITAKER
HOUSE

deepercalling

This novel is a work of fiction. References to real events, organizations, or places are used in a fictional context. Any resemblances to actual persons, living or dead, is entirely coincidental.

WINDS OF EVIL: Book One of the Laodicea Chronicles

All inquiries regarding this publication and Sharon K. Gilbert may be made to:
www.mytharc.com
e-mail: sharon@mytharc.com or derek@mytharc.com

ISBN-13: 978-0-88368-809-0
ISBN-10: 0-88368-809-3
Printed in the United States of America
© 2004, 2005 by Sharon K. Gilbert

WHITAKER
HOUSE

1030 Hunt Valley Circle
New Kensington, PA 15068
www.whitakerhouse.com

deepercalling
www.deepercalling.com

Library of Congress Cataloging-in-Publication Data

Gilbert, Sharon K., 1952–
Winds of evil / Sharon K. Gilbert.
    p.   cm.   — (The Laodicea chronicles ; bk. 1)
Includes bibliographical references and index.
ISBN-10: 0-88368-809-3 (trade pbk. : alk. paper)
ISBN-13: 978-0-88368-809-0 (trade pbk. : alk. paper)
1. Inheritance and succession—Fiction. 2. Human-alien encounters—Fiction.
3. Missing children—Fiction. 4. Women—Indiana—Fiction.
5. Aunts—Death—Fiction. 6. Supernatural—Fiction. 7. Indiana—Fiction. I.
Title. II. Series.
PS3607.I42325W56 2005
813'.6—dc22   2004027644

1 2 3 4 5 6 7 8 9 10 11 **W** 12 11 10 09 08 07 06 05

Dedication

To Derek and Nicole

For all those days when you scrounged for your own supper, washed your own clothes, and kept the house clean, all without one word of complaint, and all the while encouraging me to write.

For all of your many sacrifices and for your patient, unending love, I say thank you with all my heart.

And unto the angel of the church of the Laodiceans write; These things saith the Amen, the faithful and true witness, the beginning of the creation of God; I know thy works, that thou art neither cold nor hot: I would thou wert cold or hot. So then because thou art lukewarm, and neither cold nor hot, I will spue thee out of my mouth.
—Revelation 3:14–16 KJV

And, behold, there came a great wind from the wilderness, and smote the four corners of the house, and it fell upon the young men, and they are dead; and I only am escaped alone to tell thee.
—Job 1:19 KJV

Prologue

Donny Alcorn slammed on the brakes. "Stupid dog!" he shouted, reaching for the car door. "Wait here while I get it off the road."

Amy Horine leaned into the dashboard of Donny's refurbished 1978 Camaro, squinting through the gathering fog, trying to watch Donny. Her mother would be mad again. Not that it mattered much. Amy had gotten used to Maria Horine's temper tantrums of late. Sometimes, she wished her dad hadn't moved to Indianapolis, but then she would remember how he'd treated her and her mother. It was better to live with a mother who cared, even if she showed it by nagging and complaining.

Still, her mother shouldn't crab too much. After all, this was prom night, and Amy was with the captain of the football team. Not bad for the school brain. As class valedictorian, Amy got the grades but rarely the boys. Donny Alcorn had been a friend since she was little, and she just knew they were meant to be together. He'd shown her the sensitive side beneath his rough football-player exterior. Consequently, she'd do just about anything for the handsome quarterback.

9

Despite weeks of anticipation, the prom had been dull and boring. The scheduled band had failed to show, so one of the parents with experience at the local radio station had filled in at the last minute, spinning a mish-mash of "eighties and nineties and today," punctuated with nonsensical banter from a bygone era.

Most of the popular seniors had left before eleven, making their way to one of several private parties scattered about town. Amy and Donny had been invited to Little Tubby's Place to party with a group of college kids she'd gotten to know during her visits there the previous fall. Preferring a quieter evening, she and Donny had chosen to celebrate their upcoming graduation parked on a moonlit road just north of the old pork factory.

Donny cursed.

"Donny!" she shouted out the window. "No swearing! You promised!"

"Sorry, honey," came his embarrassed voice, echoing eerily in the fog.

Amy glanced at the delicate diamond watch her mother had let her borrow for the night. Half past twelve. She'd promised her mother she'd be home by one. Amy could see Donny struggling with what appeared to be an animal. The dark form didn't move.

"Is it hurt, Donny? Maybe I should call the animal hospital. We could take it in."

Alcorn's lips drew into a thin line. Amy loved animals, and he knew she'd flip when she saw this pitiful mess of blood and fur. "No use callin' the vet," he said at last. "It ain't no dog anyway. Looks like...I don't know what it looks like. You're gonna have to help me move it, Amy."

"Are you sure, Donny? In my prom dress?" she asked, adjusting the bodice of the sapphire blue strapless gown she'd saved three months to buy. "I can call someone if you need help. I've got my cell phone."

Donny closed his eyes tightly and counted to ten. Amy could be a real priss when she wanted. Other times, she could handle a basketball better than Reggie Miller. She *would* choose now to get all girly. Then again, he liked the girly parts of her best.

Coming up to the open window, Donny kissed her small, gloved hand in apology. "Sorry, hon. I wasn't thinkin'. Although, I'm not exactly dressed for this either," he added, looking down at his rented black tuxedo. "You might want to see this thing, though. You know, since you like all that veterinary stuff. I think it's some kind of monkey."

Amy's blue eyes twinkled with curiosity. "No way! What would a monkey be doing around here?" She opened the passenger door to the Camaro and followed her date to the front of the car.

"See?" Donny asked, nervously fiddling with some change in his right trouser pocket. "You're the one who's gonna be a vet one day. Is it a monkey or what?"

Amy stared at the motionless pile of matted hair. A light rain had just begun to fall, and in the glow from the headlights, the drops glistened upon the dull, reddish fur. She'd never seen anything like this in any of her books. Amy's high school biology teacher had written the recommendation for her application to Eden College's Animal Science program. Mr. Turnbill had been impressed with Amy's natural gifts and intense study habits. In fact, he had helped her prepare the valedictorian speech she would be giving in just a few days. But no amount of study had prepared her for the strangely twisted creature that lay just inches from her blue three-inch heels.

"Donny, I don't know what the heck this could be. Come on, let's turn it over so we can see its face better."

The warm spring rain spattered their backs and necks as the pair knelt to turn the dead animal over. Amy had begun to wish they'd gone to Little Tubby's.

The body was heavy, and they strained to pull its shoulders toward them, both blinking raindrops away.

Suddenly, Amy screamed.

"Oh my God!" she cried wildly, dropping the thing's crushed head back into the asphalt. "It can't be! It...oh, God! This can't be happening!"

Donny, who wasn't close enough to see, stared at his girlfriend's ashen face. "What is it? You know what it is?"

Amy's hands were at her mouth, smudged pink lipstick mixing with the thing's blood on the palms of her mother's white lace gloves. "Donny, don't you see it? Don't you recognize it—I mean, him?"

Alcorn knelt closer, turning the misshapen head toward the light where he could see it better. Amy wasn't ordinarily excitable. In fact, her calm detachment had gained her the nickname "Dr. Freeze." So why should some poor animal cause her to react so violently?

Donny shifted on the balls of his feet, leaning into the thing, taking in the fullness of its strangely familiar features.

His heart nearly stopped.

"No way!" he cried, jumping to his feet. "It can't be! It can't be!"

Amy was crying uncontrollably now. All thoughts of her mother's anger, of the time, of Little Tubby's Place flew from her mind, displaced by the burning vision of this hideous mutation of a boy both she and Donny had known since they were kids. A boy who had been dead for eight months.

"It...it's Tim Kilgore, isn't it?" she whimpered, naming the thing.

Donny nodded. "We gotta call someone."

"And say what?" she snapped back, her voice shaking. "That the school's most popular student, who died last year, isn't in the cemetery? No, he's lying in a puddle of blood on County Line Road. The guy we planted a tree for last fall is some kind of undead freak?" By the time Amy finished, she was shrieking with near hysteria.

Before Donny could answer, a high-pitched howl echoed behind them.

"What was that?" he whispered nervously, his voice rising in pitch.

"What was what?" Amy asked, terrified, her eyes riveted on the strangely simian features of Tim Kilgore's face. "Donny, we need to call someone! We need to..."

The last words floated into the air, leaving only rain on an empty road. Yards away, Amy and Donny had both been slammed into a ditch by something very large and very dark.

"Donny!" cried a voice that Amy recognized as her own. But the sound died out as her small mouth filled with blood.

Amy's pretty high heels had dropped off, and she could feel the soft, red mud squishing between her toes. Above her head, she could just make out the outlines of two enormous shadows—shadows that moved.

"Help us!" she cried out, weakly raising one small hand. "Please!"

A gigantic, clawed hand lifted her chin, and Amy thought she heard a vile voice buzzing in her ears. *They're going to kill us*, she thought. *They're going to carry us away, kill us, and use our bodies like Tim's. Just like Tim's. And we'll look just like monkeys, too.*

13

Crying out triumphantly, the huge beings dragged two limp bodies toward a chain-link fence surrounding a nearby utility shed. Amy's eyes flickered open again, and she caught sight of a gigantic foot, scaly and black. Barely conscious, she thought of her poor mother, fretting as her daughter's curfew approached, and of the seven-page valedictory speech that lay waiting on her desk at home. *I'll never deliver that speech,* she thought as she was lifted high into the air.

Amy glanced at Donny, whose head had begun to ooze red from a deep gash just above his right ear. He was perfectly still and ghostly pale. Like death.

They were being moved, she realized, snatched up like carrion, taken far away from the road and toward a small white building on the far side of the field.

"Mama," she called out, tasting blood. "I'm sorry I didn't love you more."

CHAPTER One

Pump 6? That'll be $17.59 even," smiled a middle-aged woman, gold incisor twinkling in the fluorescent lights of the gas station's interior.

Katherine searched the depths of an aging brown leather handbag, retrieved a twenty, and handed it to the woman, noting the nametag. "Thanks, Rosie. Do you have a restroom?"

Rosie returned the change, leaned into the register's open drawer to close it, then shoved a pencil into a lacquered thatch of unnaturally red hair. "Oh, yeah. In back, behind the video machines. It's just been redone, brand new."

Katherine found the door marked *Private* and passed through a short hallway. At the end was a battered but clean green door sporting the international symbol for women. After knocking, she entered and closed the door behind her. The sliding lock shone brightly, new and secure, and Katherine hastily shut out the world. "You can do this," she whispered to herself, closing her road-weary eyes. This trip had been far more stressful than even Katy had imagined. *Katy,*

15

she thought. *That's what Aunt Celeste always called me—her little Katydid.*

Glancing at her pale reflection in the cheap mirror, Katherine beheld a woman of thirty-nine years and counting. Sable brown eyes now looked dull and bloodshot from the strain of the unplanned six-hour drive. Katherine had been living near St. Louis for the past ten years, and this unexpected trip back to Indiana might have been a lovely drive were it not for the reason.

You should have been there for Aunt Cissy, Katy thought as she combed her short auburn hair into place. *God knows, she practically raised you, and you weren't even there to kiss her good-bye. You could have visited her, could have made her last days less lonely, but your career came first. Worst of all, Katherine, you didn't even bother to write or call most months.*

Opening her purse, Katherine fumbled through a knot of pink tissues and found an amber-colored plastic bottle. *Take one tablet every six hours,* the label stated in clean black type. Dr. Evans insisted she needed them, but Katherine couldn't bear the thought of being dependent on anyone or anything other than herself. She had depended on David. She had allowed herself to become vulnerable.

"Never again," she said aloud, her teeth clenched.

Shaking off the bad memory, Katherine returned the pills to her purse and snapped the closure. *Never again—not even if it means going cold turkey.*

Ready to face the drive into town, Katherine ignored the nagging thought that keeping the pills might be dangerous, too much of a temptation. She would not allow anyone or anything to control her. She would remain her own woman. Perhaps coming home to Eden was her chance to prove just how independent she really was.

Returning to the counter, Katherine grabbed a pack of breath mints and a cup of coffee for the road. Only a few more miles to go before facing that large empty house. Although she felt heavy with the lack of sleep, she knew she couldn't give in to the feeling. Years of traveling to promote her books had taught her to fight jet lag, and she could fight this. All she had to do was stay awake until bedtime. Then, she'd get back on track.

"That's $2.46," Rosie said as Katherine added a newspaper to her purchases. "Make that $3.96, hon. Pity about those two kids, huh?"

Katy nodded without knowing why she did. "Kids?"

"Page one, honey. Been there for more'n two weeks. Two high school kids disappeared over on County Line Road by that electrical shed. Car was runnin' and all. Not a sign of either of 'em, exceptin' for the girl's pretty blue shoes, all covered in dried mud. Prom night. Ain't it awful? It's just not safe anywhere anymore."

Katy tucked the paper beneath her left arm and pocketed the mints. Taking the coffee, she made a mental note to visit the newspaper for the complete story. Maybe she would find something here she could use in a book. Maybe she could actually write again.

"Thanks!" Rosie called as Katherine pushed past the front glass doors, heading toward her car. "Welcome to Eden, hon! You come back now!"

CHAPTER Two

The Gas n' Go had been perched on a hill just outside the Eden city limits. Katherine drove slowly, obeying the thirty-five miles per hour limit, passing the Eden Memorial Cemetery just outside of town and a small white church building adjacent to the graveyard. Next to the white clapboard structure stood a wooden sign, proudly proclaiming the name:

EDEN BIBLE CHURCH—ENOCH JONES, PASTOR.

Just beyond the church, a wooded knoll rose up from the valley below, and Katherine beheld Eden for the first time in over ten years. Below her, a town of 9,700 plus citizens and nearly 3,000 college students stretched along the Ohio River like a quaint, Norman Rockwell village. Antebellum houses mingled with more modern structures to form a perfect patchwork, intersected by clean, square lines that Katy knew to be perfectly maintained streets.

Eden had been named an All-American City in 1976 during the nation's bicentennial, and Katherine recalled standing in City Hall as a twelve-year-old, staring wide-eyed as President-Elect Jimmy Carter presented a plaque to Mayor Sturgill, proudly proclaiming Eden to be the rarest of flowers in the entire prairie. Never mind that Eden lay two states east of the prairies. Carter had been big news, and the town had boomed into a tourist bonanza.

Katherine's mother, the widow of the former mayor, had stood on the podium along with the Sturgills, representing the former administration, which had been a stark contrast to Sturgill's newer, more prosperous one. As mayor for six years, Katherine's father had led the effort to restore Eden to its former antebellum glory, while Mayor Sturgill had sought new industry and progress. Evelyn Adamson had clenched her daughter's slender hand for strength, and Katherine had given all she had in return.

Three months later, Evie Adamson died. Shortly after leaving a meeting at the college, she had been struck down by a passing car, later dying in the ambulance on the way to Eden General. Katherine, an only child, had been placed with her maiden aunt, who had just retired from twenty-seven years of teaching English to sixth graders.

Flooded with memories, Katherine wiped a tear from her cheek and pulled over. Ahead she could see the town's city limit sign, proudly proclaiming Eden's historic status. *Eden, Indiana—All are welcome to our All-American town! Edward Sturgill, Mayor.*

Edward Sturgill, thought Katy, her mind reaching back to high school. Eddie. A prom date from ages past. Son of Ted Sturgill, Eden's mayor for as long as Katy could recall, and one of the meanest men ever to take a breath. She wondered if Ed hadn't fallen far from that rotten old tree.

Returning her thoughts to the road, Katy drove past the sign and took a left onto Main Street. Aunt Celeste's house stood on one of Eden's finest corners, Broadway and Main, three blocks from the library her great-grandfather had donated and six blocks west of the town square.

The elegant Georgian graced a generous corner lot with all the charm of an aging princess. Three-and-a-half stories tall with its native brick exterior decoratively painted in a rich russet and trimmed in creamy white and navy, the patriotic house represented all that had once been good in Eden. Ivy-entwined maples and tall oaks anchored the landscape of the front gardens, and a brick pathway wound through gently aging flowerbeds filled with primroses and pansies. A prize-winning rose garden stood sentry in the backyard, waiting for an errant lover or a dreamy-eyed damsel to wander among the fragrant rows. Bordering the proud home stood the very fence that Katherine's great-grandfather had built with his own hands to protect the family's growing tribe of ten children.

Katy pulled into the brick drive that circled behind the house. The gate, usually closed to keep out unwanted foot traffic, was open, and Katherine pulled in beside a bright red Caddy with the vanity plate I-SELL4U and an Eden Realty sign in the window.

"Hello," Katherine called, shutting the driver's side door. "May I help you?"

A tall woman had just exited the rear of the house. Upon hearing Katherine's voice, the woman started, her heavily made-up face revealing surprise at being observed.

Katherine called again. "I'm Celeste Adamson's niece. She isn't here."

The woman's face became a mask of welcome. "You must be Katherine," she sang back, her mellow alto a practiced and polished sales tool. "I'm Rhonda Coleman." An outstretched hand with perfect nails in jungle red greeted Katy's with a firm shake.

"Your Aunt Cissy, rest her soul, asked our little firm to make your task a bit easier," the woman continued. Her bleach-blond hair didn't move much, and Katy thought she caught a whiff of jasmine. The agent's slim figure was perfectly accented in a trim suit of white linen, and her teeth gleamed like a uniform row of polished marble.

"Thank you," Katherine managed, looking past the woman and into the rose garden. "I wasn't aware that Aunt Celeste had contacted a realtor."

The woman followed Katy into the garden, dogging her steps with the clickety-clack of four-inch heels. "Oh, her wishes were quite clear. She spoke with Carlton Whitehead only a few days before she...passed. Carl promised to help you unload this old place. I mean, you won't want to spend too much time in a hamlet like this. You have a life in St. Louis, and we're here to help you with all the details."

"How did you know I live in St. Louis?"

Rhonda halted along with her prey. "Oh, I'm sure Cissy mentioned it to Carl. You're a writer, aren't you? Conspiracy theories or something like that?"

Katherine thought of her last conversation with George McMahon, her literary agent. How he'd pleaded with her to get back to writing, promising her the moon if she would only string a few words together. Moon or not, Katherine felt washed up as a writer. David had sapped her creative energies when he'd ripped open her heart. She'd love to spit on him most days, but David's new home in California kept him out of range. For now.

"I used to write," Katherine replied.

"Oh, my friend Linda Kemp loves your books. K. C. Adamson, right? Your pen name?"

Katy sat on a curved stone bench, nestled between a stand of bearded irises. "It's my name, and I write under it. It's not really a pen name."

Rhonda laughed, forced and nasal. "Silly me! It shows to go ya'! I was never good at English. Better at making friends, I suppose. Like I always tell Linda, when it comes to books, don't take me literally!" The laugh wheezed through her nose like air through a noisemaker on New Year's Eve.

Katy sighed, longing for a moment alone. "Clever," she returned with a brief smile. "So Aunt Cissy left you with a set of keys?"

"Yes, but maybe we should hang onto them until the place is sold. It's so much easier than a lockbox."

"There's no need for either," Katherine replied matter-of-factly. "I've no plans to sell. At least not yet."

"Don't wait too long, Miss Adamson. The housing market is due to drop soon, and there aren't that many buyers who could afford this place. I mean, it's just about the biggest home in Eden."

"The keys?" Katherine asked again, her sable eyes narrowing with suspicion. This woman was beginning to raise Katy's radar to maximum.

"Keys! Oh, yes. Silly me!" The laugh again. "Here you go now. There's a whole ring of them, so I'd be happy to take a tour of the house with you to familiarize you with..."

"No thanks," Katherine interrupted. "I grew up here. I know this house and all its secrets. I'll be able to work through the keys myself. Thank you for meeting me, Miss Coleman."

"Rhonda!"

"Rhonda," Katherine continued. "And please thank Mr. Whitehead for me as well. I promise to contact him if I choose to sell. Oh, can you tell me if Joshua Carpenter still works at the newspaper?"

Rhonda had already begun dialing a number on her cell phone, but looked up at Carpenter's name. "You know Josh?"

Was there a hint of jealousy there? Katherine wondered. "Since we were pups," was her short reply.

The real estate agent flipped her phone closed and pursed her lips into a pout. "Well, yes, he's still there. He's the publisher now, since his dad died last year. But I guess if you're so close, you'd know that already."

Katherine knew this woman's kind. She'd met them often on her many travels, and she found their games wearisome. "Oh, he probably mentioned it. I'm sorry to hear Sam died. He was one of the good ones."

Rhonda sniffed. "Yeah, he was. Too good for his own well-being."

"Hmm?" Katherine asked, unable to imagine anyone making such a thoughtless comment.

"Truly good," she answered, making a note in her PDA. "Gotta run. Now, you call me when you're ready for an open house. I'll take care of all the details. I'll even book a room for you at the Eden Inn. Here's my card."

"I'm not sure if I want to sell!" Katherine called to the woman's retreating back. Ignored, she breathed a heavy sigh at the woman's departure. The white suit swayed with the rhythm of the woman's gait, and the clickety-clack of her heels faded into memory beneath the roar of the Caddy's engine.

The card felt oddly warm in Katy's hand, and she glanced at it involuntarily.

RHONDA COLEMAN—
MAKING DEALS SO HOT,
THE DEVIL TAKES NOTES.
Eden Realty, 666 South Broadway

CHAPTER Three

J oshua Carpenter had spent his entire life in Eden. Since his father's death, he'd tried to run the Eden *Chronicle* with the same integrity, but he often felt at a loss to live up to his legacy. Over the past eight months, the paper had lost nearly seven hundred subscribers, and the merchants' ads were disappearing as fast as they could make the phone calls. Everyone seemed to be deserting the ship for *The Watcher,* Eden College's newer, hipper paper.

This Monday hadn't started out any better than any other in recent weeks. First came a phone call from Harry's Tasty Treat, canceling his daily coupon, followed by a leak in the pipes over the press. Fixing that had taken most of the morning, leaving Josh no time for lunch. His only remaining full-time reporter was chasing down leads on the missing high school kids, even going so far as to help with the search. This left Josh to cover the normal stories of birthdays, hospitalizations, and obits. Birth and death were always part of the news, and in between, perhaps, lay a life of quiet dignity and honor. But lives of quiet dignity seldom sold papers. Maybe he just wasn't cut out to be a newsman.

Deciding to rumble through the break room fridge for possible remnants of yesterday's sandwich, Josh checked his pocket for loose change. He'd need something to wash down the stale cheese on rye. A Big Red cream soda would do nicely.

"Looking for my phone number?" called a woman's voice from the other side of the news desk.

Josh squinted past the glare of overhead fluorescents and into the bright panes of the front windows. Silhouetted there stood a nicely rounded woman wearing trim slacks and a short-sleeved blouse with a cotton sweater tied around her shoulders. She looked to be about medium height with boyishly short hair that shone like copper in the backlight. Joshua recognized the voice, even after ten years.

"And why should I invite you to lunch? As I recall, you owe me, Katy Celeste."

The woman moved closer to the desk, the overhead lights reflecting her strong Irish features. "From what I heard about your dad, Joshua, I owe you a lot more than that. I'm really sorry for your loss. And I'm sorry for the town's loss. Samuel Carpenter kept this town on its collective toes, and he never compromised on a story."

"God help me, Katy, you're a sight for sore eyes!" Josh said, jumping over the desk and landing with a light thud. Throwing his long arms around Katherine's shoulders, he pulled her into his chest. "I'm sorry it took your Aunt Cissy's death to bring you home again."

"Thanks," she said, pulling back a bit after a moment to break the embrace. "So, you're running the *Chronicle* now. Have you elevated Eden's level of societal awareness? Won that first Pulitzer yet?"

Suddenly feeling awkward, Joshua lowered his arms and shuffled his size thirteen feet absentmindedly, hoping an impression would break the sudden tension. "Ah, gee, Miss," he answered. "It's not much. Just doin' my job."

"That's the worst Jimmy Stewart I've ever heard!" she laughed, enjoying the sense of relief that washed over her. She had so dreaded this encounter, and now it was like old times. How she had missed their banter! Joshua was always so comfortable to be around. Why had she let him go?

"Well, you always said when it came to acting, I'd make a great newspaperman. And here's your proof. I stink at both."

"Nonsense," she said. "Come on! Take me to lunch at Sandy's, and I'll tell you why you're the best newsman west of the Cumberland Gap!"

"How about the hotel? Linda Kemp runs Sandy's, and well, she's not one of my greatest fans right now."

"I thought Linda worked at the library."

"She left last year after Dad died. She tried her hand at reporting for a while before starting at Sandy's," he replied, giving her a look that pleaded for an end to the subject.

Katy found she couldn't resist the soft hazel eyes or the little boy look.

"OK. I'll let it go for now. But you owe me a story for the trouble."

Josh grabbed the keys and flipped the front door sign to read "Gone fishing for news." Turning out the lights and locking up, he switched to Katy's right, taking the protective side toward traffic.

"You always were a gentleman," she said as they approached the light at Main and Howard. "I'm glad some things never change."

"Yeah, it's a nice way of saying I'm stuck in the past. That's OK, Katy Celeste. Just for that, you buy."

Several miles from the corner of Main and Howard sat a man who was anything but stuck in the past. Richard Gibbons had worked for the Mount Hermon Institute since its opening six years before. As head of security, Gibbons conducted periodic surveillance checks using the elaborate computer systems that had been installed three years before by a New York outfit. Cameras and microphones, stationed at over a hundred different locations, allowed Gibbons and his team of two dozen to keep track of not only the current residents but also each member of the medical staff.

The head of the Institute, Dr. Apollo Bell, had personally hired Gibbons for the prestigious post from a pool of nearly fifty applicants. With the closing of the old pork factory, jobs had become scarce in Eden, and nearly every man with computer experience had clamored for Gibbon's position. Since the opening of the Institute, Eden had prospered as never before, and Dick Gibbons walked tall as a man of influence. Rather than hire old high school cronies, he'd chosen instead to hire from the college, which had forced him to cut ties with his old drinking buddies but elevated him into a far more elite circle of educated friends.

Rachel, Dick's former wife and mother of his two children, still lived in Eden, but her Second Street address kept her secluded from his new life with his new wife, Diana. Rachel may have been a good cook and mother, but she had been boring. Diana, with her knock-your-socks-off looks, made Dick feel like a real man, especially when he took her out on the town.

Other men envied Dick Gibbons for his wife and his job, and he figured he owed that to Dr. Bell. Consequently, Dick wouldn't hear a bad word against the Syrian-born doctor, and that extended to keeping his mouth shut about certain activities his surveillance screens showed him.

As he leaned back into the supple leather chair that came with his corner office, Gibbons knew he shouldn't be seeing what he was. Inside Area 15, the same shadows Dick had watched all too many times before moved back and forth within a room designed for genetic research. Dick knew the advertised purpose of the Institute was to conduct research into the prevention and treatment of diseases such as Alzheimer's. To that end, a steady stream of foreign doctors, patients from all geographies and social strata, and a host of college-age test subjects flowed through the halls, but the shadows didn't seem to fit in with any of these groups.

Now, as he watched the malevolent shapes working with two figures laid out on stainless steel tables, Gibbons knew turning a blind eye would mean a fat bonus in his paycheck. What he didn't see didn't hurt him, and what didn't hurt him didn't bother him. He had, however, learned to keep the volume turned off when watching Area 15. While Gibbons managed to forget most of what he saw, he still had nightmares about what he sometimes heard.

Gibbons clicked the remote to show Area 7, glad to see a knot of curious students lined up for pre-trial testing. Stupid preppies. Eden College was a private school with an out-of-sight tuition, and still these rich kids had to get richer. It'd serve 'em right if the shadows got hold of them.

Gibbons checked his Rolex, a Christmas gift from Dr. Bell last year. It was nearly two, and he had a meeting at half past. He'd make a quick call to Diana to see if she wanted to meet him at Rowdy's over on campus for a cocktail. He grinned at the thought of her in a tight black something. Time to make the college kids drool some more.

Before switching his main screen to monitor the lobby, Gibbons returned once more to the mysterious room in Area 15. The two shadows had been joined by a third, this one taller, who had begun some kind of procedure that involved the insertion of a cylindrical object into the left ear of each of the two test subjects.

Gibbons knew these two weren't part of the college volunteer pool. These two, like so many others in this room, had been brought here by the *others*. Dick shuddered, recalling his one glimpse at the hideous winged creatures that scoured the area for perfect victims. It had taken nearly two six-packs and a quart of whiskey to erase that horrible vision from Gibbons' mind. He had never forgotten the screams. It was the nightmares that drove him away from Rachel—it wasn't her fault. He had come to hate all kind, normal people.

Diana was different. As long as he kept her well dressed and iced with diamonds, Diana didn't care if they both went to hell.

Looking at the shadows now, Dick began to wonder if they weren't already there.

CHAPTER Four

The Tulip Tree Hotel had been built at the turn of the century by Jasper Etherington, a self-made millionaire from Pennsylvania. Although Eden had been founded in 1814, two years before Indiana had become a state, the thriving river town had never had a quality hotel until 1904, when Etherington constructed his masterpiece on the corner of River Drive and Tulip Tree Lane.

Overlooking the Ohio River, the massive hotel had been built of Indiana limestone in the heavy Romanesque style that was popular in Etherington's native Pittsburgh. At seven stories tall, the Tulip Tree towered over most of Eden's surrounding buildings. Featuring sunken gardens, a clock tower, and two grand wings, the hotel had been hailed as the showpiece of southern Indiana through the late 1930s.

Decorated throughout with lighting and windows from Tiffany's and textiles from Schumacher's in New York, the hotel had served as an elegant retreat for the robber barons Etherington had called friends. No Saturday night passed without a party in the grand ballroom, and no Sunday morning without a host of hangovers.

The end of the hotel's golden age had come during just such a typical raucous weekend, late in the fall of 1937, when several partygoers had chosen to take a midnight stroll along the banks of the Ohio.

Etherington and two friends, men of grand political reputation and small conscience, had insisted upon an ill-conceived rendezvous with three ladies from the hotel's guest list, intending to cruise the river in Etherington's spacious yacht, *Serena*. But a new moon and a low river had conspired against the sextet, and the yacht's engines had joined the conspiracy, refusing to ignite, despite all efforts by Etherington.

The inquest that followed never truly resolved who had possessed, much less fired, the pistol, but Etherington had died the next day of a most embarrassing wound, and the hotel had declined into that languid existence shared by many old, unloved buildings.

That is, until the recent purchase by an eastern collective. Now restored to her former glory, the Tulip Tree Hotel once again embodied elegance and opulence.

It was into this rarified air that Joshua escorted Katherine at one thirty-seven that Monday afternoon. Katherine, whose last glimpse of the hotel had been at her farewell party ten years earlier, could hardly believe the difference.

"It's incredible! It's as grand as any of the hotels in Paris or London! Who is this mysterious collective that took over?" she asked as they were seated in the Etherington Room.

Josh shrugged broad shoulders and donned a pair of reading glasses. "No one's really sure," he replied as the waiter brought water and two menus. "We'll need a minute," he told the waiter. "Unless you know what you want, Katy."

"Hardly," she answered, opening the calligraphed menu. "This place is nothing like I remember it. Whoever the new owners are, I have to admit they've done a wonderful job."

Josh moved his silverware to one side and leaned in close. "I wrote a series on them when the hotel first opened up two years ago. I even drove out to Pennsylvania on a hunch that it was Etherington's granddaughter Alice who had done it, but she had just died, leaving all her assets to some outfit called The Temple. Search me as to who they are, because I couldn't find anything about them in LexisNexis or anywhere else. They're supposed to have headquarters in Italy somewhere."

"Italy? That doesn't make much sense. Why would some Italian cartel want to buy property in a little town like Eden?" asked Katherine.

The waiter came to take their orders.

"May I suggest the veal, Mr. Carpenter?" he asked Josh with a forced smile.

"Sure," Josh answered. "She's buying, so bring me your best."

Katherine raised an eyebrow and ran a finger down the list of chef's specials. "The cordon bleu, I guess. Asparagus tips and a small salad with Ranch."

"Ranch?" The waiter's lips curled ever so slightly. "Very good," he said at last with a theatrical bow, then turned to exit toward the kitchen. The kid couldn't be more than twenty.

"He's from the drama department at the college," Josh explained with a suppressed laugh. "Most of the waiters here are. Now, let's forget all about Eden and talk about you, Katy Celeste. It's so good to see you, but I am sorry about your Aunt Cissy. She was good people."

"Thanks. Cissy was one of the best people this town ever knew, and I didn't appreciate it until now. When I was growing up, I pegged her as a meddling old lady with blue hair and support hose who constantly corrected my grammar. Later, I realized she loved me more than anyone else on earth. God help me, I let her down, Josh. I really let her down. I didn't even make it to the funeral! Of course, no one called me until it was all over."

"Honestly, Katy, she wanted it that way. Gerry Anderson told me that her will specified some odd requests, but he'd honored them. If no one told you, it's because she wanted it that way."

Katy faked a smile. "I suppose I deserved that."

"You look tired," he told her, hoping he hadn't been insensitive. Her eyes were puffy with dark circles, and the sparkle had left her soft brown eyes. *She's still beautiful, though,* he thought, wishing he could somehow comfort her.

"I got up early to drive here," she answered, wishing she could turn the conversation away from herself. "Mr. Anderson called me last night—around ten, I guess—and I didn't really sleep after that. Look, I'll tell you all about my life over dinner one night this week, OK? For now, what's all this about two high school kids going missing?"

Their food arrived, and the waiter offered freshly ground pepper, while a dark-haired busboy tended to their water. Once they were alone again, Joshua bowed his head silently for a moment. Katherine looked from side to side, slightly embarrassed and not sure if she should start eating or wait.

Raising his head, Joshua smiled. "Sorry. I should have asked you to join me."

"Was that a prayer?" she asked, settling her napkin into her lap and eyeing the cordon bleu.

"Oh, yeah, you know me. Always give thanks. I know you always used to pray before meals."

"Well, uh, I guess it's been a while since I thought about it. If it works for you, more power to you," she answered, feeling her cheeks flush. He was still smiling, but his eyes pierced through her to all her secrets. No wonder they had never married. Who could take the constant examination? He hadn't changed at all.

"So, tell me about these kids."

"You really haven't heard about it? It's been all over the national news."

Katy recalled the last few weeks, the last few months, with bitter regret. Since David's sudden departure, she'd watched no television, read no books or papers, and had barely eaten. A prescription had kept her in a fuzzy state of uncaring, but the call from Gerry Anderson about Cissy's death had brought her back to the world of the living and made her face life again.

"I've been out of touch," she answered softly.

Wiping his mouth, Joshua shot her a knowing look but chose to let it go for the moment. "It happened over two weeks ago on a Friday night. Eden High prom night. Donny Alcorn and Amy Horine were apparently parking near the old powerhouse on County Line Road. Amy's mother said she had promised to be home by one, but when three o'clock rolled around, Mrs. Horine started to worry. She tried calling Amy's cell phone. No answer, so she called Sheriff Branham's office. He was out on a call, but she talked to Deputy Walker. Remember Alvin Walker? He was a year behind us in school. Well, anyway, Al promised the mother he'd drive around. It was Al who found the car, still running and abandoned. Amy's phone was on the front seat along with her purse and jacket, and her shoes were discovered lying in a nearby ditch. Donny and Amy were nowhere to be found."

Katy made mental notes, inwardly wondering how she could be so detached about such a terrifying story. *The curse of a writer,* she told herself. *Everything is a possible plotline.* "No bodies and no real clues?"

Joshua swallowed a bite with a swig of water. "Nope. Teams of searchers have scoured the woods, the fields, and every nook and cranny of town and the outlying areas since the morning after they disappeared. The only bit that doesn't fit is the blood spot on the road in front of Donny's car."

"Blood? That's a pretty big clue!"

"You'd think so, but it's not human. Or at least it doesn't match human characteristics. That's what the science guys at the state criminal lab said."

"So, it's animal blood?"

"Not exactly."

Katy's internal antenna shot up, and her writer's senses began to hum. "Not exactly? What on earth does that mean?"

Josh swallowed hard and took a deep breath. "Don't take this and run with it, OK, Katy? I mean, if this got out, it could be all over the news, and even though I'm a newsman, this isn't the kind of thing I want our town known for, which is why I haven't printed it."

"Spit it out, Carpenter. What do you think I'm going to do with it? Call Dan Rather?"

"I know the kind of books you write, Katherine. This is the kind of thing your readers eat for breakfast."

Katherine stared at him, her dark eyes no longer dull with weariness but dancing with curiosity. "I'll ignore that little jab at my genre. Now, let's have it, Carpenter."

Leaning very close, Josh whispered as softly as he could, taking Katy's hand to make it look as though their conversation were merely romantic. "The blood appeared to contain elements that weren't human or animal. In other words, the blood didn't match any type known on earth."

Katherine nearly pulled her hand out of Joshua's grasp, but he held on tightly. She struggled to keep her face a mask of calm. "No one outside of the sheriff's office and the state boys knows about this?" she asked, suddenly aware of how many people sat in the restaurant.

"No one else. Except, of course, now you. Promise me you won't hop on this, Katy. This probably has some reasonable explanation, so it's pointless to get the local folks all riled up about it, and heaven help us if some of the New Agers at the college hear about it! Professor Fields and his bunch would be on it like a fly on sugar! He's been all but preaching to his students that aliens are the new man, and all we have to do is welcome them with open minds. He's crazy, but a lot of people are buying into his theories. And he doesn't need much more ammunition to set off an explosion that would rip this town, if not our country, apart!"

Joshua's voice had begun to carry, and Katy worried that their conversation had ceased to be secret, so she did the only thing she knew to stop his momentum.

She kissed him.

CHAPTER Five

Maria Horine hadn't really slept in days. Ever since her daughter Amy's disappearance, Maria's world had become a timeless whirl of interviews, searches, telephone calls, sympathetic neighbors, and endless crying. Looking back, she couldn't remember not crying. Her deep brown eyes sagged now with the wet-rag exhaustion that only a mother can know. Maria looked far older than forty-one years.

Amy had been Maria's only child, born three weeks premature with a high bilirubin count and a low chance of survival. A terrifying week of incubation followed by months of nightly bed checks had formed a bond between mother and child that no human could break, not even Amy's worthless father.

Maria had been captivated by the "Greek god" in her political science class at Eden College. Stan's prowess with a basketball, coupled with his natural ability to win friends, had assured him a future in local politics. Maria had been dazzled by promises of afternoon teas with the mayor's wife and a prime box at EC's Memorial Stadium. The Horine family had earned a sterling reputation in nearby Wellington, Indiana, and Stan stood to inherit all the clout that came with being Ernie Horine's only son. Their Christmas wedding had been covered by all the regional papers, and there had even been a write-up in the *Indianapolis Star.*

The first year of their marriage had been storybook perfect. Stan had joined a local law firm as a clerk in preparation for his admission to Indiana University Law School in Bloomington. His LSAT scores had been impressive, and the school had shown a keen interest in Stan. Stan had a trust fund to take care of all his expenses, courtesy of his maternal grandfather's estate. To help integrate Stan into Eden society, Maria had begun to volunteer with local charities. Their life together had seemed perfect.

Until she got pregnant.

It wasn't a planned pregnancy, but Stan's surprise and subsequent anger had mystified Maria. He'd blamed her for ruining their future, and soon he was spending more and more time at Rowdy's Bar. By the time little Amy had turned three, Stan's second extramarital affair was in full swing, and Maria and Amy had moved to a small apartment on Elm Street. Stan Horine had given his daughter a name and little else.

Although raised Roman Catholic by her Mexican mother, Maria welcomed the divorce, refusing to be tied to a man who didn't truly love her or their baby. Three months later, after using up his entire trust fund, Stan left town bankrupt and owing nearly forty-five thousand dollars in gambling and credit card debt. Maria hadn't heard a word from him since.

Until last week.

Last Sunday afternoon, following a WRTV piece on Amy's and Donny's disappearance, Maria had found herself staring into the television at the well-dressed image of her very successful ex-husband.

Now living northeast of Indianapolis in Lawrence, Stan had cried a river of crocodile tears and bemoaned the loss of "those wonderful years" with his darling daughter. Now the owner of a string of grocery stores, Stan and his third wife, Ingrid, had used the time to promote Stan's Warehouse grocery chain by parading their three perfect children, all under the age of five, before the eager press. The publicity made Stan look like the grandest father since Abraham.

Maria had very nearly downed an entire bottle of Prozac that night, but a chance phone call had stopped her. It had been Joshua Carpenter, calling to ask how she was doing. He hadn't wanted an exclusive or even a teaser for the next edition. He'd just wanted to help her make it through the night.

Maria longed for such strength every night, but she feared any moment would bring the confirmation of her daughter's death, and then what?

As she blinked mindlessly into the afternoon sun filtering its way through the gauzy lace window sheers, Maria wondered if her small strength hadn't all but left her. She prayed to find solace in her mother's rosary, but saying the words felt too much like weeping, and her heart could stand no more of that. Perhaps, she should call Father Mike in Wellington. No, he'd only scold her for not coming to him sooner. And he'd remind her that she hadn't been to confession since her divorce.

The jangling of the telephone jarred Maria back to reality, and she raced for the receiver, hoping against all hope that this was good news about Amy.

"Hello?" she answered, breathless and expectant.

"Mrs. Horine?" asked a resonant, male voice. "It's about Amy."

"Yes! Do you have news? Please, tell me! Is she...is she alive?"

"Your daughter is well. That's all you need to know for now. She'll be returned to you—if you remain quiet. You cannot tell a soul about this phone call, otherwise Amy will never come home."

"What do you mean she's...Do you have her? Have you taken her? Hello? Hello?"

Click.

The man had ended the connection.

"Dear God!" Maria cried, falling to her knees. "Don't let her die! Please, oh, please let it be true that she's alive! Please, God, please!" she wept, burying her face in her hands.

She remained that way for hours, on her face, prostrate before God, searching her soul and seeking God for a miracle. She confessed her sins, wailing as her heart bled anger and distress until there was nothing left. Her small form, bent and penitent, traced a tiny silhouette against the window, now stained with the rouges and soft purples of sunset. Finally, as night fell, she slept an exhausted sleep of deep and untroubled dreams. For the first time since the nightmare had begun, Maria Horine had found a moment of peace.

CHAPTER Six

All the way back to her aunt's house, Katy had mentally kicked herself. How could she have kissed him? Dear God, how embarrassed he had looked! How foolish she had felt! *An impulse,* she told herself. *A stupid impulse, like something one of my characters would do.*

Walking back to Aunt Cissy's where she'd left her car, Katherine fought the urge to reach for the pills. She could use the uncaring calm they brought right now. But the truth was she would only be running away. *Running never solves your problems,* she lectured. *It just makes your legs tired.*

Late afternoon on the river had brought her great joy as a child. Katy could remember running from park bench to tree and back again, happily playing tag with her father. She could still hear his melodic laughter as he'd scoop her into his strong arms and kiss her flushed cheek. Paul Adamson had walked tall among men, although he'd stood only five feet ten inches tall. Katy recalled photos of his high school basketball days, when her father had appeared like a grasshopper among giants.

Genetics, she figured now, but as a child she'd often asked about the many tall men in their small town. Why, she remembered now that there had even been a national news story about Eden's Amazing Men of Renown, a local group that had a requirement that members be over six and a half feet tall. The group boasted of having thirty-seven members on its rolls, and many of those men stood over seven feet tall. One man, Henry Ferguson, had been officially measured at eight feet, four inches! Henry had worked for the pork factory, loading trucks, and it was said he could lift and load an entire skid of boxes without breaking a sweat.

Stupid memories, Katy thought. *I'm deliberately letting myself get off the real subject—just why am I here?* Truthfully, since Cissy's funeral had already occurred, Katherine could have had someone like Rhonda Coleman handle most of the details of Cissy's estate. What details were there, anyway? Closing up the house, checking off a list of belongings, donating Cissy's items to charity, and hearing the will.

Katy shuddered at the thought. No, Aunt Cissy had been a mother to Katherine after her real mother's death. Cissy deserved better.

Turning north on her walk, Katherine noticed for the first time how much the town had changed. Not in overt ways as so many other Midwestern towns had begun to change, but in subtler, more sinister ways. The architecture had remained the same. In fact, the town had never looked better. Josh had mentioned a revival of sorts when the younger Sturgill took over the office of mayor from his father. New businesses had taken root, and the fruit of their labors brought forth the original pleasing aesthetics of the town, with every building restored to its antebellum appearance. Even the streetlamps stood straighter, prouder. In some ways Eden appeared to be a perfect world.

Yet something about this perfect world nagged at Katy's inner self. Who was she to judge, though? She'd abandoned

Eden for the broader ways of St. Louis. And why? Because of David. He had led her there, and he had left her there. Maybe that was why she'd kissed Joshua. Just to prove she could still do it.

Ahead, she could see the friendly outline of Cissy's house— *no doubt my house now,* Katy realized with regret. Fortunately, she had a lot to occupy her mind inside the house. Reaching into her purse, Katy found the large ring of keys Rhonda had given to her. *These are the keys to your future,* she told herself. *Hold on to them tightly. Because, if you're careful and don't blow this, you might just be able to begin a new life here. Right back where you started.*

Nearing the house, Katherine spied another of the many posters that had been stapled to light poles around town. MISSING, the sign declared in bold black print. Two faces, smiling brightly with the carelessness of youth, stared out at her from the white paper. "Amy and Donny," the words read. *God help them, they're probably dead. That's how these things play out,* Katy thought darkly.

Opening the gate, she headed toward the front door. She'd not yet been inside the house since her return. She'd chosen instead to go straight to Joshua. *Why was that?* Taking a deep breath, Katherine inserted the largest key into the lock and turned it. Even after all these years, the tumblers worked smoothly, and the door swung open to reveal a foyer that hadn't changed since Katy was a child.

Inside, the late afternoon sun shone softly through clean lace curtains, dancing lightly upon highly polished oak floors. In the center of the grand open foyer stood a large round Rococo table with claw feet, dressed, as always, with a hand-embroidered scarf made as a gift for Aunt Cissy by a former student. Beyond that, the foyer opened to several rooms on either side of the great oak and marble staircase that dominated the home.

All around her, Katherine could actually sense Aunt Cissy's presence. Everywhere she looked stood physical manifestations of her walk upon this earth: knick-knacks from her summer travels, photographs from the remotest corners of the globe, and crocheted doilies made by Cissy's arthritic hands, each one a living testament to the kindest woman Katy had ever known.

Ahead, the grand staircase ascended to seven bedrooms, but Katherine had no desire to go there yet. She needed to drink in the memories, breathe them in like a rich and exotic perfume. To the right, Cissy's courting parlor awaited visitors to share tea and cookies. To the left, the music room tempted the wayward traveler to come in and rest while listening to the soothing tones of the magnificent old Steinway that graced the center of the room. In a far corner, a harp and violin longed for the touch of a master, but Katherine, who could play only the most rudimentary tunes, touched the smooth wood and moved on, leaving them for another time.

To the left and behind the staircase, a friendly hallway led to the kitchen where rapturous smells had so many times beckoned Katherine to breakfast on a snowy winter morning. To the right of the staircase, a library, filled to the ceiling with books about dragons and victorious knights, tempted her to come and shut out the world of reality.

This house is magical, Katy thought, suddenly feeling years younger. She had grown smaller in her mind, lighter, and she felt as though the years had all but faded into the past of a perfect childhood. The sun shone only for her. This house and all its treasures were a puzzle that only she had been privileged to solve, and she had all the power in the world!

Running a hand along the foyer's graceful table, Katherine knew she was home. All her wanderings were behind her now. David could have California and his wife. She would retreat into the loving embrace of the familiar. No more pills, no more publishers, at least not for now. She would write again, yes. She knew that now, but only after she had taken the time to read, to play, and to sip the elixir of eternal youth.

Closing the front door, Katherine smiled. "Welcome home, Katherine," she said aloud. "Welcome home."

On the other side of Eden, deep within Area 15, two tall figures had completed their work. The room smelled strongly of disinfectant, and the fans of over a dozen computers hummed a dissonant tune. Four overhead lights glared down onto the sleeping subjects, who lay as still as death upon the two tables. Two IV bags connected to the sleepers' arms sagged now with only traces of the clear fluid each had once held.

The shadows moved silently, their tall thin bodies reflecting no light, although they craved it. Long fingers, stretched and wispy, probed the teenagers as though they were nothing more than cattle.

"We must release them tomorrow," the taller of the two shadows said without a word spoken. Language had long ago been lost to their world, although they longed to experience it once again. "We must complete the transformation by midnight if we are to remain on schedule."

The smaller shadow nodded, recalling the sensations of long ago: touch and smell and sight and hearing, and the taste of food with all its savory delights. Oh, to be embodied once again, to share in the sensual delights that flesh and blood would bring! This girl's form, though not the most pleasing shape the shadow had ever used, would suffice to entice and

45

enthrall. Soon, this girl and her unworthy boyfriend would be reborn, and the shadows, along with their new identities, would join the others already embodied, and the true mission that had brought the shadows to Eden would begin.

I will soon walk the earth again, thought the taller shadow, recalling a golden age when great men strode between mountain peaks, and forbidden knowledge had been taught to the children of men. Soon, that great and mysterious knowledge would once again find utterance, and the shadows would be shadows no more. Victory was within their grasp.

"It is nearly time," the taller shadow reminded the smaller one.

"We must prepare ourselves for the transformation."

CHAPTER Seven

Katherine awoke with a start. She had fallen asleep in the middle of unpacking and woke to find herself sprawled half-on, half-off the big canopy bed she'd slept in as a child. Her mouth had that cottony texture that she remembered from her nights of partying in college, but she couldn't remember having had anything to drink.

Where was she?

Oh yes, the corner bedroom, third floor of the nicest house in Eden.

Katy glanced at the cuckoo clock mounted just over the fireplace. Nearly ten o'clock. Since it was dark outside, she assumed that meant it was ten at night. Her head felt like a small elephant had climbed up her nose and set up camp in her sinuses.

She had kissed Joshua Carpenter.

Fool!

Sitting up, Katy frowned at the crumpled clothing that lay draped over her brown leather luggage. The casual viewer wouldn't know that these wise old suitcases had seen the world's greatest cities—twice. Katherine had done a great deal of traveling during her twelve years of writing. She'd made countless personal appearances and signed her books in a variety of

47

venues and conventions from coast to coast and sea to shining sea.

Stepping down from the high, antique bed, Katy began putting away the clothes in an old walnut wardrobe that stood between the windows on the south side. The nine-foot-tall wardrobe had come over from Germany with Katherine's paternal great-grandmother as a wedding gift. Hand-carved and lined with cedar, the wardrobe greeted her with a strong whiff of mothballs, Aunt Cissy's answer to nearly every textile trouble.

The oppressive quiet of the empty house pushed at Katy's eardrums, and she decided to turn on the old 1929 Crosley radio. Dialing for a local station, Katherine was surprised to find a strong signal at a familiar frequency. 770 AM had been the home of Katherine's favorite top forty music station when she was in high school. Crazy Jack Jones had been the top deejay then, and most of Eden had tuned in regularly during his afternoon timeslot.

"...and that's why we won't be undersold," droned the first voice she heard. "Because if you can find it cheaper than here at Howard's Auto Plaza, then it's just plain cheap!"

Katy smirked. Arnie Howard was still hawking cars. He should know cheap—his picture was in Webster's right next to the word.

"WEDN radio!" sang a quartet as a bumper to the ad. "News, news, news!"

Saccharine and off-key, she thought, but it was just like she'd remembered.

"Two local Eden High teens still missing. I'm Terrence Wilson, and this is the ten o'clock news. According to Eden High School Principal, Daniel Cheatham, Sunday's graduation ceremonies will include a tribute to missing class valedictorian Amy Horine and Angels football quarterback Donald Alcorn.

The ten-minute memorial will fill the time allotted for Miss Horine's valedictory address. The search for the two teenagers has reached a standstill, says Sheriff Kit Branham, but the hotline remains open for anyone who may have information regarding what happened to the two teens over two weeks ago. Anyone with information should call 1-855-EDEN KIDS.

"In other news, Eden Hospital reports another record birth! Eden residents Max and Charlene Childers announce the birth of a baby boy, born at a whopping fifteen pounds and challenging the records at a lengthy twenty-seven inches. This is the second child for the Childers family, and big sister Carol says her little brother isn't little at all! Mother and son are reported to be in satisfactory condition.

"And what was that in the sky over Miller's farm last night? The phones at Sheriff Branham's office and this radio station have been ringing off the hook with reports of a glowing object that hovered over and then appeared to land near Miller's south cornfield. Professor Adrian Fields of Eden College's folklore department, a man who has gained local celebrity as a UFO chaser, led seven of his students to the field this morning to search for artifacts. Although no definitive evidence was found, Fields insists UFOs have been targeting our area. Stay tuned for more news at half past the hour. Now, it's time for *Ask Dr. Phipps*."

Katherine shut off the radio. Perhaps quiet was better after all.

Somewhere in the house a phone was ringing, but where? Katherine stumbled sleepily toward the staircase, following the sound down two flights to the main floor. Dashing into the parlor, she grabbed the familiar old black receiver.

"Hello?" she asked, breathless from the mad dash down the stairs.

"Gee, Katy C., I hadn't realized my good looks had such a profound effect on you. You sound positively out of breath!"

Joshua.

"Just finishing my nightly calisthenics. Fifty push-ups, followed by a hundred crunches. You should try it."

She could imagine his endearing smile on the other end. Endearing and oh so maddening.

"Sounds like work to me," he laughed. "But I guess that's how you manage to keep that pretty figure. Listen, I was wondering if you have a minute to talk shop?"

Ten-seventeen. Although still weary, she doubted if she could sleep through the night. She kept expecting to see Cissy coming into the room, an unsettling feeling at best. Maybe spending some time on the phone would be a good idea.

"Katy, are you all right?" came Joshua's genuine concern—almost as good as a hug.

"I'm fine. Just tired. You know how traveling can take it out of you. What sort of shop talk, Carpenter?"

"It can wait if you need the sleep," he insisted.

"Spit it out. Besides, I'm restless. Is it about the missing kids?"

Joshua waited a beat. He was thinking. She could almost hear his mind working.

"No, although I wish it were. Their families have taken all the bad news they can, and the national press is having a field day in Eden. No, it's...well, it's about UFOs."

"You mean the bit at Miller's farm?"

"How did you know about that?" he asked, his voice half-surprised, half-filled with admiration.

"I keep up," she replied, sitting as a smile crossed her pale face. "Don't you believe in little green men?"

She expected him to laugh, but he didn't. This must be serious.

"Katy, there've been some very strange, disturbing things happening around here, and...well, as much as I want you to stay, you might consider heading back to St. Louis. Let's just say, Eden is not the town it used to be."

"What do you mean?" she asked, leaning forward. "Josh? Joshua?"

Nothing.

"Carpenter? Hey! Joshua!" she called again, but the line had gone dead.

She heard an ominous howl—a dog or a wolf. Outside, the wind moaned like a woman in labor, wailing as though in agony.

Hanging up the telephone, she shuddered. Lines in Eden probably weren't state-of-the-art. Just a bad connection, that's all. She'd call Joshua back tomorrow. For now, she'd take one Dr. Evans' magic pills. Tomorrow, in the comforting light of day, she would begin her new life.

CHAPTER Eight

TUESDAY

Morning broke with a splattering of rain and the howling of a dog. Katherine hadn't slept well anyway, but being awakened before six by the incessant noise from the mutt next door did not promote a neighborly attitude in her sleep-deprived brain.

Donning Cissy's favorite blue chenille bathrobe and matching scuffs, well-worn but comfy, Katy made her way down the two flights of stairs to the kitchen, where she hoped she would find coffee. She didn't even care if it was good coffee. Just as long as it was strong.

After turning on the copper-framed overhead lights, she scoured through the cupboards for any sign of beans. Not a one. *Silly,* she thought. *Cissy wouldn't have kept beans. She always used pre-ground, and that was usually whatever was on sale.*

Turning toward the larder, Katy sighed with relief at the discovery of an unopened can of regular coffee, which she happily poured into a filter and popped into the coffeemaker near the sink. By now the sun was up, and the neighbor's dog had switched from howling to a constant, sharp bark.

Remembering morning routine in Eden, Katy checked the front door for the morning edition of the *Chronicle*. Sure enough, Joshua hadn't let her down, and she found a crisply folded newspaper waiting for her with an envelope tucked into the rubber band, no doubt his apology for rudely hanging up on her last night.

Returning to the smell of java heaven, she poured a cup of black gold with three sugars, but sans cream due to the lack of anything in the refrigerator. She made a mental note to stock the fridge and settled into one of a quartet of Windsor chairs at the round breakfast table. She put her feet up on the next chair, crossing one scuffed foot over the other.

Before opening the paper for the morning's headlines, she turned her attention to the white number ten envelope with her name printed in blue block letters. She imagined that Joshua had put the note there this morning, personally leaving the paper on her doorstep. *He could have rung the doorbell, the little coward,* she thought sleepily. *Maybe he really is angry over the kiss at lunch. Stop second-guessing, Katherine. Open it.*

Using her thumb to rip open the seal, Katy saw that the note wasn't from Joshua at all. The block writing continued on the inside, written in somewhat stilted language.

MISS ADAMSON:
    IF YOU WANT TO KNOW WHAT IS REALLY HAPPENING HERE IN EDEN, MEET ME TODAY AT SANDY'S BAR AT 2:00 PM. SIT IN THE FIRST BOOTH. ASK FOR A LUNCH MENU. I WILL JOIN YOU.

The letter wasn't signed. This could be from Joshua, but it wasn't his style. Josh had always been pretty direct, and this letter seemed pretty darn ambiguous. Besides, Josh had always called her Katy. This had to be from someone who did not know her well, if at all.

Two this afternoon gave her plenty of time to see Cissy's attorney at ten, fill the fridge, stock up on donuts, and still make it to Sandy's.

I hope this isn't going to be a secret meeting with Linda Kemp, she thought ruefully. *Although she might be able to tell me why Joshua is avoiding her.*

Deciding a second cup of coffee would steel her for the busy morning, Katherine filled her mug and headed upstairs to shower and dress. Someone out there wanted to meet her, so she should probably make an effort to look nice.

Two hours later, Katherine left the house, dressed neatly in a turquoise-blue cotton sweater and matching linen slacks. Her auburn hair, painfully short since last month's rampage with a pair of dress shears, was at least easy to care for now—a bit of styling mousse and a few scrunches, and she was set to go. Katherine's chocolate brown eyes needed little makeup, but she had donned a bit of matte brown shadow and some mascara. Her skin had always been good, as was her bone structure, both inherited from her mother. Strong cheekbones rising out of light olive skin spoke of her checkerboard ancestry: German, Irish, English, and a smattering of Cherokee. The mix was not atypical for southern Indiana, but Katherine's strong features often stood out in a crowd.

May had been a dry month until today, but the early morning rain had finally stopped, and Katy walked out into a clear morning filled with sunshine and flowers. She'd need to drive to the attorney's office, but that wasn't until ten, so she decided instead to walk to Margarita's for breakfast.

The little restaurant sat directly across from the newspaper. It was owned and operated by a couple from Juarez who'd come to Eden to pick tobacco thirty years before and decided to stay. Gomez and Angelina Ramirez had applied for citizenship and been sworn in on July 4, 1976. Since that time, eleven Ramirez children had grown up in Eden, each one taking his or her turn in the kitchen.

The restaurant, named Margarita's for Gomez's mother, served American food, but with a Mexican twist. Eggs Angelina, a casserole that included hash browns, eggs, jalapeños, and jack cheese, drew a crowd every morning. Margarita's had been one of Katy's favorite haunts during her high school and college years. She and Joshua had eaten more than their share of Angelina's enchiladas.

Katy had lost forty-three pounds over the past few months on the "my boyfriend is a jerk" diet. David's sudden departure for California and his revelation about a wife and three children had left Katy unable to sleep, eat, or write. Now at one hundred and twenty-nine pounds, her five foot, four-inch frame felt lighter physically, but the heaviness of having been duped by a man who wasn't even that good-looking had never left. Sometimes she fantasized about appearing on a sleazy tell-all talk show with David and showing the whole world what a true worm he was.

Locking the door behind her, Katherine was glad for the light sweater. The temperatures had cooled with the overnight rain. Walking east, she crossed Broadway and passed by the house with the dog. Years ago, the Lynch family had lived there, but now Katherine noticed a freshly painted sign in the front yard. Apple Tree Inn—Bed and Breakfast.

Perhaps the dog belonged to guests. Katherine prayed it did, since she didn't wish to have her next appearance on television be as the wild woman who strangled a poor poodle with its own tail.

The morning sun brightened as she headed downtown, so Katherine donned a pair of sunglasses. Although she had earned a place as a local celebrity due to her success as a writer, Katherine rarely tried to hide her identity. She felt a little bit phony wearing the shades. Her path took her past Davis's Bookstore, and she noted that her last book, written two years before, decorated the front window. *The Widow's Son* had taken her two years to write, and it had nearly broken her spirit.

Like all her novels, the story was based on truth, or at least truth as Katy's research had uncovered it. Truth with a capital T had become a nebulous notion to Katherine lately. As a child, she had embraced a world of black and white, always knowing what was right and what was wrong, but now she saw only gray.

Seeing the book now with its red and blue cover startled Katherine, reminding her of the strain of writing. She wasn't sure why she opened the door, but her feet took her into the small shop and straight into the path of owner Jean Davis.

"Excuse me!" the tiny woman said softly, her blue-tinted hair pulled into a neat chignon. "Welcome to Davis's Bookstore. I don't believe we've seen you here before—Oh! Wait! You're Katherine, aren't you? Katherine Adamson? Yes, you are! A trifle skinnier, but you're Katy. I'd know you anywhere!"

"Miss Davis, it's so good to see you again," Katy answered honestly, leaning down to kiss the older woman's cheek. "You haven't changed one bit."

"You have, child! You've lost so much weight! And what happened to all that glorious hair?"

"It's a long story, Miss Davis. If you've got time for breakfast, I'd love to tell you all about it."

"You haven't eaten yet? Oh, honey, you aren't going to put that weight back on that way. Sure, I can ask Nancy to watch the store while we go out. Nancy!"

From the back of the store, a tall young woman emerged, holding a small box of books marked Balsam House. "Yes, Miss Davis?" the girl asked.

"Sweetheart, you won't mind taking over out here while I have coffee with an old friend, will you? You do recognize our hometown author, don't you?"

The girl donned a pair of cat glasses that hung from her neck by a silver chain. "Hometown author? Oh my! You're K. C. Adamson, aren't you? I've seen your photo every day since I've been here! It's an honor to meet you, Miss Adamson!"

The girl's freckled face flushed as she crossed the floor in only three strides, reaching out to shake Katy's hand. The girl must have been six feet tall if she was an inch. Her hair was dark, but her eyes were a light, almost iridescent blue. The glasses, old-fashioned in a hip sort of way, didn't appear to alter the size of the girl's eyes the way a strong myope's might. *Maybe her glasses are a fashion statement,* Katy thought.

"This is Nancy Cheatham, the high school principal's daughter. She's been working here since Christmas, and I must say she's been an answer to prayer!" Miss Davis said, pulling a sweater around her slight shoulders and reaching for a beaded purse that was hanging over a chair behind a rolltop desk.

"It's a pleasure to meet you, Nancy. Have you read any of my books?" Katy asked, noting how the immense size of the girl's hands dwarfed her own.

"All of them!" she gushed. "*Children of Anak* was my favorite, although it seemed a little far-fetched."

Katherine laughed. "Well, that has been said about all of my books at one time or another. The notion of an unknown planet crossing paths with earth and seeding humanity isn't all that out there, though. It's pretty well documented in ancient Sumerian texts."

"Oh, I know, I know! But don't you think those texts could have been faked?"

"Nancy, honey, you have to save your questions for later. It's nearly eight-thirty, and this poor girl hasn't even eaten!"

"Oh, I'm so sorry, Miss Adamson! But I would love to talk more. I'm studying folklore at the college, but I hope to be a writer one day. You're one of my favorite authors, so I'd love to bounce some ideas off you, if that's all right."

The girl looked genuinely smitten with the idea of chatting with a published author, and part of Katherine was flattered, as it always was in such circumstances. But a small part of Katy thought otherwise. A tiny voice, calling from a past Katy had nearly forgotten, was crying out a warning, and the sound of the voice was unsettling.

"I'd love it," was her reply, and she and Miss Davis left for Margarita's.

CHAPTER Nine

Maria woke that morning to the patter of rain hitting the tin roof of the shotgun house she now called home. After moving from the apartment on Elm, she and baby Amy had rented space in a variety of tenement houses. Sometimes she'd earned the rent by cleaning houses, and other times she took in laundry to pay the bills. When Dr. Prosser had offered Maria a job working in his satellite office on Pear Tree, she had jumped at the chance to build a better life for her daughter.

That had been nearly thirteen years ago, and Amy had been able to grow up in a normal home, as normal as possible without a father. Dr. Prosser had taken a shine to the child early on, and he'd often been a stand-in at social functions. His wife had died during the birth of their second child, and Robert Prosser had chosen to remain a widower. Maria had grown close to the kind physician, earning his trust while he earned her loyalty.

Now, as she lay in bed, listening to the rain slapping lazily against the tin, she thought of how God had blessed her. Their house, though small, was walking distance from the clinic, and Amy had loved playing in the backyard as a girl. The neighbors were helpful, and many of them had children Amy's age, so friendships had blossomed, helping to ease Maria's loneliness.

Donny Alcorn's parents had originally lived only three houses from their little bungalow. Two years earlier Donny's father had been promoted to vice president of the advertising firm where he worked, and the family had been able to move to the Willow Tree Farms subdivision. Things were looking up for the Alcorn family. Within the year, Donny had been named all-state in football.

Maria rarely saw Meredith Alcorn any more, but she had spoken with her several times over the past two weeks. The tragedy of their children's disappearance had forced them together, both personally and in the press. Meredith had remained stoic and barely shed a tear as the cameras from Louisville and Indianapolis stations had rolled. Harold did all the talking for the three parents, accustomed as he was to dealing with the public.

Maria had often felt invisible in the maze of reporters and microphones. Sometimes she wished she really could disappear.

Outside, the rain was slowing, and the gradual brightening of the room told her the sun was nearly up. She knew the morning would bring another group of reporters to her front door, fishing for some tidbit they could feed to their voracious viewers. Maria considered telling them about yesterday's horrifying phone call, but the Voice had ordered her to remain silent, had said that her daughter's survival and ultimate return depended on it. Should she have called Sheriff Branham? Should she tell the Alcorns?

Closing her eyes, Maria turned over in bed. She would shower, then she would decide. But first, she must pray. She would not make any more decisions without consulting God.

After her divorce, Maria had left the church, scarcely even attending on Easter, but now she felt an overpowering need to talk with God. She didn't want to have to go through a priest. But her childhood memories demanded she do so.

Perhaps she would call Father Gregory from St. John's. His parish extended to East Eden, although the cathedral was located closer to the college. Father Mike in Wellington was too far away. Father Gregory would hear her confession. Yes, she would call him.

Right after she took a shower.

Joshua Carpenter opened the front doors to the paper, wondering why he even bothered. The readership had declined steadily for the past year until he was lucky to sell a thousand copies in a day. Circulation had once been over fifteen thousand, including the issues mailed to former residents. Now, the paper that had once brought news to all of Eden lined birdcages and puppy boxes.

Exhausted from a long night of working to get the morning edition out on time, Josh looked forward to a quiet day. He would have to make the daily phone call to the Alcorns and Mrs. Horine for their latest quotes about the missing teens. There was the hospital beat to cover and, this being Tuesday, he'd need to call the local churches for the titles of the upcoming Sunday sermons. Tedious, yes, but Josh had never been afraid of what others might call routine. He knew people relied on him, even though that number kept dwindling. He would not let down those who had been faithful.

Josh knew Michael Denton, his only remaining full-time reporter, should be in soon. He'd see if Denton wanted to cover the so-called sighting over Miller's Farm. It seemed lately that real news took a backseat to more sensational claims, but Josh had promised his father to cover all the news, and he'd be shirking his duty if he ignored this simply because he didn't believe in aliens.

"Mornin', boss," Denton called from the doorway. "I stopped by the college on the way over, and boy is that place hopping! End-of-the-world types are all over the place!"

Dropping two quarters into a red soda machine, Joshua pushed the button for Big Red and popped the top. "Armageddon Andy?"

Denton laughed, fishing in the pockets of his Dockers for his own quarters. Coming up empty, he nodded. "Yeah, he was there, holding court outside the student union. Enoch Jones was there, too. Of course, his crowd was considerably smaller."

Josh handed Denton fifty cents and began to sift through the mail. "His crowd is generally a small one. I'm surprised his church doors stay open. But they manage to keep the bills paid and the services going."

"You still go there, boss?"

"When I can. I try to make it to all the churches over time, but truthfully, I'm not so sure about a lot of them. Like that Church of the Higher Power that took over the old building where First Presbyterian used to meet. Do you know what they do on Sundays? They chant. They all sit around, and they chant. And I'll tell you, they are not directing that chant toward heaven."

Denton popped open an orange soda and sat opposite Carpenter. "You ever read the Bible, boss?"

Joshua looked up, his hazel eyes bloodshot. "Sure, don't you?"

Denton looked embarrassed. "Well, I've cracked it a few times. I mean, who hasn't had to learn a verse or two in Sunday school? But this Armageddon stuff, it's a bunch of hogwash, right?"

Raising a dark eyebrow, Carpenter took a sip of his drink and shrugged. "It's in there, I can tell you that much, Mike. And it's something to think about. You ought to read it."

Denton was about to answer when the phone rang. Answering it, the seasoned reporter's mouth went slack, and he muttered something about a miracle. Putting down the receiver, he stared at the desk for a moment, then at his boss, wide-eyed. "You won't believe who just walked into the SuperMart asking for a can of Coke and a sandwich."

"Don't tell me it was one of Ben Miller's aliens?" asked Joshua.

"Better. Donny Alcorn."

Katherine pushed her plate away. Two biscuits, gravy, and a helping of Angelina's special egg casserole rumbled in her tummy. Breakfast with Jean Davis had been a healing experience. Jean had been a good friend to Aunt Cissy since they were girls, and Katy had reveled in tales about Cissy's repeated attempts to chop down the big maple in the back of their house and the time she had tied a scarf around her cat's neck to see if a cape could help it to fly.

"The cat survived," Jean finished with a wry grin. "Which is more than can be said for Cissy's backside. Your Grandpa Adamson doted on that cat."

"Jean, you're a dear," Katherine said as she motioned to the waitress for another round of coffee. "You and this town never change."

"Oh, everything changes, honey," the older lady said matter-of-factly. "Especially Eden. Oh, Eden's very different now. You know, all the new people coming and going. And the way some of the older folks act now. All different. But not me. I'm all right. Cissy and I used to talk about it a lot. I miss her. I always knew I could trust my little Cissy."

Katherine smiled. Jean Davis stood four feet eleven, if she stretched and wore a hat, and Celeste Adamson had towered over her at five ten. Almost a foot difference. Yet, because Jean had been born three months earlier, she had always referred to her friend as "little Cissy." It was Jean, in fact, who first called Celeste *Cissy*. Jean, an only child, had figured Celeste with three brothers needed a sister, too, so she'd called her Sissy. Somehow, over the years, the spelling changed to Cissy, and soon the whole town called her simply Aunt Cissy.

"I miss her, too," Katy admitted, finding the memories more painful now than ever before. "Why was it no one called me until after the funeral?"

Jean pushed back her coffee cup and shook her head at the waitress. "No thanks, hon. I've had my caffeine quota for the day." Once the waitress had finished refilling Katy's cup and left the table, Jean leaned forward and answered Katy's question.

"You can't be too careful," she said in a whisper. "She may be listening."

"Who? Aunt Cissy?"

"No, that girl. You have to watch what you say, honey. Eden's changed. And it's not for the better. But as to the funeral service, well, that's the way Cissy wanted it. She had it all written out in her will long before she died. She didn't want more than twenty-four hours to pass before being cremated. And no one was to be told about her death until the cremation was done. Except me, of course. Dr. Prosser told me, and he told Cissy's lawyer, Gerald Anderson. The three of us contacted Pastor Jones."

"Enoch Jones? He's with Eden Bible Church, right?"

"That's right. How did you know?" Jean asked, her light gray eyes rounding with surprise. "He's been with Eden Bible for, oh, I'd say twenty-five years or more, but Cissy and I only started going there four or five years ago. We used to go to Miracle Baptist, remember? With Pastor Wright. You probably remember him. I think he baptized you when you were a little girl."

Katy nodded, remembering the cold water of Skunk Creek. She could still feel the slippery mud gushing between her toes. She'd nearly forgotten that whole part of her life. She'd been ten years old, and life had been in that comforting black and white stage. Giving your life to Christ had seemed so right then. Now, she wondered what it was she'd really done.

She certainly hadn't lived the way she knew a Christian was supposed to. One live-in boyfriend in college and a string of broken relationships, then the whole David mess. She wanted to think she would never have dated him had she known he was married, but the truth was, she couldn't be sure. Had she loved him? Probably not. Had he loved her? Definitely not. But the need for each other had been real—like an addiction. Katy doubted that Cissy would have understood. Maybe that was part of the reason Katy had avoided calling her.

"Pastor Wright resigned, oh, just before Easter about five years back. His wife had left him, and he wasn't very happy. The very next week, Easter Sunday, the church burned to the ground. So, Cissy and I switched to Eden Bible. I think it was Josh Carpenter who started us going there." Jean winked. "Pastor Jones is really quite nice, you know."

"I saw his name on the sign outside the church as I came into town yesterday morning. This Enoch Jones, did he conduct a service for Cissy?"

"Oh, yes. He preached a good one. Of course, there were only the five of us there."

"Five? You, Dr. Prosser, Gerry Anderson, Pastor Jones, and who?"

"Oh, Joshua Carpenter was there. Didn't I mention that?"

"No. Neither did he."

"What?"

"Never mind, Jean. Say, do you know if Cissy ever contacted a realtor in the weeks before she died?"

The small woman's face turned dark. "No. She never did. But your asking makes me wonder. Are you talking about Eden Realty?"

Katherine sat back, amazed at the older woman's perception. "You're quite a little detective, aren't you, Jean? Yes, a woman from Eden Realty met me when I first got here yesterday. Do you know Rhonda Coleman?"

Jean clucked her tongue, her ageless eyes rolling. "That sneaky witch? She'd been nagging Cissy for months, trying to get into her head, you know? Believe me, Celeste Adamson would not have turned your family's home over to that piece of work!"

"Then how did she get Cissy's keys?" Katherine wondered aloud.

Jean leaned forward, taking the younger woman's hand in hers. Jean's papery skin was warm, and her small hand felt reassuring, like a mother's touch.

"Katherine, dear, if Rhonda Coleman had Cissy's keys, then she stole them. You mark my words! Take careful inventory of the house, and especially look into Cissy's papers. That's all I can say here. I'll check in with you in a day or two. Oh! I nearly forgot! I was going to call you anyway, since—well, I'm not sure how to say it, but I have Cissy's ashes."

Katherine paled. She hadn't expected this. "Her ashes?"

Jean opened her small bag, an opulent opera bag decorated with hundreds of delicate glass beads. Withdrawing a pressed, white handkerchief, she dabbed at her small nose. "I have her urn at my home, locked up safe and sound. It's a beautiful urn, Katherine. It was actually an antique, and it was my friend Ethel Winston who found it last year, at that little shop where McGinty's furniture store used to be—you know the place—so I bought it as a gift for Cissy—oh, my dear, you look worn out. This has been too much all at once, and my going on and on isn't helping. Now, you should go back home, take a lovely morning nap, and I'll drop off the urn at your house just as soon as I lock up the store at six."

Katherine had started to object, but stopped when she saw Joshua Carpenter dash through the front door of the restaurant. He'd come in for a rushed take-out order of breakfast. Seeing Katherine, he headed straight for their table.

"I'm glad you're here," he said quickly, handing a ten to the waitress who had followed him with a bag of bacon and egg burritos. "Keep the change, Bonnie."

"I was just about to leave," Katy explained.

"Good. You can go with me to the Alcorn place."

Katherine paid the bill, while Joshua helped Jean on with her sweater.

"Thank you, Joshua. You are always such a gentleman," Jean said with a darling smile.

"I can't go anywhere right now, Josh. I have a ten o'clock with Cissy's lawyer, Gerry Anderson. We have to talk about the will."

"It can wait! Gerry won't mind, trust me. You can call him on your cell phone from my car."

Puzzled, Katy shouldered her purse and started toward the door. "Give me one good reason why I should postpone hearing Aunt Cissy's last wishes?"

"Because Donny Alcorn is back, and he's talking a blue streak!"

CHAPTER Ten

Meredith Alcorn couldn't stop gazing at her son and hugging him to make sure he was really there. Outside their home on Willow Tree Lane, a knot of reporters clamored for quotes, and the doorbell hadn't stopped ringing. Harold, who had always handled the press with ease, had spent the past hour writing and rewriting his comments aided by his friend and attorney, Kurt Richardson.

Richardson's unsuccessful bid for Eden district attorney some years back had looked like the end of his political aspirations. Now with all the publicity he'd received as Alcorn's staunch legal supporter, Kurt felt sure his next run would be just the beginning.

Meredith remained oblivious of the political wrangling taking place in her living room. She only knew that her son was home again.

"Still hungry, baby?" she asked. Donny, who had already eaten two sandwiches at the SuperMart snack bar and a plate of spaghetti with meatballs plus two slices of apple pie at home, wiped his mouth with a linen napkin.

"Maybe a milk shake, Mom. Chocolate?"

Meredith kissed her oldest child and dashed toward the kitchen to find the syrup.

Unnoticed in the far corner of the room, Grace Alcorn watched her brother's eyes. Something didn't seem right to her, but she didn't dare mention it. Maybe it was the ravenous way Donny looked at their parents, as though he longed to consume them. Maybe it was the way he had no recollection of Amy's whereabouts—unbelievable for Donny. He'd been mad for Amy since their freshman year, and now he didn't seem to care that she was still missing.

Grace walked quietly to the window, gazing thoughtfully at the herd of reporters wandering about on their front lawn. The tulips she'd helped her mother plant last fall now sagged from the abuse they'd taken during the two-week siege. The grass, although still green, had grown sparse in spots. Grace wondered where the unwelcome swarm would go next. They were like locusts, she thought. Like a plague of locusts, taking all that lay in their path and giving back nothing in return.

Suddenly, her green eyes brightened. A brown Chevette had pulled into the circle drive in front of their home. She knew the car. It belonged to Joshua Carpenter. Throughout the last two weeks, Joshua had been the one ray of light in Grace's drab life. Something about the gangly newsman made her smile inside.

It wasn't a crush—at least, she didn't think so. It was more like deep admiration and trust. But he was pretty darn cute.

Rushing to the door, Grace opened it a crack and motioned to Joshua. *Drat,* she thought, *he isn't alone.* A woman who looked to be about her mom's age walked beside him. Grace thought she looked familiar, but she couldn't be sure.

"Mr. Carpenter!" Grace called, careful to keep the insistent pushing of the other reporters from bursting the door wide open. Pulling Katherine along, Joshua burrowed through the writhing knot of microphones toward the open doorway.

With Katy's hand firmly in his, he threaded his way through the tight opening and into the Alcorns' foyer.

Behind the pair, the swarm of reporters rushed toward the opportunity, but Joshua helped Grace squeeze the door shut before they could get in.

"Thanks, Grace!" he gasped.

"Oh, you're welcome, Mr. Carpenter. Mom's feeding Donny, and Dad's with Mr. Richardson in the living room. Who's this with you?" she asked breathlessly.

"I'm Katherine Adamson," Katy said, smiling. "You must be Grace Alcorn. Joshua didn't tell me how pretty you are."

Grace blushed, her red hair and freckles making the blush seem even more intense. "Thanks," she managed. "Come on into the dining room. It'll be more private in there. Dad won't care. He barely knows I'm here."

They followed the girl into the vaulted dining room. Taking a seat next to Katherine in matching Queen Anne side chairs, Joshua gave Grace his broadest smile. "How's Donny doing?"

Grace warmed herself in the smile Joshua gave her. Shyly smiling back, she said, "He's okay, I guess. He doesn't look like he was hurt or anything."

"Did he say where Amy is?" Katy asked, noting the admiration on Grace's freckled face. *Twelve years old,* she thought ruefully. *I remember twelve.*

"Nope."

"Has he said anything about what happened to them? Where they've been?" Joshua asked, deliberately choosing not to take out his notepad.

Grace shook her head. Katy watched her eyes. There was something there that disturbed her. Grace's eyes darted about nervously with the painful, dry look of someone who didn't dare cry. She was scared, but she didn't want to admit it.

"Joshua, perhaps we should hold back on the third degree for a moment. Grace, is it too much to ask for a cup of coffee?"

Grace looked relieved. "Oh, I'd be happy to get you some coffee. Black?"

"Tea for me, with a little milk, if it's not too much trouble," Joshua chimed in, not sure why Katy had shifted gears, but trusting her instincts.

"And I'll take three sugars and creamer, if you've got it."

"I'll only be a minute," Grace replied with a grin, jumping from the table and heading toward the kitchen.

"OK, so what's your gut say?" he asked Katherine once Grace had left the room.

"She's terrified of something, Josh. Didn't you see it? And this house, there's something way off here. Why didn't her dad come over to say hello or even order us out of his house? And why isn't the sheriff here?"

"Your writer's nose smell something amiss?"

Katy smiled. She hadn't realized until this moment just how much she missed writing. Who knew a trip to her hometown would spark the inner fires once again? Yes, something was wrong in Eden. Katy had sensed it from the first day, but her writer's nose, as Josh called it, smelled more than a story. It smelled the stench of something evil.

"You'd laugh if I told you what I think. But isn't it a fair question? I mean, shouldn't Sheriff Branham be here interviewing Donny, trying to find out what happened and where Amy is?"

Josh nodded. "Well, I think the sheriff did interview Donny when he picked him up at SuperMart, but Donny's parents refused to allow further grilling without Kurt Richardson's presence. I imagine Branham will be paying a call here later. Hey, wait a minute, I think Harold's heading outside."

Both rose as they watched Harold Alcorn, his attorney at his side, motion to reporters from within the half-open doorway.

"We'll be giving a statement in a moment. If you'll please have the podium ready with the microphone," Richardson directed. "Mr. Alcorn only wants to say this once."

"Podium?" Katy asked, leaning toward Josh in the shadow of the dining room's archway. "Is he kidding?"

"Look outside, Katy. Channel 6's satellite truck is here, and if I'm not mistaken, that big box truck behind it is the satellite feed to WNN."

"Wow. I didn't think the story was big enough for World News Network," Katy commented.

"Here's your coffee and tea," Grace said sweetly, coming up behind them with a large silver tray. "Daddy's going to be busy talking to the reporters, and Mom's gone upstairs to help Donny pick out an appropriate outfit for the cameras. So, we have a few minutes to talk."

Rejoining Grace at the mahogany table, Josh helped her push aside the dried hydrangea centerpiece to make room for the tray. "Looks delicious. Cookies, too, huh? Your mom make them?"

"I made them," Grace said proudly. "They were practice for 4-H, but I can bake another batch. They're snickerdoodles but with my own twist on the recipe. I add lemon extract."

"They're wonderful!" he gushed, noting the appreciative gleam in Grace's green eyes. "You are going to make some lucky guy a terrific wife."

Katherine kicked him under the table.

"Are you all right?" Grace asked, noticing Josh's sudden wince.

"Yes," he choked. "A charley horse, that's all. I've been spending too much time in the office and not enough in the field."

"You have a farm?" she asked with genuine interest.

"No," he answered, trying his best not to laugh. "Reporting, you know, in the field."

Embarrassed, Grace looked away. "Oh, yeah. I knew that. So, what else do you need to ask me? I don't know where Amy is, if that's what everyone wants to know. Donny doesn't know either. Donny doesn't seem to remember much of anything."

"He doesn't know where he's been for two weeks?" Katy asked, sipping her coffee.

"He thinks he was in a building, but he isn't sure. Daddy will probably tell it better in his speech. Did you know Daddy is going to run for mayor?"

Outside, Josh could hear a WNN producer testing the hookup and sound. Then a tall reporter who looked like he'd feel more at home on a movie set than the lawn of a small, Midwest town went live to announce the upcoming statement.

"...from the Alcorn family, who has spent the past eighteen days wondering if they would ever see their son again. This beleaguered family has put on a brave face for the nation as we've suffered with them, but the prayers of millions have now been answered. Donny Alcorn has come home."

Katherine shook her head. A typical Brent Snowden snow job. She had met Snowden, one of WNN's top investigative journalists, several years before at a book launch in Washington. Three martinis and several hundred signatures later, she'd even agreed to have dinner with him, but David had called from the road, and Katy had stayed up all night waiting for the man she thought she loved to join her. He never showed up.

I should have known then that something was up, she thought bitterly. *At least it kept me from ruining my life with the likes of Brent Snowden. He's better off married to his mirror. Baghdad Brent must be eating this up. Few stories galvanize viewers better than a missing child. Better yet, if that child becomes children, and those children are attractive and hail from the heartland, then the ratings go through the roof.*

Turning back toward the dining room, she watched Grace come to life as she talked with Joshua. At about the same age, Katherine had lost both her parents and moved in to the home of an aunt she had barely known. Twelve years isn't old enough to understand the complexities of the adult world, but it is enough to know pain. Katherine saw herself in Grace's tight shoulders and clenched hands. The girl's emerald eyes were rimmed in dark circles, and her pale skin looked drawn and stretched. She doubted that Grace had slept much during these two weeks. She loved her brother and her parents. But who was loving her?

Outside, Kurt Richardson had stepped up to the podium, and a dozen bright lights switched on. "He's about to make his speech," Katy said. "Do you want to go outside to stand with your father, Grace?"

Grace joined Katy at the window. Her small frame had begun to shake slightly. "No," she answered softly. "If it's all right, I'll just watch from here."

"It's fine," Katy replied, squeezing Grace's shoulder. "Go on out, Josh. You should be there to represent the paper."

Carpenter gulped his remaining tea and dabbed a few crumbs from his mouth. "I'll slip out the back and go around."

75

As he crossed the living room, he passed Donny and Meredith Alcorn as they descended the stairs. Donny, who had earlier been wearing his disheveled prom tuxedo, now wore light gray pants and a cream cotton sweater over a light blue oxford. As he passed by Joshua, Donny turned to face him, glaring at the newsman, his eyes dark with some unvoiced rage.

"Come on, Donald," his mother urged him, straightening her peach jacket. "It's national television, dear."

Donny turned from glaring at Joshua and followed his mother like an automaton.

"Weird," muttered Josh as he made for the back door. Coming around the swimming pool and through the privacy gate, Carpenter found his way to the back of the herd. Seeing no need to move up, he took out his notepad and listened.

"A miracle has happened in Eden," Richardson began. "Those of you who have been following this tragic story can now rejoice with our small town, for our prodigal son has come home. Donald Eugene Alcorn returned to us this morning, when he found his way to the SuperMart on Garden Drive. Now with a summary of what has happened since then, and with a statement of how the family is handling all of this, is a man many of you have come to think of as family over the course of these two weeks. Mr. Harold Alcorn."

Applause echoed through the subdivision, bounced off the satellite trucks, and filled the homes of millions of wide-eyed viewers. Harold Alcorn, dressed smartly in olive green trousers and a dapper fisherman's knit sweater in pale yellow, cleared his throat and spread several pages out before him on the podium.

"Before I get into the details of how Donald came back to us, I would like to thank all those Americans who have been praying with us. My wife Meredith and I, along with our daughter Grace, have felt your prayers and gained considerable strength through them. I also want to ask you to keep praying. Pray for Amy Horine, who is still missing, and for her mother, Maria Horine. Maria could not be here this morning. She wanted to remain at home in case there is word of her own child's return. It is our prayer that Amy's return is but moments away. Amy, honey, if you can hear and see us, your mother misses you, sweetheart. Come home to us."

Turning pages, Alcorn ran a hand through his thick, sandy hair and continued. "As Kurt said a moment ago, Donald returned to us this morning at SuperMart. Although he is still in a mild state of shock, my son is in relatively good health, and I'm happy to say, has an appetite befitting a college quarterback."

Several reporters pressed forward at this last comment.

"Did you say college?"

Holding up his hands in a calming manner, Alcorn smiled proudly. "That's right, we heard only an hour ago from Indiana University. Donald has been offered a full scholarship to attend IU as their second string quarterback for the upcoming fall. This deal's been in the works for several months, and Donny had hoped to be first string. However, with a summer spent training hard, we feel certain that Coach DiNardo will be using Donny a great deal this fall."

Katherine shook her head. Didn't this man even care that his son had undergone a terrifying ordeal? And what about Amy? What was he thinking? Was this really the right time to announce college plans?

"Daddy's really proud of Donny," Grace said, turning her head to one side to look for Joshua. "He's been working with Donny for years on his passing style. He says IU isn't great shakes as a football program, but it gave Trent Green a chance to show his stuff, so maybe Donny will get picked up by a major pro team. Daddy wants the Bears first, then maybe the Rams. He's not sure."

What a father, Katy thought, glancing at the antique mantel clock that graced the top of the buffet table. Eleven o'clock. She could make it to the lawyer's office for a quick meeting, then be at Sandy's in time for her mystery date at two. "I need to go, sweetheart. Is it all right if I go out the back, too?"

"Sure. I'll show you the way. May I call you Katherine?"

"I'd like that. And I'd like to see you again. What are you doing for lunch tomorrow? Would you be free for a movie? Oh, wait, do you have school?"

Grace beamed. "You bet I'm free! Daddy took me out of school right after Donny disappeared. And Mom won't care. Could we see *The Two Towers*? It's playing at the Encore Theater. I've already seen it lots of times, and we have the DVD set, but it's not the same as seeing it in the theater."

Katy had seen the movie, too, but she loved Tolkien, and Grace was right about the theater experience. "Done," she replied, shaking Grace's small hand. "I'll pick you up here at eleven-thirty. OK?"

"Done," Grace said with a giggle. "I'll wear my Frodo shirt. He's hot."

"Done and done." Grace then led her new friend to the pool entrance, where Katy waved good-bye and headed toward the circus on the front lawn. With a word to Joshua, the two agreed to leave early, but Katherine continued to watch the dog and pony show as Josh cranked up the old Chevette.

Donny, who had suddenly come to life, charmed the crowd, while his mother and father looked on with polished pride and synthetic smiles.

Unseen and unnoticed, Grace looked on from the dining room window, her small face pale and tense. As the reporters broke into spontaneous applause, a solitary tear slid down her freckled cheek. The Chevette turned out of the drive, and she waved, glad to have made a friend. Now there were two people to trust.

CHAPTER **Eleven**

TUESDAY AFTERNOON

The waiting room clock was just striking twelve-thirty as Katherine walked through the frosted glass doors that led to Gerry Anderson's suite of offices. Katy had left Joshua at the *Chronicle* building, walking back to Cissy's house where she took her car and drove across town as quickly as she could without breaking any laws.

"Good afternoon," the brightly attired receptionist said. She wore a headphone/microphone combination over perfectly coifed chestnut hair, so she could type while answering phones. The unmistakable scent of L'air du Temp filled the air, and Katherine was sure she recognized last year's Chanel suit. The woman looked right at her with an ear-to-ear smile that would put Miss America to shame.

Katy returned the smile, shuffling her purse from her left shoulder to her right. There was something about law offices that always made her jumpy.

"I'm Katherine Adamson, and I..." she started.

"We've been expecting you, Miss Adamson. I'm Paige Wilson, Mr. Anderson's paralegal. And may I say your book jacket photos don't do you justice. Mr. Anderson is the last door on the right."

"Thanks," was all Katy could manage, and she walked past the woman, who had buzzed the back office to notify her boss of Katherine's arrival.

"You're very welcome, Miss Adamson. And I love your new haircut."

"Thanks again," Katy said, running a hand through the short thatch of auburn. "Maybe I'll keep it."

"Katherine!" the pudgy attorney gushed, meeting her in the hallway with a gap-toothed smile and a firm handshake. "Come in! Come in!"

She followed him into the walnut-paneled office, wondering why Aunt Cissy would choose an attorney with such garish taste in clothes. Katy had known men with poor taste, and she'd known men who were color-blind. Now, she was certain she'd met a man who suffered both afflictions.

"Sit down, please. Would you like a soda? Coffee? We have a great coffee cake in the back," he said with a jovial laugh.

OK, so he won't win any fashion shows, but he does come off as genuine, although he seems more like an insurance salesman than a lawyer. "No thanks. I had a big breakfast. And I just had some coffee at the Alcorn place."

Anderson's bushy eyebrows shot up as he sat down. "You were at the Alcorns' today? Big news, right? I heard Donny came home."

"He did," she answered, lowering her purse to the floor. "That's why I'm late. Josh Carpenter is an old friend, and he asked if I'd accompany him there. It's really incredible, don't you think?"

Gerry looked like a man torn between the truth and a lie. Katy knew that face well. Generally, David had chosen the lie.

"I don't know if I should say this, Katherine, but I'm not sure about that whole business. Now, I don't know the Alcorns all that well—I meet them now and then at the country club, but we don't really travel in the same circles as a rule. Anyway, Harold Alcorn hasn't shown—well, he just hasn't seemed all that torn up, if you catch my meaning."

Katy knew just what he meant. Harold Alcorn had seemed more caught up in his own public image than in his son's welfare. He'd make a great politician.

"Well, I did notice some of that when I was there, but, as you say, I don't know him. He has been under a great deal of stress, though. It's hard to say how one might react to such a trial."

"You've got that right, Katy. You don't mind if I call you that, do you? I mean, after meeting with your aunt so many times, I've heard a lot of Katy stories, and I feel I know you. I hope I'm not being too forward."

He meant it. Maybe Aunt Cissy wasn't such a bad judge of character after all. "Not at all, Mr. Anderson."

"Gerry. Everyone calls me Gerry. I'm just a regular guy who happens to have a law degree, Katy. My wife picked out this office. Me, I preferred the old office. One room and a convenience. That was enough for me. And Doris picked out the gal out front. Paige Wilson is her name. She's studying pre-law at the college, and Doris thought she'd class the place up. I guess she does. Anyway, I'm just an old Kentucky boy with his feet in Indiana. You ever been to Letcher County, Kentucky, Kate?"

Katy laughed softly. She was beginning to like this man. "Gerry, I can honestly say no to that. I take it you're a Letcher County native?"

"Born and raised," he said happily. "I met Doris during law school in Lexington. She's the one who wanted to move to Indiana. Her grandparents were here. Oh, I don't blame her, and she's happy enough. She hangs out with Jean Davis and that Historical Society bunch. Me, all I need is a stout leather Lazy Boy, a John Wayne movie, and a bag of pork rinds."

"You're a charmer, Gerry. No wonder Aunt Cissy chose you as her attorney."

"Why, thank you, Kate."

"My pleasure, Ger."

Gerry grinned from ear to ear, his balding pate glowing with pride. "You are every bit as generous a lady as your aunt said. Now, I know you're pressed for time. You have a late luncheon engagement, if I remember from your phone call. It's too bad. I'd be happy to take you to one of my favorite haunts, Emmy Lou's Diner on Third. Best beans and corn bread this side of Whitesburg."

"I'll have to make that another time, Gerry. But I'll hold you to it. Now, as you say, we'd better get down to business."

Anderson plucked a fat file from the drawer to his left. "Let's see," he began, settling a pair of half-glasses on the end of his bulbous nose. "Your aunt had a sizable estate, considering she didn't give a fig about money. There's the house, of course, and all the property associated with it, which amounts to about an acre. Nice place. Did you know that house was built by the founder of Eden, Stromie Amburgey?"

Katy nodded. "I've heard the story. My great-great-grandfather won the house from him in a card game. Stromie moved west after that, leaving his wife and seven kids without support or reputation. He passed through Illinois and ended up near Cape Girardeau in Missouri. Seems his gambling ways caught up with him one night, and he was shot dead by a sixteen-year-old kid. Supposedly, the kid was his own seventh child, who'd been bought from his mother by an Indian named Walking Tree."

Gerry's eyes lit up, and he leaned forward, his leather chair creaking with the weight. "That's right! That boy'd been a handful for poor old Widow Amburgey, as she called herself. I guess she figured callin' herself a widow brought a smack of respectability. Do you know the whole story?"

"There's more?" Katy asked, fascinated.

"Her youngest son, Jackson, had been a pill from day one, and his poor mama bore up as long as she could, but this Indian passed through town—let's see, it was sometime around 1814 or '15, I think. His name was Walking Tree, a name he'd been given 'cause of his being over seven feet tall—a mighty big size for anybody, but particularly big for an Indian. This feller claimed to be descended from an ancient tribe that had come from a hole in the ground down south somewhere.

"Anyway," he continued, clearly delighted to share his treasury of town lore, "Walking Tree taught Jackson all he knew about survival and even taught him to read and write. The pair decided to track down Jackson's father, so they followed news of him through the Vincennes settlement and on into St. Louis. It's said they finally caught up with him in Cape.

"The story goes that Jackson, who'd gone from being a pill to being just plain nuts, challenged his dad to a poker game, putting up a considerable stake. Old Stromie couldn't resist—he was tapped out and owed everybody in town, including the undertaker, who had promised to collect one way or the other. Stromie won the first hand and the second, but he should've stopped there. You see, he was placin' a bet on the third hand—the pot bein' up to five thousand dollars at this point—when a trim and perky woman waltzed into the saloon, catchin' Stromie's eye.

"He gave her a wink and tipped his hat—Stromie fancied he was a ladies' man, you might know, but he was pretty well dried up by this time, and the most any woman saw in Stromie was an easy way to get a free drink. Stromie, like I was sayin', he tips his hat, and the lady gives him a smile. 'Hi there,' he says to her, no doubt thinkin' how he'd spend the five grand on showin' her a good time. But that pot didn't have his name on it.

"Nope. Jackson, who was in fact the common-law husband of the perky little lady, took advantage of his daddy's distraction to draw his gun and shoot the smile right off old Stromie's face. As he lay dyin', Stromie asked why, not recognizin' his own kin, and Jackie spit in his face. 'I got you,' he was heard to say. 'Just let the papers say Crazy Jackie finally caught up to his no account pa!'

"With that, Jackson scooped the pot into his hat, grabbed his wife's hand, and was out of town before the blood had dried on Stromie's waistcoat. The undertaker had his day, though. He used Stromie's stuffed and wax-covered corpse as a dummy in his window for the next two-and-a-half years."

"I'd never heard that bit before!" Katherine said. She hadn't laughed this hard in a long time, and she wiped her eyes, not caring at that moment that her eye makeup had begun to run. "Gerry, you are not only a fount of information, but a great storyteller to boot!"

Gerry smiled, blushing slightly. "It's just tellin' the truth, that's all. There's a whole lot more about Stromie and his brother Stuffley, but I wouldn't want to make you late for your lunch meeting."

Katy glanced at her watch. One o'clock. She would have to go soon. Sandy's was downtown, nearly a thirty-minute drive from Anderson's west county office. "I do need to leave soon,

Gerry, but you must promise that we'll get together again before I leave town, OK?"

"My pleasure, little lady. Now, let's get back to it. I'll give you a copy of the will, and you can read through it. What it amounts to is that you are the sole heir. Cissy had several accounts at Eden Home Bank, as well as a couple at Eden County National. She made some sound investments. In fact, the total of her cash and investments adds up to over a million dollars."

Katherine's jaw dropped. "Did you say a million?"

"Oh, yeah. Cissy hardly ever spent on herself. She gave a lot to charity, but she also squirreled a lot away. She told me she just wanted to give you the nest egg your daddy would have given you if he'd lived. How about if I stop by Cissy's, I mean, your house tomorrow morning? I'll give you all the bankbooks, and we'll finish up the paperwork so you can claim your inheritance."

"Well, uh, tomorrow morning isn't the best, unless it's before ten or so. I'm meeting Grace Alcorn for an early lunch and a movie."

Gerry smiled, closing the folder and removing his glasses. "Good. That little girl needs a friend right now. OK, then. How about if I were to come by after the movie? Say, just after suppertime? Seven o'clock be all right?"

"Make it eight, and that will be fine, Gerry. I'll see you then. And thanks—for everything. I am so glad we met."

Katherine left the office, and Gerald Anderson returned to the file. Suddenly, he slapped his head, rolling his eyes. He had forgotten to tell her about the diary! He'd have to do his best to recall it later, because he didn't dare make a reminder note. He couldn't risk anyone else knowing about it. Not after all Cissy's careful planning. He just hoped this little lady would know what to do with it.

CHAPTER Twelve

Maria Horine had spent most of this agonizing morning either on the telephone or answering the front door. As reporters slowly abandoned their posts in front of the Alcorn home, their numbers had inversely accumulated in Maria's cramped front garden.

She'd called Father Gregory to see if he could come by, but his housekeeper had explained that he had driven to Indianapolis that morning to meet with Bishop O'Brien and that he would return her call as soon as he checked in that afternoon for his messages. Since Father Gregory's meetings were scheduled to last through the weekend, he might not be able to meet with her personally until Monday.

In other words, Maria thought gloomily, *you're on your own.* She shouldn't have expected much more; she wasn't really one of his flock. But how could she go to Mass? She had been divorced. She couldn't take communion or go to confession until the Church had formally approved the divorce and granted her an annulment. An annulment would mean her beautiful daughter Amy would be considered an illegitimate child. That would never do.

Maria had raised Amy in a local Methodist church. The minister had been kind and the sermons soothing. Amy had gone through confirmation in junior high, and she had even shown an interest in going to Wesleyan University in Indianapolis.

Maria had failed as a Catholic. How could God listen to her? Yet, she felt that He heard. She had taken to reading the King James Bible that Amy had been given on the date of her formal confirmation. The small white book with its delicate gold edging had comforted Maria in the dark hours of waiting. She wanted to believe what it said in Romans 8:28, that God could work even this horror into something good.

The strange Voice on the phone had promised her that Amy would come back. Had the Alcorns received a similar call? Would Amy just as suddenly reappear in some local store, dazed and asking for help?

The sharp jangling of the blue princess telephone jolted Maria from her inner dialogue. Running to the threadbare armchair that sat near the phone, she grabbed the receiver. "Yes? Amy?"

The deep, resonant, nearly mechanical voice startled her. "You have been faithful, haven't you? You have not revealed my presence?"

"Who is this?"

"Maria, you must keep believing. I will return her to you, but you must not waiver. Do you believe in me?"

She began to tremble, her eyes darting to the window where a small crowd of reporters chatted, sipped at coffee cups, and nibbled on sandwiches. The WNN satellite truck had pulled into a neighbor's driveway, and several technicians tumbled out of the cab, followed by an elegantly dressed man with a neatly trimmed beard.

"Why should I believe in you?" she asked the Voice, clutching the small white Bible to her heart. "Tell me! Is Amy alive?"

Silence.

"Do you have her? Send her home, please! You can take me, just let her go!"

Silence.

"Please, please, please," Maria sobbed, slumping to her knees. "I'll believe anything you say, just please let me talk to my daughter!"

"That's better," the Voice answered huskily. She could hear a wheezing in the background and a sharp, high hum like the sound emitted by big transformers. "Do you believe in *me*?"

"I believe," she whispered tightly. "I'll believe anything."

Soft laughter. "Good. You will hear from me soon, Maria. Very soon. Tell no one. My time is not yet."

Click.

She dropped the phone into her lap, fear and grief raining down her pale face. A maniac had her baby. And she could tell no one.

Not even God.

In a small house not unlike Maria's, across town on the west side of Eden, a shriveled man wrote unsteadily in a notebook. His tobacco-stained fingers gripped the yellow barrel of his number two pencil so tightly his nails had blanched, nearly drained of blood.

With his left hand, he flicked a long cigarette ash into a green, frog-shaped ashtray—a gift from his only grandson, made proudly at scout camp. The unfiltered smoke tasted of death, but his cravings shouted far louder than the cries of the grave. Coughing, his fragile body shook with the spasm in his

89

lungs. He would have to turn the oxygen back on, suck up a bit of life.

But first, he had to finish the entry.

The point of the pencil had dulled to near worthlessness, and his words were scratched into the page as much as written. "Blast!" he cried out, the effort sending his lungs into painful cramps. "No time for this," he said aloud. In the seventeen years since Elizabeth's death, he'd learned to talk to himself, ever hoping she might hear.

Next to his duct-taped recliner stood an adjustable hospital tray on wheels, laden with packs of cigarettes and sharpened pencils along with half a dozen Clark Bar wrappers. The old man reached for a new pencil and continued his entry. His writing, though small and shaky, was legible. The words ran out of the pencil in a steady stream, graphite testimonies of twenty years of watching.

He would die soon, he knew that well enough. But not without leaving the truth for someone else to find. He may be old and barely able to breathe, but he knew a dragon fighter would come, and his diaries—prophetic paintings in scribbled words—would guide the slayer to his prey.

...the unholy child must die. Watch for the virgin with the belly of death. She must not be allowed to live. The false Elijah will be a lie and a liar. You mustn't trust. You must only act. See what isn't there. See...

The coughing seized him again, tossing him backward and forward like a rag doll. The old man dropped the pencil, snapping the lead. Time for a break. He reached for the slender, clear tube that hung from his neck, fitting it into his nostrils. *There, suck on that,* he thought. *Live another day and write another day and pray another day.*

The old man's faded brown eyes filled with water. *God, please, don't take me yet. Let me live just one more day.* Gradually, the spasms in his lungs passed, and his frantic heart settled into an uncertain sinus rhythm.

He wiped his eyes, glancing through the dirty picture window that formed his only eye to the outside world. The unmarked truck was still there. Nearly two hours had passed, and the two men lingering by the truck's side door hadn't moved an inch. They wore gray uniforms without writing, but the old man knew who had sent them, as well as why.

Time was running out.

Pushing against the arms of the tattered chair, he reached for another pencil. Behind him, the walls were lined with bookcases, filled with identical green plastic binders, each labeled in the same hand, a hand that had grown shakier with each passing year.

The old man settled the pencil against the clean white page before him. The green three-ring binder in which it rested was nearly full.

One more page, he thought. *Then, I can rest.*

CHAPTER Thirteen

Where had the day gone? Katherine pushed open one of the glass doors that led into Sandy's Place. Located downtown near the county courthouse, Sandy's was the most recent incarnation of an old brick factory. Once the home of the Ohio River Brick and Ironworks, the three-story building had been built in 1827, when Eden was young.

Through the years since then, the voiceless walls had echoed to the ring of hammers, the clatter of sewing machines, the hum of generators, and the endless clicking of typewriter keys. With the closure of Imel's Shoe Factory thirty years before, the immense rooms on the first and second floors had been subdivided into a trendy antiques mall called The Ironworks. The third floor, accessed by a circa 1930 Otis elevator, hosted a brightly painted sports bar called Sandy's and a snobby coffee roaster called Stromie's Blend.

During the day, the interior of Sandy's seemed bright and garish. The high ceiling tiles had been painted black so the dozens of neon signs that hung there appeared to be suspended from nothing. Two grand oak and brass bars flanked the interior, sandwiching a sunken main floor lined with private booths and dotted with twenty highly polished round tables, each surrounded by at least four wooden chairs. Irish music filled the air during most afternoons. At night, however, the lights dimmed and the flickering screens of six big-screen televisions came to life, broadcasting football, basketball, and baseball, as the season demanded.

Katy hadn't been here since before Sandy Emerson's death in 1994. Sandy had been well loved by most of Eden's locals as a welcoming host and a genuine gossip. If it walked, talked, and drank, Sandy knew its darkest secrets. His untimely demise on the eve of his fiftieth birthday had been a tragedy that continued to baffle the sheriff's office.

Sandy, it seemed, had remained behind to count the night's receipts after bidding good night to the last of his waitresses, Jessica Goodyear. Jessica's police statement indicated she had left early to study for her final exam in biochemistry.

No one knew exactly what happened after Jessica's departure, but Sandy Emerson had been found by the assistant manager the following morning at nine-seventeen, folded into a position quite foreign to human anatomy, lying atop the southern bar, precariously poised upon an unnatural bed of thirty-three green beer bottles.

Since then, the bar had only become more popular.

It was just before two, when Katy followed the gum-chewing hostess to a non-smoking booth. "I'll be meeting someone," she explained, not sure how she would know this stranger. "Is Linda Kemp working today?"

"She's in the office. Did you have a complaint?" the girl asked, giving Katy a menu and a suspicious glance.

"Oh, no! I'm an old friend from college. If she's not too busy, could you tell her Katherine Adamson is here. I'd love to see her again. It's been a while."

The girl smiled, obviously relieved. "I'll be right back. Your server will be Rachel. She'll be with you in a moment."

While she waited for Rachel, Katherine checked her cell phone for messages. As she'd feared, there were three from George McMahon and one from David, his third that week. She deleted David's without listening to his packs of lies. As to George's pleas, she made a mental note to return the calls that evening.

"Katherine?" asked a woman's voice.

Katy looked up, returning the phone to her purse. "Linda? Can that be you?"

Linda Kemp had never been a prize during her years in the Liberty-Thayer Journalism School at Eden College. Tall for a girl, a somewhat heavy six feet, she had towered over many of her male classmates. Thick glasses covered the possible beauty of chestnut eyes, and although her dark blond hair had a certain loveliness, she had paid little attention to its arrangement, preferring to wear a severe ponytail at the nape of her neck.

Linda's manner with boys had always been brusque and contentious. Katherine, who had been two years ahead of Linda, had felt a deep compassion for the ugly duckling but had enjoyed no success in changing her feathers.

Apparently, someone else had.

Before her eyes, Katherine viewed an amazingly transformed woman. Naturally, time and maturity might have a positive effect on anyone's appearance, but in Linda's case, time had performed a miracle. Seeming taller than ever, she had slimmed considerably, and her formerly dark blond hair was now bleached to near platinum and cut in a flattering blunt cut near her jaw line. She wore a sleeveless navy turtleneck over a red linen pencil skirt, showing off her slender hips to perfection. She could easily have graced the cover of any fashion magazine.

"You look wonderful!" Katy gushed honestly, shaking Linda's hand firmly. The bar's owner smiled, showing off an expensive smile of perfectly matched white teeth.

"You think so?" she asked, her voice sounding genuine. "I've had a little work done. Age takes a toll. You look as slim as ever."

Katy laughed. "Maybe I do now. You should have seen me a few months ago. I looked like a short round balloon from Macy's parade. Too much traveling and too many fried chicken luncheons. The woes of a writer, I guess."

"You're anything but that now," Linda replied. "Like I said, you've hardly changed. Except for your hair, of course. I like the short cut."

"I'm getting used to it. So, you own Sandy's now?"

Sitting, Linda flashed the perfect smile again. "It's not what I had imagined for myself back in school. You know, I'd always pictured myself slaving away for some small but honest newspaper, digging out the stories that matter to real people. But here I am, dispensing beer and sandwiches to armchair jocks. Honestly, it's not as bad as it sounds. I actually like it. I'm making money, and I've even met someone."

"I'm glad, Linda."

"You're doing well!" she said. "I've read all your books. I especially liked the one—oh, let's see, what was it called? The one made into a movie? Oh, yes! *The Jonas Diaries*. That one kept me up at night for weeks!"

Katy laughed. "It kept me up for months! Getting into the mind of a serial killer, especially a real one, is not exactly restful."

"Didn't you interview Thomas Allen Stroud for the book?"

"Seven times. He gave me more information than I ever wanted. I still have nightmares about it sometimes. He's in hell now, if there's any justice."

Linda looked up as Rachel, the waitress, arrived. "Good afternoon, Miss Kemp. Will you be eating as well?"

"Oh, no. I need to get back to work," she answered with a nod toward the office.

Rachel looked puzzled. "I was told this table would be for two," she mumbled, her head cocked to one side. "It's for one then?"

"It's for two," a man's voice answered from behind Rachel.

The three women turned to look at the new arrival.

The man stood a few inches shorter than Linda, and his form was hardly that of an athlete. He wore glasses, perched on the end of a sharp, thin nose, and he looked to be in his mid to late fifties. He wore no wedding ring, and his tweed sports coat spoke of quality but showed fraying at the cuffs. He had small eyes behind the horn-rimmed glasses, but his mouth was wide, and his square face showed the lines of a man who had once loved to laugh but had forgotten how.

"Miss Adamson?" he asked, looking anxiously toward Katherine.

"Yes," she replied tentatively. "Won't you join me?"

Linda moved aside, making room for the man to pass. "Professor Fields! So this is your mysterious lunch guest, Katherine. Rachel, give them whatever they want. It's on the house."

"Linda, that's not necessary," Katy protested.

Kemp raised a manicured hand. "I insist. In return, maybe you can sign a copy of one of your books."

"I'd have done that anyway. Really, you don't have to..."

"No, no! It's done. Rachel, whatever they want. Just send the bill to my office."

With that, she left the pair alone. After taking their orders, Rachel headed for the kitchen, giving Katherine a chance to discover the reason for the professor's clandestine request.

"So, Professor Fields, do you always come on to women this way?"

The shy man shook his head. He had a graying comb-over that barely hid the shine of his crown. An obvious bachelor, but a seemingly kind man. "Oh, Miss Adamson, I hope you don't think I would—I mean, I would never..."

"Relax, Professor. I'm only kidding. What can I do for you?"

Wiping his forehead, he glanced around the room furtively. "I don't wish to be overheard, you know. And I have no doubt you'll find my story outlandish, but I assure you what I have to tell you is perfectly true."

"And what is it you have to tell me?"

"That—that, our little town is being visited, Miss Adamson," he whispered, his voice barely audible.

"I don't doubt it, Professor. The tourist trade in Eden has grown by leaps and bounds since my last trip home."

He shook his head so sharply, his glasses nearly fell from his nose. "No, no! I'm not talking about tourists! Good heavens, who would care whether or not tourists were visiting Eden? God knows they're rude and contentious, but even they have their place. No! It's the other kind of visitor I'm speaking about. The—the unwanted, undesirable kind. I am sure you of all people will understand. You did, after all, write *Gray Anatomy* and *Cydonia's Child,* did you not?"

"Guilty of both, but I don't see what those books have to do with Eden."

"They have everything to do with Eden!" he half shouted, growing red in the face.

Fields glanced about quickly, clearly embarrassed. "Do forgive me, Miss Adamson. I am not a nutcase, as you must be starting to think. I've lived and taught in Eden for twelve years now, and I have seen things."

Had Katherine met this man only twenty-four hours before, she would certainly have put him down as a lunatic. However, the Eden she had seen since her arrival was a changed city, and she wondered if there might not be some semblance of truth to his beliefs, no matter how irrational they might sound.

"Professor, I do not think you're a nutcase. In fact, I would like to speak to you about the specifics of your suspicions. Can you tell me exactly why you think Eden is being—uh, visited?"

"Didn't you hear what happened at Miller's Farm two nights ago? And there have been dozens of other landings. I have over a hundred photos taken of crop circles that have appeared in corn and soybean fields locally. And I have..."

He stopped as Rachel arrived with their meals. "Is there anything else?" she asked.

Both shook their heads, and she headed off toward the kitchen. Fields stared at his reuben on rye, his button eyes glazing over.

"Did she get the order wrong?" Katy asked. Her own cheeseburger and seasoned fries had arrived with no problem. Did he need ketchup or something?

"Professor? Should I call her back?"

"No—no. It's just—it's just that, I've remembered I need to grade some papers. I should really be going, Miss Adamson. Good heavens, here you are trying to spend some time enjoying your hometown, and I'm blathering on about foolishness. I hope you haven't believed anything I've said. I'm always making a silly fool of myself. Please, please, forget all about it. And I hope you have a pleasant visit."

He rose suddenly, snatched up his scuffed leather satchel, and made directly for the glass doors.

Puzzled, Katherine searched the room to see if someone might be staring in the direction of their booth, but everyone else seemed to be caught up in their own conversations. She then took a look at the professor's plate. His demeanor had changed drastically when the food had arrived. Perhaps a clue lay somewhere in or on his plate.

Pulling the blue and white china closer, Katherine saw nothing out of place at first. The reuben looked well grilled, and the accompanying fries were hot and crisp. Then she saw it. Buried beneath the fries, plainly visible, were three words, written in small capitals, apparently in grease pencil, upon the white face of the plate.

WE'RE WATCHING YOU.

Katherine looked up, but the professor had disappeared. Waving to Rachel, she asked the waitress for a box for her sandwich.

"Is there something wrong, Miss?" the girl asked, her unlined face growing dark with worry. "The professor left suddenly, and now—it isn't the food, is it?"

"You know the professor?"

"Sure, doesn't everybody? He teaches at EC. My boyfriend had him for mythology last semester. Should I box up his sandwich?"

"Can you tell me who prepared this for him?" Katy asked.

"Oh, it is bad, isn't it? We have a new cook today, and we've had a few complaints. I'll take it back."

"No! Leave it here. I'll—I'll box it up for him. The professor will want it. He just had to hurry back to grade some papers. Can you tell me what building he's in? I'd like to take it to him."

"The humanities building on the south side of campus. It's on the riverside, overlooking the cliffs. Should I get Miss Kemp?"

Standing, Katherine gave the poor girl her best smile. "Please don't. Thank her for me, will you? And tell her I'll sign that book when I see her next. I'll be staying in Eden for a while. All right?"

Rachel nodded, heading off to fetch two Styrofoam boxes.

While she was gone, Katherine reached into her purse and removed her PDA. Last Christmas, after years of getting by with pen and notepad, Katy had finally purchased the combination handheld and digital camera. She'd thought the added camera an extravagance at first, but the salesman had convinced her that an author should always have a camera handy. He'd proven it by having his manager snap a photo of himself with Katherine. The compact Sony also featured a digital voice recorder and a wireless interface for accessing her e-mail. Although she'd had little need for the camera since then, she silently thanked the persistent salesman as she surreptitiously snapped several photos of the plate and the lettering.

"Here you go," the girl said upon returning. "Is there anything else I can do for you?"

"I don't think so," Katherine answered, pocketing the small computer and scooping the meals into their respective boxes. "Oh, would you have a grease pencil in the kitchen? I'd like to mark the Professor's box so I don't mix them up."

"I don't think so," the girl answered. "We have some markers, and I have a ball point, but I haven't seen any—wait a minute! Dennis was using a grease pencil this morning to checkmark the orders. He's the new cook. We're supposed to get them marked by the cook, so we know who prepared each plate."

"Could you ask Dennis if I might borrow it—just for a minute?"

Rachel headed to the kitchen but returned quickly. Her face was red, and she panted from the pace. "I'm so sorry!" she said, catching her breath. "Dennis apparently left early. I can get you one of the markers."

Katy shrugged, proud of her sleuthing skills. "Oh, that's all right, Rachel. I'll just put the professor's on top of mine in the car. I don't know why I didn't think of that before. I appreciate your help, though. Here, I'd like to give you a tip."

"Oh, no! Miss Kemp said this was on the house!" the girl objected.

She looks thin, Katherine thought. And there was something about her run-down shoes that reminded Katy of so many other students she'd known back in school. "No, I insist. You earned it." She gave Rachel a twenty.

"I can't!" she whispered, trying not to attract attention.

"You can, and you will. You know, I might be writing a book about Eden College and what it's like to be a student nowadays. Would you be available for an interview sometime?"

The girl's eyes sparkled. "Oh, yes! I'll give you my phone number." She wrote her number on the back of a blank guest check and handed it to Katy. "I've only read one of your books, Miss Adamson, but I thought it was wonderful. If you ever make another film of one, I'd love to be considered. I'm an actress, you know."

"I thought so," Katherine replied, glancing at the girl's fine handwriting and mentally comparing it to the china plate words. No similarities.

"Call me anytime. You can always leave a message on my machine if I'm not in," Rachel said happily.

"I will," Katy promised and grabbed the boxes, heading for the exit. She would take the professor's box to the college later. For now, she intended to head home. The morning had exhausted her, and she had a feeling she would need energy for dealing with the perplexing Professor Fields.

CHAPTER Fourteen

It was nearly three-thirty by the time Katherine pulled in to the bricked driveway behind Aunt Cissy's house. Turning off the engine, she noticed the dog next door had started his nightly concert several hours early. She would have to visit the owners of the Apple Tree Inn and see if anything might be done about the dog's woeful and very annoying howls.

Nearly forgetting the take-away boxes, she leaned back in to retrieve them from the front seat, then closed and locked the car's doors. She would have her lunch, much delayed and no doubt cold, then she'd return George McMahon's call, giving him the good news that she had found a new story. Tonight, K. C. Adamson would begin her thirteenth novel, and it would be centered around people she had grown up with, people she thought she had known, but who were proving to be stranger and stranger with each passing moment.

Letting herself in the back door, Katherine kicked off her shoes as soon as she hit the kitchen. She set her handbag down and turned on a small transistor radio near the sink for noise. Last night's station had faded, so she dialed until she found another, noting the music had a classical sound. That would be nice background music while she had a quick bite. Perhaps she'd take a long hot bath, too. Her creative juices were flowing, and she had a hunch this would be a long night.

"Aunt Cissy, why didn't you own a microwave?" she asked out loud, looking everywhere for signs of modern touches to the old kitchen. *Note to Katy: Head over to SuperMart and buy a microwave and a new radio.* There were groceries to buy, too. Katherine knew writing a book could mean months of hard work, so she might as well stock up. After all, like Gerry Anderson said, this was her house now.

It felt strange even thinking it.

Anderson was right. Celeste had wanted her to have this house, and the least Katy could do was spend some time here. What was there in St. Louis to call her back? No one and nothing. She had no pets. She owned a small 1920s bungalow in Kirkwood, but she had a neighbor checking in on it now and then, so that would be fine. As a writer, she took her office with her—a notebook, a pen, and a laptop were all she needed. She'd need a printer, and she'd definitely need access to the Internet. *Additional note: Ask Joshua if Eden has broadband.*

A Mozart piece had begun to play on the small yellow radio, fading in and out, but audible enough, so Katherine sat at the kitchen table and opened the Styrofoam box. She gulped down the cold cheeseburger and fries, then poured a tall glass of water from the tap. Chasing the big meal with the cool water, she felt revived. Her internal radar had been signaling for the last hour, and she itched to start writing. She'd need to talk to Joshua about the missing teens again. She'd need background material.

Then she remembered Brent Snowden and WNN's remote truck. Dashing into the TV room, a small but cozy space that was actually a four-season porch, Katy prayed Aunt Cissy hadn't cancelled her cable service.

Sitting on a three-legged table, perched oddly upon a hand-crocheted doily, was a small but relatively new 13" color set with a happy little cable coming out its back panel. "Yes!" Katherine cried out in victory. She turned on the set and fished around for a remote, which she found tucked into a wicker basket next to the television.

The little television hummed as it warmed up, and the screen flickered a couple of times before popping on with full picture and sound. The home and gardening channel's afternoon line-up met Katherine's eyes, and she pressed the remote's channel up button, past the home improvement channels, past the shopping channels, and stopped at the first news station. Two more channels up she found a story about the North Korea stalemate.

It looked like the UN would declare North Korea in violation of the resolutions passed by the security council in September, leaving it no alternative but to give the signing nations permission to disarm the small country in much the same manner as the Alliance of the Willing had disarmed and deposed Saddam Hussein under the leadership of Bush and Blair. The commentator droned on and on about the drain on the nation's unbalanced budget and whether or not the U.S. should take on a new front while still policing both Iraq and Syria. Since Russia's saber rattling about Israel had begun, it looked as though World War III was approaching, or so most of the pundits proclaimed, and President Shepherd's military measures against North Korea might have to wait.

Although she usually consumed foreign policy, Katherine had no interest in international preludes to war. Not tonight. She wanted news from Eden.

Clicking the up button once more, she found WNN and discovered the beginning of the very story she had been looking for.

Brent Snowden stood in front of the Alcorn home with mic in hand, his hair perfectly coifed, and his voice perfectly modulated. "...However, there is still no word of Donny's girlfriend and classmate, Amy Maria Horine."

From the WNN studio, a blond anchorwoman asked, "Brent, does law enforcement there have any clues as to where Donny was being held?"

Adjusting his earpiece, the reporter shook his head. "I had a little trouble hearing you, Sheila, but if I got your question right, Sheriff Branham is still looking into Donny's account of the kidnapping. Apparently, there are certain aspects that don't add up so far. Of course, Alcorn had undergone a terrifying ordeal, and doctors here agree that it's quite possible that his memory might have certain gaps."

"On a lighter side, Brent, have you had an opportunity to investigate the other big story coming out of Eden, Indiana? Have you seen any UFOs?"

The seasoned reporter laughed. "Well, Sheila, locals will be quick to tell you the night skies around Eden have been filled with strange lights lately, but many of the more skeptical among them also remember a time seventeen years ago when similar lights were reported. The cause was finally determined to be an unusual southerly display of the northern lights."

"Thanks, Brent. We'll see you back here tomorrow."

"That's right, Sheila. I'll be back in Washington for Vladimir Putin's visit to the White House, but I understand you will be replacing me here in Eden, taking us live to cover the Eden High tribute to Amy Horine."

"That's right, Brent. Save me a seat at Sandy's, OK? I understand that's the place for fries in Eden."

"I'll put in your reservation. For now, this is Brent Snowden, reporting live from Eden, Indiana."

Sheila Van Williams shuffled the papers on her desk, turning from the big screen to her left and toward the camera. "Now, to Tony Thompson in New York City with the latest on the terrifying school shooting last week."

Katherine turned off the set. She considered calling the Tulip Tree to see if Snowden had checked out yet, but dismissed the notion. It had been several years since they'd met, and she wasn't sure he'd even remember her. Besides, her instincts were screaming that Eden's quiet, rolling hills were hiding a story of immense proportions, and she didn't want to tip her hand to a seasoned newshound like Snowden.

She weighed her options. The time was nearly five-thirty, and her belly was full, but her eyes had grown weary with the meal and the brief rest. *An object at rest tends to stay at rest,* she thought ruefully. That was how she'd packed on the pounds before. Better get up and do something.

Phone calls.

Dashing toward the front of the house, she found the stylish 1955 black telephone sitting in its usual position atop a gate-legged cherry table near the south bay window. Cissy had installed the phone here, rather than in the kitchen, so she could sit in her front window seat and keep an eye on her cat while talking to friends.

Cissy had spent a good part of each morning chatting back then. Living alone, and using a walker most days, the retired schoolteacher had loved checking in with her old cronies every morning between nine and eleven.

Katy wished she could see her there now, exchanging recipes with Frieda Howell or discussing flowers for the altar with Nedra Ison, all the while tapping on the window to keep Mr. B., her spoiled Siamese, out of trouble. The cat was gone now, and so was Cissy.

Willing herself back to the present, Katy picked up the phone and dialed. She'd call George McMahon first and give him the good news about the new book. Then, she'd see if she could arrange another meeting with Professor Fields for that evening. She should call Josh as well, she thought, making a mental list.

Somewhere in Lenexa, Kansas, a cell phone picked up, announcing the owner was away. *George must be either napping or in the bathroom,* she thought. Those were the only two times he didn't answer. Leaving a short message, she dialed again, this time the *Chronicle*.

Again, she got an answering machine. Joshua must be hot on another story. "Josh, Katy here. I'm beginning to see why you said Eden has changed. If you get this message before the end of the day, meet me at Cissy's house for dinner. I'll cook."

She hung up, knowing he couldn't resist that last bit. Katherine had been notorious in college as the worst cook in town. Although her skills hadn't come up to master chef quality, she had learned a trick or two while working on *The Serpent's Egg* in Germany and England. She had plenty of time for grocery shopping, and whether or not Josh made it, she'd enjoy the relaxation cooking brought her. Besides, steak and salad and a nice merlot sounded like the best nourishment for her right now. Keep the carbs low, and the protein coming. Now that she had made it back to fighting trim, she wanted to keep it.

Perhaps she'd start her shopping at SuperMart, where microwaves were well priced, and information about Donny Alcorn might be available to the right customer.

———

Amy Horine opened her eyes to darkness. Her eyes felt crusty and swollen, and her stomach ached. Where was she? Her last clear memory was of hunching over some hideous thing in front of Donny's car. Had she flown? Her head throbbed, and it grew worse with each breath she took.

Where in God's name was she?

As her eyes adjusted to the darkened room, she could just make out shapes. The room didn't appear to have windows, but she saw the faint outline of a door on the wall opposite where she lay. The bed beneath her felt cold and hard. A light blanket of some thin, metallic material covered the upper half of her body, but her lower torso and legs, though uncovered, felt warm.

She realized then that she was naked.

Panic hit Amy, and she jerked her head up, intending to sit up. She couldn't move. Though she felt no straps or other binding anywhere, she had no mobility other than a turning her head slightly and blinking her eyes. She tried to open her mouth, but something got in the way.

No, not something—someone. As her mind grew more wakeful, Amy's returning senses telegraphed a horrifying message to her groggy brain. Someone or some*thing* lay on top of her. She was being methodically and clinically raped by a cold, dark shape. As the shadow moved rhythmically, Amy's frozen eyes caught occasional glimpses of dim light beyond the black hole that was violating her. She felt nothing, yet she knew it was there.

Her ears had wakened now, and she imagined a clicking sound, like that of an insect. And for one hideous moment, she thought she saw the face. Inside an ever-blackening wisp, she could just make out the outlines of a mouth—a gaping maw, and a tongue, an inky ribbon of slavering hatred that writhed toward her own.

Her small mouth jerked open, as though pried apart by claws, and Amy's brain shot electric signals to her vocal cords.

She heard her own screams echoing in the cold darkness, and she remembered every prayer she'd ever been taught in confirmation class. Nothing then had seemed real to the growing teen. God had grown irrelevant with the dawn of the Internet, if He'd ever really existed at all. Now, she knew He existed. He must, or else this Evil had no master.

"Help me, please! Oh, God, help me!" she screamed aloud, tears stinging her swollen cheeks. "Help meeeeeeeeeeee!"

———

Miles away, Maria Horine was weeping, her knees bent in prayer, her head bowed against her aging hands. Somewhere, her baby needed her. Somewhere, God alone could save her. If He only would.

CHAPTER Fifteen

Dr. Apollo Bell paused before addressing the board. As called for by the Institute's charter, the executive board met once a month on the second Tuesday. Although the agenda for May's meeting had already been set, Bell had plans of his own. Before him sat Eden's finest and brightest, or so they thought. *Twelve men and women, good and true,* Bell thought with a silent laugh. *Morons.*

At the end of the magnificent cherry table sat Ed Sizemore, owner of a chain of carpet stores with headquarters in Eden, a man whose homosexual exploits in college back east could lose him a wife and all chance of election to the town council next fall.

Next to Ed sat Anthony Wayne Jasper, principal investor in the Paradise Park golf course and backstabbing embezzler.

Following Ed was Tim Collins, a Kentucky hick with sizeable pockets and a penchant for young, impressionable girls.

Making his way around the table, Bell considered the others:

Harry Gates, owner of the Tasty Treat and several Internet pornography sites.

Gaylord Jackson, outstanding defense attorney and online sex chat aficionado with a special interest in boys.

Judge Patrick Davis, who had warmed the bench of Eden County for seventeen years while greasing his palms to the tune of nearly sixty-three thousand dollars in bribes.

Medora Crabtree, headmistress of Eden's most exclusive private school, The Tree of Knowledge. Medora had never married, saying her students were her life. Bell wondered what the elite academician would say if he trotted out his photos of her in leather, chastising one of those naughty male students.

Dr. Patricia Dixon, Chief of Surgery at Eden General, head of missions at Paradise Community Church, and killer of over three hundred unborn babies. Although most of her murders were considered legal by human standards, Dixon's side business of murdering for hire had gone unnoticed due to the complicity of her benefactors, seven husbands with mistresses who demanded too much. Each expendable woman had died during or within months of a supposedly harmless D & C procedure. Dixon's bank account had grown fatter with each new death.

Daniel Cheatham II, principal of Eden High and grandson of the late Daniel Cheatham, whose airplane engine factory's contribution to WWII had been to use the cheapest materials on the Asian market, resulting in the loss of over three hundred pilots' lives when their engines burned up after three hundred hours of flight time. Young Daniel, though not complicit in his grandfather's ill deeds, had inherited the blood money and the secret of the fortune. He'd chosen to remain silent rather than admit the company's involvement in the soldiers' deaths. Two hundred and six widows had been made along the way, all thanks to the cheap parts used by Cheatham.

Forest Erickson, upstanding head of Eden County National Bank was next. His homespun hospitality and down-home charm had made the bank into one of the largest in southern Indiana. His gambling addiction had siphoned over three hundred thousand dollars from his investors' portfolios, and he was ever on the lookout for the next big score that would help him replace the missing funds.

Next came Kyle B. Lilly, no relation to the famous Lilly family of Indianapolis, but a player in the game of pharmaceuticals nonetheless. Owner of six KB Pharmacies, Lilly used his connections to obtain illegal, controlled substances, which then found their way into the arms and noses of some of Eden's finest, while over a million dollars in drug money had found its way into Kyle Lilly's Swiss account.

And finally, the board's newest member, Howard Miller, cousin to the farmer whose south field had hosted the mysterious light show two nights before, and owner of five all-night convenience stores called Howie's Stop n' Shop. Howard's biggest claim to fame lately was that his small stores boasted the greatest number of lotto winners in all of Indiana. Six major winners in as many years, and Howard got a nice slice of the pie each time. Howie had smiled before the nation's cameras, claiming ignorance as to the source of the amazing luck his little stores had enjoyed, but knowing the truth all the time. None of his customers had ever seen the altars Howie had erected in secret rooms beneath each store. Nor had anyone ever noticed that the locations of Howard's stores formed an interesting polygon when marked on a map of Eden County. Five points, spaced equidistantly, with the fifth store at the southernmost point, formed a curious star, which Dr. Bell knew very well.

"Good afternoon, to all of you," Bell began. "I wish to thank each of you for taking time out of your busy schedules to attend this month's meeting. As you see from the agenda, we have several important matters to discuss. However, before we get started, I wish to introduce some new business."

Dixon looked over her glasses, leveling her gaze at Bell. "That's a little irregular, isn't it, Doctor? I have afternoon rounds to make."

"Ah, yes, Dr. Dixon, I am sensitive to your needs, but I assure you this change is paramount."

Cheatham shrugged. "Let's get to it then. There's a rehearsal for the commencement exercises this evening, and I'm a key player, you know. Those diplomas won't get handed out without my being there!"

Bell smiled. "As you say, your presence is required, Principal Cheatham. By the way, may I congratulate you on your election to superintendent? Oh, I do hope that news wasn't private."

Daniel blanched. He had gotten the phone call only that morning. How could anyone, let alone someone outside the school system, know already? "You have excellent sources, Dr. Bell. Thanks. The new position doesn't begin until the fall semester, but I am looking forward to it."

"I am sure you are," Bell agreed with a grin. "Now, to the additional points for this afternoon's meeting." Someone knocked. "Excuse me," he said, turning toward two elegantly carved doors that enclosed the mahogany-paneled board-room. "Please, do come in, Miss Prynne."

Bell's assistant, Esther Prynne entered, carrying plain white folders, each marked with the name of a board member. "Do not open these folders yet," Bell explained. "We will begin as soon as Miss Prynne returns to her desk. Thank you, Miss Prynne. You may go home now."

The small woman returned a broad smile to her boss and benefactor. Esther Prynne had been born with a clubfoot, and although her brain ranked high on the intelligence scale, her halted gait had made it nearly impossible to secure a position with any reputable company until Apollo Bell had approached her with his offer.

Now, because of his generosity, she worked in the finest of offices for a handsome salary and enough perks to make any big city executive assistant green with envy.

"I'll turn on the machine before I leave, Doctor," she said as she closed the doors behind her.

The twelve men and women turned to the man who sat at the head of the table, waiting for his next words. "I have a tempting proposition for each of you—an offer that will be given only once. And I assure you, if declined, you will certainly regret it."

Each one looked to the others, muttering about bonuses, profit sharing, and the like. Their greedy faces gleamed with anticipation spurned on by the lust of their hearts.

"Go on," said Medora Crabtree, anxious to open her folder. "Is the offer in here?"

Bell nodded, steepling his long fingers calmly, waiting for them to quiet down.

"In each of these folders, you will find an individual offer. I have designed these offers specifically for each one of you. I am quite sure you will all be pleased, and no one should wish for more. But before you open the folders, let me tell you the small price I ask in return for the bounty promised to you within these folders."

Every eye looked toward their leader. Bell waited a beat, until he was certain of the perfect moment. "Very well. The small price I ask you to give me, in return for the answers to your hopes, your dreams, and your desires, is simple. Each of you must offer up to me your complete loyalty, your unwavering faith, your fidelity, and oh, yes—your soul."

CHAPTER Sixteen

The electronics aisle at Eden's east end SuperMart was situated in the middle of the store, just to the left of the home furnishings department. Katherine had stopped first at the snack bar for a lemonade and a bag of chips. While there, she'd struck up a conversation with Brenda Ellis, the snack bar's manager, asking the perky twenty-something for her impressions of Donny Alcorn's demeanor the previous morning.

"Oh, he looked like he'd been through hell and back—and you can quote me!"

Katherine had tried for more specifics, but the girl had already sold her story to the *National Star* magazine for an undisclosed amount. Tossing her lemonade bottle into the recycle bin, Katy imagined the front page of next week's rag: Local Waitress Claims Donny Alcorn Father to Her Love Child!

Threading her way through the midafternoon crowd of soccer moms rushing to finish up errands before that evening's game, Katy headed for Household Goods. Aunt Cissy had spent very little money on modernizing the house, so Katy grabbed an empty cart that had been abandoned near bedding and began filling it with necessities: an electric can opener, a toaster oven, a coffeemaker with an automatic grinder (now she could stop by that snooty coffee roaster next to Sandy's for a few pounds of Kenya AA), a bread machine, and a 1200-watt microwave with turntable.

With her cart loaded, Katherine made for the checkout lanes. There she ran into Joshua.

"Imagine meeting you here," he laughed. "I didn't know you shopped for anything that didn't have a hard drive or a dust jacket."

"Only when necessary. Did you get my message?"

He shook his head. "I've been here, trying to get quotes for tomorrow morning's edition. Boy, that gal in snacks is tight-lipped."

Katy edged toward the shortest line. "I guess we can read about it in the tabloids," she shrugged. "The message you missed was an invitation to dinner. I'm grilling steaks."

"You're cooking?" he asked. "You?"

"Me, and maybe you, if you want to toss a salad. Got a better offer?"

"Well, I could spend the whole evening at the paper, banging my head against the desk and nibbling on a dried cheese sandwich. Ah, but I can do that anytime. Consider that salad tossed, Katy Celeste. You do have bleu cheese?"

"Who doesn't?" she retorted. "Wine? Yes or no? I'm off to The Garden Grocery to dance through their veggie aisle."

"Big Red on your list? It's my current addiction."

"Ooh! That will be perfect. I haven't had cream soda in a long time. And what's the rule? Red always goes best with beef," she laughed. "I'll buy a case. Just on the chance you drop by more than once."

Josh's hazel eyes twinkled. "If you throw in a banana cream pie, I may just marry you."

"Drat! I had a hankering for apple."

"Not in Eden," he laughed. "Apple is just not on the menu. I'll see you at eight? I have to finish up at the paper if I want to spend the evening being treated like a king."

"Eight is fine," she answered. "Come earlier and you can cook, your majesty."

"Who me? I'm the perfect guest!" he said as he scooted past her and out the exit.

Katherine began loading her items onto the belt. He *was* the perfect guest, she thought with admiration. In fact, Josh always seemed to say and do the perfect thing. Maybe she would let him marry her. After the book was finished.

———

In the small church that sat atop Paradise Hill, Enoch Jones wandered through the pews, gathering up bits of trash left over from Sunday and making sure each hymnal rack had the requisite number of pencils and visitor cards, and one copy each of the old blue Baptist Hymnal and the hardcover edition of the NIV Bible. As he scooted through the narrow aisles formed by the smooth wooden pews, Jones reflected on Sunday's two services.

Thanks to the new visitation program, attendance had spiked to over a hundred for the first time in years, and three adults and one teenager had come forward to claim the amazing gift of grace that Jesus Christ offered to all who would only believe. That evening's baptisms had taken place at a small creek that ran past the church property, aptly named The Little Jordan by the church's former pastor, Harlan Collins.

Miracles were happening at Eden Bible Church, and Enoch praised God for His amazing gifts each day. Since his wife's death seven years before, Enoch had dealt with his grief by pouring his strength into the good people that formed his congregation.

As he finished straightening the last hymnal, Jones perked up his ears. Outside, the wind had begun to blow in from the west, and the front double doors rumbled. Above, he could hear the stunted ding of the old church bell, swaying in the sudden gust. Enoch shuddered. Something about this wind struck him as highly unusual. It sounded almost human, as if some unseen entity rode upon the rushing air, controlling it, owning it.

Ever since he'd accepted Christ at age eleven, Enoch had studied the many Scriptures that dealt with the end-times. Following in his deceased father's footsteps, Enoch had earned an engineering degree from Purdue by age twenty, then gone on to complete a master's in less than a year. Government work had failed to fill the aching hole in the young man's heart, and Jones soon looked for a way to serve a greater cause.

His mother had despaired of his choice to leave a steady job in Ohio to attend Bethel Bible College. At thirty years old, Jones had left behind a promising career and become a freshman again. Jones had saved little money, but he'd chosen to believe the calling genuine. Somehow, he had told his precious mother, God would provide funds for yet another round of schooling.

His trust had not been in vain. One day before classes began, the first of a series of mysterious checks had arrived in Enoch's mailbox, an amount just large enough to pay for his tuition, room, and board for one semester. Upon graduation, he had learned that his mysterious benefactor had been the little church of Eden Bible, which had found his name on a list of needy students and had been praying for him from his very first day to his last.

Just two weeks after learning of this remarkable yet small congregation, Jones had also learned that their pastor, Harlan Collins, had succumbed to cancer and gone on to meet the Lord at the age of seventy-one.

Jones had moved to Eden the very next day. He smiled now as he recalled the shocked faces of the Eden Bible congregation when they'd first met their new pastor.

They had not expected a black man.

Although several members were African-American, and many others were Hispanic or Asian, the surprise had been unmistakable. Still, within only a few weeks, both congregation and preacher had settled into a mutually respectful relationship, which eventually led to an all-out, familial love.

Enoch had never felt so welcome or loved. Before long, he'd met and married Ruth and begun a love affair with her and with Eden Bible that lasted until this very moment.

He missed Ruth from the bottom of his feet to the top of his graying, old head. Every day had an unspoken heaviness to it, but Enoch had learned to deal with it. Since they had never had children, their small house next to the church seldom echoed any voice save his own, but he survived. Day by day, he survived. He knew he'd see her again—soon.

Listening now to the wind, Jones steeled himself for what he knew must lay ahead. Throwing open the double doors, he squinted into the reddening sun, setting now behind the line of pines that crowned the hills west of the church. The wind rushed into his face, slapping at the lenses of his reading glasses, nearly knocking them off his nose. Enoch stood his ground, letting the wind whip against his skin, stinging the flesh and raising welts.

Voices called to him from within the whirling wind. Images of Ruth rose into his mind, and a dark fear began to claw at his heart. *She's in hell,* the voice hissed. *And she hates you for lying to her.*

Enoch forced the images—the lies—from his brain.

"You cannot win!" he cried into the winds. "You have already lost! Don't you know that? Our Lord and Savior Jesus Christ won the victory on the cross, and we are saved by the blood of the Lamb!"

At the name of Jesus, the wind slammed Enoch into the west side of the church, bruising his shoulder, but as he spoke the words *blood of the Lamb,* the wind abruptly ceased. The disheveled pastor raised himself up, repositioned his glasses, and smoothed his clothes. While others might have been terrified at such a scene, Enoch had grown accustomed to them. Since his childhood, Enoch had seen and heard many things not sensed by others.

For we wrestle not against flesh and blood, he thought, recalling the words of the apostle Paul in Ephesians 6, *but against principalities, against powers, against the rulers of darkness of this world, against spiritual wickedness in high places.*

Closing the doors behind him, Enoch returned to the church's interior and fell to his knees. This would require much prayer and fasting. The time of the end was near. For now, the Enemy owned the air. It was his domain, his kingdom.

But not for much longer. Soon, all the world would change.

CHAPTER **Seventeen**

K atherine grabbed a cup of coffee and sipped it with great satisfaction. "Oh, that's the stuff!" she sang, dancing around the kitchen. With her fridge well stocked and the larder teeming with chips, Big Red, Coke, and homemade salsa from Angelina Gomez's busy kitchen, she was beginning to feel at home.

The shiny new appliances she'd purchased at SuperMart were proudly lined up on the counters, and outside, two men from Prince Cable Systems were switching out the old analog cable line to a digital line that would double as her broadband access for the Internet. In a matter of two days, Katy had succeeded in bringing the old house her great-great-grandfather had won in a card game into the twenty-first century.

Maybe she'd even put in a big-screen television.

Half past six, she noted. *Just enough time for a quick shower and makeup job before starting supper.* Katy had taken to wearing less makeup than when she was younger. Back then, she dolled up her eyes with half a cake of eye shadow, hoping it would transform her into someone else—someone confident. Nowadays, she wore very little even when she went out. For some reason, though, she wanted to put a bit of spark into her pale skin tonight.

The black telephone in the front parlor jangled noisily.

Katherine rushed to catch it. Why hadn't she called the phone company today? She'd need new lines run into several rooms, and she'd have to buy some new phones. *Back to Super-Mart,* she thought happily.

"Hello?"

"Katherine?" a familiar voice asked.

"George? Georgie Porgie? Is that you? You got my message!"

The man on the other end sounded doubtful. "This is Katherine Adamson, right? I've reached her aunt's house in Indiana?"

"Well, you're partly right. This is Katy Celeste, and I'm in Eden, but hey, Georgie, this is my house now. She left it to me. Can you believe that?"

"Are you kidding me?" he answered. "Katy, tell me you're not staying there!"

"I may, Georgie. I may—at least for a while. I'm installing digital cable and broadband as we speak, so I'll be able to post chapters. Happy?"

"Chapters? Did you say chapters? Dear God in heaven, Katherine, don't tease me!"

"Not a tease, my friend. Truth. My nose detects a story right here in River City. I should be able to have a rough outline of my ideas for you in a week. How does that sound?"

"Like I'm dreaming. Katherine, is there any chance you could have this book finished by June? Because your publisher says if we can get a manuscript to them by the end of June, they could have a new offering for your fans by Christmas. Please say yes."

"June? That's only a month and a half. There's a lot of research to do first—well, maybe. No promises, George. Don't overpromise—comprendé?"

"I wouldn't dream of overpromising," he lied. "Send me an e-mail with your ideas. And it would be nice to have the first three chapters by the end of next week."

"Slave driver. Call me next Monday, not sooner. And try to relax, George. Good-bye."

He hung up. George McMahon had a superstition about saying good-bye, so he simply didn't. Katherine had learned to live with George's many idiosyncrasies over the years. He always found a terrific publisher for her books and got her top dollar. Of course, he hadn't done too badly on his fifteen percent.

Katy finished up her Kenya AA and set the blue and white mug into the right side of the old porcelain sink. Time for that makeup. As she passed through the foyer to go upstairs, she glanced outside to check on the cable men. She had nearly forgotten that they'd need a signature from her.

Pushing open the front door, she stepped into the warm evening air and waved to the neighbor across the street. She loved small-town friendliness. Though her present hometown of Kirkwood, Missouri, was relatively small, it had begun to lose some of the independence of a small town. As payment for belonging to metro St. Louis county, most small towns in the area had become little more than neighborhoods of the greater St. Louis metropolis. The days of small-town identity were slowly dying there.

Not here, it seemed. The lady who had waved, clad in midcalf jeans and a flowered, long-sleeved shirt had taken a moment from tending her irises to send a little bit of human-ity Katherine's way. Katy made a mental note to stop by there later in the week. Maybe she'd even bake cookies!

"We're nearly done, Miss Adamson," the shorter of the two men told her. "Pete, there, just needs to check the signal inside, if that's okay. Then, if you like, we can install those extra outlets you asked about."

Katherine calculated the time. There seemed little point in having them come back later just to install the outlets upstairs and in the parlor. "That'll be fine. I'm having company for supper at eight. Will everything be done by—say, seven-thirty?"

The man nodded. "No problem, Miss. I'll just let Pete know. You said you wanted outlets in the front bedroom and in the parlor—that'd be the front eastern corner, right?"

"Right. Unless you need me, I think I'll make a quick visit to the Apple Tree Inn to say hello to the owners. Do you know them?"

"No, Miss. They're from upstate, I heard. Noblesville, or Anderson. I'm not sure. We'll be quick and take care not to disturb anything."

"Thanks," she said, waving to Pete. Looking both ways, she crossed Broadway and turned into the walkway that led to the front porch. The majestic old Victorian that now served as an inn welcomed Katy with a brilliant display of flowers and a brace of willow rockers. Watering the many geraniums that dotted the gray-painted porch was a small, friendly look-ing woman. As Kate approached, the woman looked up and offered Katherine a gentle smile.

"Hello!" she called, setting down a watering can and wiping her small hands on her pants. "You're Katherine Adamson, aren't you? I'm Helen Markham. My husband, Bill, is inside working on one of the fireplaces."

Helen offered a hand, which Katy grasped happily. "Call me Katy," she said, stepping onto the porch. "I love your flow-ers. I should do something like that on my aunt's portico."

"I'm sorry about her passing. We only met her a couple of times, but she seemed like a very special lady."

"Thanks, Helen. She was that and much more. She raised me after my folks died. I guess the house will always feel like hers, you know."

Helen's husband emerged from within the house, and he reached out for Katherine's hand. "Bill Markham," he said with a wide grin.

"Katherine Adamson," she replied. Bill stood at least a foot taller than his wife.

"Oh, you don't have to tell me!" he said, wiping a brown lock of windblown hair. "I've read every one of your books. It's nice to know we have another conspiracy theorist on the street. I'm honored to meet you, Miss Adamson."

"Katy," she said, thinking what a cute couple they made. "As to the theories, let's just say I've learned to trust very few people, especially those in government. Tell me that you're not in government."

"Lord, no! The closest I come is an uncle who was an alderman in Noblesville. That's where we're from originally. We vacationed here last year and fell in love with the town. We talked with Eden Realty about moving, and they called three weeks later about this place. The former owners had moved to Colorado, so we jumped on it! Being on Main Street, it seemed like an ideal spot for a B&B. We even plan to have a murder mystery night each fourth Saturday night starting next month, if you're still in town then."

"I probably will be. I've got a new book in the works, so I'm thinking of staying here to finish it," she told them, deciding to omit the fact that Eden's latest mysteries were at the heart of her new novel. She'd found such confessions often spoiled any hunt for the truth.

"Won't you come in, Katy?" Helen asked. "We don't have any guests right now, so it's a nice time to get to know a new neighbor."

Katherine pointed to the men in her yard. "The cable company's here right now, so I'll have to take a rain check. Also, I'm having a guest over tonight for supper. Have you met Joshua Carpenter from the *Chronicle*?"

Helen's blue eyes brightened. "He goes to our church sometimes! Eden Bible Church. Have you been there?"

"No, but I'd like to try it," Katy answered. "You know Enoch Jones?"

Bill nodded, holding Helen's small hand. "He's a great man. We've been taking his class on the tribulation. In fact, he's starting a new section next week. Maybe you can go with us?"

"Maybe." Katherine knew a bit about the period Bible students called the tribulation, but it couldn't hurt to learn more. Besides, she'd feel closer to Cissy there. And, she could ask Pastor Jones about the rushed cremation. That story Jean Davis had told still nagged at her.

"We'll remind you," Helen said with a genuine smile.

"That'll be great! Say, while I'm thinking of it, do you have a dog?"

Bill shot Helen a gentle, but clearly disapproving, glance. "We do," he said. "Helen's sister asked us to look after her Husky mix for the week. She's kept up half the neighborhood, I'm afraid. We apologize if you've lost sleep. I promise you, she'll be gone by Sunday."

Katherine was glad to hear it. She liked dogs as much as anyone, but she also liked her sleep. She could suffer through a few more days. "No problem. I'll buy thick earplugs and turn on the radio."

"It's funny," Helen said, "Heidi only barks at night. She's inside right now, happy as a clam and not a peep out of her."

"Heidi?" Katy asked, surprised.

Helen laughed, glancing up at Bill. "Our niece Hannah named her. There's a good chance Heidi's half wolf. My sister and her husband used to lived in Alaska, and they bought her there from an old musher named Travelin' Jack Horner. Horner claimed Heidi was sired by a wild timber wolf. Horner told my sister he'd wanted to try to tame the wolf, but a local pilot shot it during one of those land and shoot flyovers. I think it's illegal there now, but not in time to save Heidi's dad.

"Anyway, Hannah heard that her cute little puppy, whose name had been Chaser, was half wolf, and it scared her. So, my sister Brenda told Hannah to give the puppy a new name, since naming an animal gives you power over it. Hannah had just seen the movie *Heidi* with Shirley Temple. That's been the dog's name since. Not very scary, is it?"

"It helps," Katy admitted. Suddenly, her peripheral vision caught sight of a shadow crossing to her right. Beside her, out of nowhere, the dog had appeared. She was only inches from Katy's right hand and looked just like a wolf.

"Heidi, sit!" Helen spoke sharply. "It's OK, Katy. She's friendlier than she looks."

Katherine turned to see the dog, facing her squarely. Heidi was beautiful, and she did look like the wolves Katherine had seen at the St. Louis Zoo, except for the eyes, which were ice blue. "Hello, Heidi," Katy said gently, slowly lifting the back of her hand toward the dog's muzzle.

Heidi watched Katy's eyes, sniffing her hand.

"Good dog," Katy said, keeping her voice friendly.

Suddenly, the dog lunged forward, threw her weight into Katy's arms, and began licking her face wildly, nearly knocking Katy off her feet.

"I think she likes you," Helen said, relieved.

"I guess so," Katherine laughed, stroking the silky fur. "Hi, Heidi. I'll have to keep you on my side, huh?"

"Down, Heidi! Sit!" Bill commanded. The dog obeyed, sitting inches from Katherine's feet.

"I'd better be going," Katherine said. "It was nice to meet you. Let's do lunch one day, Helen."

"Great," the shorter woman said. "I'd like that."

"So would I. Good-bye! Good-bye, Heidi!" she called, walking back toward her side of Broadway. The dog whimpered as she left. Funny, she thought, as she reached her own front door, the dog hadn't frightened her. In fact, she'd felt quite safe with her. Imagine that.

CHAPTER Eighteen

Joshua arrived early, only a few minutes after the cable men had left. Katherine had found The Garden Grocery's head butcher, a rotund and cheerful man named Gary Bunch, very helpful. With Gary's help, Katy had selected a large, two-inch sirloin cut, which she was now braising in Aunt Cissy's old but reliable electric skillet. She'd found the recipe for cooking the meat in Cissy's Eden Bible Church Cookbook. She'd also found a recipe for a homemade bleu cheese salad dressing there. She figured that would make Joshua happy.

"It smells wonderful," the newsman said, sliding into one of the kitchen chairs. "I'll be happy to help in a minute, but I really need to sit and stare for a little while first. Whew! This has been one long day. Oh, these are for you."

Katherine took the bright bunch of wildflowers and headed to the sink. "They're really pretty. Did you pick them yourself?"

Josh blushed slightly. "At least they're fresh. Not like that first bouquet I gave you in college."

"Well, we'll not rehash that old argument," she laughed, recalling a stale bunch of daisies that Josh had pinched from the dumpster behind a floral shop. "You should have told me you were bringing me posies, Carpenter. I'd have bought a special vase. Oh! That reminds me! Jean Davis was supposed to come by here, but she didn't make it. I should call her."

Katherine left Joshua in the kitchen while she located the phone book and made a quick phone call to the Davis residence. When she returned, she looked puzzled. "That's funny. No one's home. I'm sure she said she'd be stopping by this evening. Just after six was what she said."

"Maybe she had something come up. She probably tried to call you, Katy. Didn't she leave a message?"

"No answering machine," she said aloud. "I tried to get Cissy to buy one. I even sent her one for Christmas one year—she gave it away. I don't know why she thought they were so evil."

"Funny word to use about an answering machine!" he laughed.

"Yes, well, Cissy had her odd moments. I'll pick up a machine tomorrow. So, what happened with Donny today? Is there anything more that I missed? Any news of Amy?"

Joshua really did look tired. "May I eat first?"

Katy slumped into the chair next to him. "OK, so I'm pushy. The steak should be finished in about fifteen more minutes. Come out onto the porch, and I'll show you my new toy."

She tugged his long arms, leading him into the TV porch. Picking up a shiny new remote, Katherine pressed a button, and the television blinked to life. "Digital cable!" she crowed. "And I've got digital online service, too. I've already ordered an AirPort from the Apple Store online; it should be here in a couple of days."

"An AirPort? No kidding. I have an old TiBook in my car. It has an AirPort card. I'll be able to work really well here," he teased her. "How about pork chops tomorrow night?"

"You wish. I also ordered a new printer and scanner. The printer will be Ethernet-ready, so I can network that. Then I won't have to do anything but sit and write."

Joshua's forehead knotted into a worried frown. "Katy, are you planning to stay here?"

"Maybe," she said, heading back into the kitchen to tend to the flowers. "If you're nice."

Joshua joined her at the sink, taking her hand. "I'm serious, Katy. I'd like you to stay, but well, Eden's a funny place now. I'd rather you were safe, even if that means you have to leave."

She leaned toward him, her deep brown eyes narrowed. "Listen, Carpenter, I am not going to be scared out of my own hometown. Your concern for my welfare is appreciated, but I can take care of myself."

"So, you are staying?" he asked, a smile playing at his wide mouth.

"I'm staying. Like it or lump it."

Joshua's mouth widened into a positive grin. "I like it."

"Me, too," she confessed, smiling as well. "Me, too."

———

Enoch Jones hung up the phone. Sarah Bellows had given birth to a baby girl. He'd be expected at the hospital next morning. All was well, otherwise he'd be on his way there now. Norm, Sarah's husband, had reported that both mother and child were fine. Was the baby delicate—like her mother? Jones had asked, not wanting to arouse Norm's suspicions. Seven pounds, six ounces. Nineteen inches.

Jones had breathed a silent prayer. He'd be there the next day, Jones had promised Norm. No reason to rush. Not this time.

Turning on the television, Jones settled into the creaky embrace of an aging leather recliner Ruth had bought him for his fiftieth birthday. "You'll need a place to put up your feet," she had teased him. "Retirement's around the corner."

She had died the following spring.

Somehow, the recliner now felt as warm as Ruthie's arms. Sitting there made Enoch feel closer to her.

Clicking the remote, Enoch scanned through the news channels. He found the more conservative tone of the local station less jarring than WNN, but he needed to hear the awful truth of world events. Events he had long expected and dreaded. *It's a world of death and decay,* he thought as the news reader for WNN began a story about Syria. *And it's no more apparent than right here in Eden.*

Enoch tried to remember when he'd first noticed the changes in Eden. It was before Ruthie's passing, probably more than twenty years back. Ruthie had noticed it, too. She called it an ill wind. Enoch knew better. The wind was far worse than just ill—it was pure evil.

Enoch dropped a handful of cashews into his mouth, wondering if he had any root beer. The only way to find out meant getting up, so he closed the lid on the nuts, shutting his eyes. He would stay put tonight. Gather his strength.

On the television screen, one of WNN's blond, surgically enhanced newsreaders was talking about Iraq. Since Hussein's removal from power, the Middle East had changed dramatically. The Iraqi transitional government was about to hold elections, supervised by the US, Poland, and England, and it looked as though Iran and what was left of Syria were grudgingly content with the changes. The massive earthquake that had hit Damascus just before Christmas last year had devastated most of Syria, virtually decimating the central control for Hamas.

India and Pakistan had patched up their border differences, but the peace had grown shaky since the Syrian earthquake.

And despite the tentative peace agreement between Israel and the Palestinian Prime Minister, the PLO had grown even more ruthless. With each concession Israel made, the terrorists demanded more. The world danced on a perilous pin, and the slightest movement could send everyone crashing into a third world war.

Notwithstanding the military changes in the past few years, or perhaps because of them, the Dow Jones Average was nearing 12,000. The housing market had taken a slight hit the previous year, but continued low interest rates and a reduction in the unemployment rate had strengthened the economy. Amidst continued war talk, business boomed and the average American saw more money in his pocket. President Shepherd's approval ratings soared to nearly ninety percent.

Science and economics were the new gods. Cloned humans, cancer vaccines, super-antibiotics, face transplants, and sentient computers filled the headlines when war news lagged, while credit cards and insurance schemes snatched the average man's paycheck. Second and third mortgages were all the rage—but not to worry!—interest rates were low and money was cheap! The only dark cloud domestically was the ever-growing fear of the super-flu that had infected China, but rumors of a miraculous vaccine soon chased away those fears, and Americans ate, drank, and laughed, secure in their belief in science.

And in the midst of all the latest fashion crazes and X-rated television, cries of peace now rang throughout the nations. Man had grown worse with the passing of two millennia, and Enoch knew Christ's return could not be far off.

Peace.

Enoch closed his eyes, the lines of age and weariness that tracked his face smoothing for a moment. The peace-loving pundits were dead right to fear war, but not for the reasons they gave, he thought wearily. A storm was coming that would soon drive the world to the brink of destruction—but only the brink. A man of false peace would then enter the world stage, and all bets would be off. The Prince of the Power of the Air would touch ground, and his time would be short. Enoch believed he wouldn't be here to see these happenings, but he sometimes prayed he might be spared the agony of witnessing their beginning.

Unfortunately, his life—his destiny—required his presence.

Enoch reached for his Bible. He'd need to spend the next few hours in prayer and reading God's Holy Word, he thought. *Dear Jesus, give me strength to stand in the latter day.*

Turning to the last book, Enoch adjusted his reading glasses and settled in for a long night. *As it was in the days of Noah,* he recalled. *The sons of God and the daughters of men. Angels who kept not their first estate. Nephilim. The fallen ones. The Watchers.*

"Dear Lord," he whispered. "Please, look after that poor girl, Amy Horine. And help us to see what is all around us."

———

Maria Horine closed Amy's little white Bible. She'd tried reading it, strained to understand it, pored through every gospel, hoping to find an answer. Nothing.

The Voice hadn't called her again, and she thanked God for it. Since the last call, she'd huddled in the corner of her bedroom, alternately weeping and praying her rosary. She'd failed as a Catholic, and she was being punished. Amy had been taken as a warning. The Voice could be a sign from God or a sign from the Devil, Maria could not be sure which.

She remembered her first communion, her first confession, her confirmation, and her wedding. She had loved the

Church then, needed her, and she had often prayed to the Blessed Virgin for aid and intercession. Stan hadn't cared one bit for the Church. Raised an agnostic, he had sworn to Maria that he had changed, that he had taken the Savior into his heart and trusted in the Holy Church to guide their family.

He had lied.

Now, Maria knew she must pay penance for her sins and his. Taking up the rosary, Maria fingered the beads, returning to her prayers: *Hail Mary, full of grace, the Lord is with thee; blessed art thou among women, and blessed is the Fruit of thy womb, Jesus. Holy Mary, Mother of God, pray for us sinners, now and at the hour of our death. Amen.*

Maria considered the words for a moment: at the hour of our death. *Blessed Virgin,* she prayed, *keep my baby safe. Take me, but let my Amy live.*

CHAPTER Nineteen

WEDNESDAY

Forest Erickson closed the door to his office. The bank hadn't even been open for five minutes, and already he had a headache. People. How he hated people. Two tellers had called in sick, and one of the loan officers had said she'd be late due to a dead car battery.

This would be another rotten day.

Sitting alone now, he thought about the wife he'd left asleep at home. He and Emily he had gotten married right out of high school, sweethearts since fourth grade, a match made in heaven. Now she looked like a beast. With the birth of each mewling child, Emily's figure had drooped a little more. Four brats later, she'd lost all semblance of her former hourglass shape. Now she looked like a shot glass.

Forest thought about the women he'd had over the last six years. Theresa had been the first. Trim and willing, she had started as a comely teller and ended as a well-paid loan officer. Marriage to the football coach from Wellington had ended their affair, but Forest still hummed when he thought of Theresa's special talents.

Then there had been Dolores. He'd met Dolores at the movies. She'd been sitting two rows back during one of the many times Forest had ducked a night with his family for a bit of solitude in the darkened interior of one of Eden's lesser known theaters. Dolores had moved to the seat next to Forest during an intermission. Forest had never enjoyed a double feature more.

Their fling hadn't lasted, though. Emily had begun to suspect, so Forest had ended it. Four children and a ball-and-chain with a double chin. That was his life. Pointless and empty.

No wonder he'd resorted to embezzlement. Financing a bloodsucking family and a mistress could tap any man dry.

Forest stared at the street below his fifth floor office. He'd inherited the bank from his father, a thankless man with an anchor tattooed on his arm and a permanent scowl etched on his face. Andrew Jackson Erickson had sired three sons, beating all three so often that he drove one into prison for felony theft and a second into a padded room at the state hospital in Madison.

Forest, the third in line, had proven tougher than his elder brothers. He had learned to take a punch without flinching, wipe his father's vodka-soaked spit from his face, and bite down hard on his tongue when his brain screamed at him to cry. Forest had earned the right to rule.

Andrew J. Erickson had died of a massive coronary on Forest's seventeenth birthday. Forest, who had been alone with his father during the attack, had called the ambulance— after he had watched his father's tongue turn purple and his gnarled fingers twitch, after he had spit in the old man's face and screamed out every swear word he'd ever learned from the old man's swollen lips, after he had laughed at him for being weak.

After he had gained vengeance for his elder brothers.

Forest hadn't cried a single tear at the funeral. His mother, Betty Erickson, had shed a torrent. Forest had comforted her. He was the man now, and he would make sure she was never hurt again.

He missed his mother. She had understood his fears and his needs.

She had not been strong enough to survive without her rat of a husband. She had been Forest's one saving grace, but his father had taken that, too. Even in death, the old man mocked him.

Opening the window, Forest leaned into the fresh breath of morning, considering the freedom that hung in the crisp, clean air. Moving closer to the ledge, Forest could feel the light breeze dancing on his face. The sun played upon his eyelids, and he smiled.

Hello, Mama, he thought, tears tracking his face for the first time since his mother's funeral. "I'm coming, Mama," he cried out as he leapt into the embrace of death. *Your little boy needs a hug.*

Katherine woke to Heidi's mournful howls. Seven-fifteen, and her eyelids were not happy about being forced open.

Moaning, Katy dragged herself to a sitting position. Joshua had left shortly after eleven the night before, needing to spend a little time at the *Chronicle* working on the morning edition. As tired as she was, Katherine knew Josh must be far more weary.

They'd spent the evening talking through the events of the past two days, including the apparent kidnapping of Donny and Amy. Donny hadn't told the police much more since his miraculous reappearance, but the police had begun speculating about a crime of passion. Joshua had told her that Branham was considering calling in the FBI.

Dinner and shoptalk about Eden's woes had nibbled away at their evening, and eleven had come all too soon. Promising to cook again, Katherine had easily convinced the bachelor to agree to another night's chatting over a plate of spaghetti and a movie. Josh had played hard to get, but Katy knew he'd been pleased to say yes.

Very little had changed in their relationship since college, save that she had learned to appreciate his small-town charm. Maybe she could thank David for that one, she thought with a smile. Maybe she was getting over that married lug.

Feet on the floor, she headed for the kitchen. Coffee and a morning of shopping again. She needed to get an answering machine and two new telephones. She'd call the phone company as well to upgrade her service and install more outlets.

FedEx should be by sometime today or tomorrow. She'd see if the Markhams would sign for any packages, and she'd leave a note on her door. *Gotta cover all the bases,* she thought. *Now, get in gear, kid. You have a hot date with a sweet girl for lunch.* Maybe she should give the Alcorn household a call to confirm.

Katy started pouring water into the coffeemaker's twelve-cup carafe, noticing again the wildflowers Joshua had brought her. She began to imagine making a life with the lanky newsman.

Stop it! It didn't work when you were in college, so why could it work now?

College! Adrian Fields. She'd drop by the college later today with Field's uneaten lunch. She'd tried to call him several times the previous afternoon, but his voicemail had always picked up. She'd begun to wonder if the reclusive professor had been a figment of her imagination. She'd thought about telling Joshua about the odd meeting, but Miller's farm and the Donny Alcorn mystery had dominated their conversation. She'd bring Josh up to speed tonight.

For now, she'd concentrate on brewing up a strong batch of Kenya AA.

Bridgette Elson had worked for MedCare since January. As a registered nurse, she could make more money using her considerable experience in the ER or ICU at Eden General, but the long shifts and heavy responsibilities no longer appealed to the fifty-eight-year-old. With two grandchildren and a husband who was about to retire, Bridgette liked being at home. The flexible hours of MedCare Home Health Service had seemed the perfect answer.

Wednesday morning meant calls to the Patterson home on Third and the Wiley apartment on Easton. It also meant a therapy session with John Thundercloud.

It wasn't that Bridgette dreaded her weekly visits with the World War II veteran. She admired military men. Her husband had served in Vietnam. Her eldest son had been a paratrooper in both Desert Storm and Operation Iraqi Freedom. It wasn't even his injuries. She had seen hundreds of amputations in her years as a nurse. She had learned to stimulate blood flow, both to the insulted area and to the heart. In addition to her B.S.N., an M.S. in psychology had given her insight into the inner demons a man or woman faces after losing a piece of himself or herself, but John Thundercloud defied all logic.

Simply put, the Winnebago Indian with the ancient eyes gave Bridgette the creeps. She had even asked Irene Steele, the owner of MedCare, to assign another nurse to deal with

Thundercloud, but Irene had insisted the old man wanted no one but her. Bridgette was stuck with him.

The hands of her pink and white nurse's watch read nine o'clock as she pulled up to the small house on Divine Avenue. As always, an American flag waved proudly from an angled pole on John Thundercloud's front porch, the single decoration on an otherwise barren landscape.

Bridgette climbed the thirteen crumbling steps that traversed the steep front yard of the Arts and Crafts style home. John's neighborhood had become a trendy one in recent years, and many of these homes, built during the 1920s and 30s, had received loving facelifts from young families. Eden's reputation as a prime school district with a gifted program, along with relatively low property taxes, had combined to renovate the aging neighborhood into a vital community of young families and swing sets.

John's home barely had house numbers.

Even though she had a key, Bridgette knocked politely before letting herself in.

"Mr. Thundercloud?" she asked, pushing the door open and entering the dim interior. "Mr. Thundercloud? Are you all right? It's Mrs. Elson. I'm here for your therapy session."

Deep within the shadows of the living room, Bridgette could make out the silhouette of John Thundercloud, apparently asleep in his battered old recliner.

"Mr. Thundercloud, you need to wake up now. It's Wednesday morning, nine o'clock. Time to work those muscles."

His head bobbed up. He'd been writing. He spent nearly all his time writing.

"Wednesday? Already? It was just Wednesday last week."

"Yes, it's here again, and they come once each week. Remember?"

John had lived eighty-seven years. And the nurse was an idiot. "Don't you think I know that? Why don't you leave me alone?"

Removing her backpack, Bridgette cleaned her hands with a squirt of alco-gel. She avoided going into client's bathrooms whenever possible. Besides, the alco-gel did a better job at disinfecting her hands than most soaps.

"Let's put down the pencil and get started."

John glanced up, peering at her over a pair of smeared lenses. "I'm busy!"

"So am I, so let's have a little cooperation. I'll sharpen your pencils for you when we're done, if that will make you happy."

Snorting, Thundercloud slammed his pencil on the tray. "OK! Let's do our exercises!"

Sliding the wheeled tray to one side, Bridgette made a quick assessment of her patient. For his age, John Thundercloud's overall health was reasonably good: nice color, pupils looked normal, pulse and blood pressure measured within normal range, his breathing was shallow, but that went along with emphysema. The ever-present ashtray hadn't been emptied in a while.

"How many times do I have to tell you not to smoke near your oxygen?" she asked, taking a moment to remove the ashtray and clean it.

"I'll go out in a blaze of glory," he snorted, fumbling in his pocket for a pack of cigarettes.

"How's your O2 supply?" she asked, ignoring his comment and making notes. "Shall I send Goliath over with a shipment on Monday?" Goliath was Thundercloud's nickname for the former Eden Angels fullback who delivered his supplies from Gilead Medical.

"Yeah, that's OK. Tell him to come see me."

Finishing up the quick assessment, Bridgette checked the condition of Thundercloud's stumps. Beneath the light blanket that served as warmth and dignity for John Thundercloud were the remains of his once long, lean legs. Cut off just below the knees, what was left had withered to inanimate vestiges.

"Nice, aren't they?" he asked, opening a Clark Bar.

"You shouldn't eat those," she scolded. "I don't know why Goliath gives them to you."

"He likes me," Thundercloud replied with a vague smile. "You're taking your own sweet time down there!"

"What time do Mr. and Mrs. Wheaton come?"

"Same time."

"And what time is that?" she pressed.

"My twenty-something, gum-popping ray of sunshine and her beatnick husband come four times a day, as if you didn't know. Eight, noon, four, and eight."

"Then why didn't Mrs. Wheaton empty your catheter bag this morning?" Bridgette asked, making a mental note to have MedCare reprimand the C.N.A. for neglecting her client.

"She did. Maybe she did. I don't know! Was she here?"

Bridgette checked the medical chart that hung from Thundercloud's mobile tray. Cassie Wheaton was twenty-three, mother of a toddler, and wife of a no-good, lazy bum. She'd gotten her job three months before, replacing Celia Anderson, who had left for nursing school in Indianapolis. Cassie needed this job, but the job didn't need someone who neglected it. Cal Wheaton came along when Cassie needed a bit of muscle, adding a bit more to the household income. Cal lifted John in and out of bed while Cassie cleaned and disinfected the small house.

Clearly Cal had been there, or else John would still be in bed. Yet, Cassie had made no notes in Thundercloud's chart.

144

"I'll change it for you, Mr. Thundercloud. And I'll call to make sure the Wheatons will be here at noon. Now, let's start with your shoulders."

Bridgette grasped his forearm just below the elbow with one hand and placed her other hand on his left shoulder. "Time to make some gentle circles," she said, her mind shifting into neutral.

After fifteen minutes, the exercises were complete, and the nurse sat for a moment. "Don't you get lonely, Mr. Thundercloud?"

The old man shifted in his seat. "Foolish question. I keep busy. Why?"

"I was trying to imagine myself in your position. You certainly do keep busy. You must have filled over twenty notebooks."

"Thirty-one," he corrected. "And they're not for you. They're for...for someone else."

"I see. May I read a bit?" she asked, leaning toward the tray.

"I said they're not for you. They're for someone who will listen. Do you have ears to hear, Mrs. Elson? Do you have eyes to see?" She shrugged. "I thought not. Most folks think 'cause I'm an Indian, I have some special spiritual connection, but you know what, Mrs. Elson? I got nothing God didn't give me. You go see Enoch Jones. He'll teach you to see. He'll teach you to hear. Then, you come back, and I'll show you what I write."

Bridgette closed her backpack. "OK, I'll let it go. Is there anything I can do for you before I leave? Would you like something to eat?"

"No...wait a minute. Yes, there is. Can you get a letter to someone?"

"I can mail it for you, if you like."

He shook his head. "No mail. Don't trust it. Hand deliver it or don't bother. Can you do it? I...I, well, it's important."

John Thundercloud's only child, Barrett Johnson—he'd changed his last name to seem less Indian—lived in Indianapolis and rarely brought John's grandson to visit. He had few friends. He had never asked for a favor in all the months Bridgette had known him. "All right. I'll deliver it."

Thundercloud's eyes softened. He handed her a large white envelope with a name written in his small script. "Deliver this to this person *only*. Then, you go see Enoch Jones, Mrs. Elson. Before the time is too late to gain eyes."

CHAPTER Twenty

J oshua Carpenter had fallen asleep. As a morning paper, the *Chronicle* demanded a lot of night work. News, however, happened twenty-four hours a day, so Carpenter had learned to grab a nap whenever a moment's peace presented itself.

He had just fallen into a lovely dream about a world where newsmen were allowed to take weeks off at a time, when the rude jangling of the news desk phone yanked him back to consciousness.

"*Chronicle*," he answered sleepily.

"Joshua Carpenter, please," a man's voice said.

"This is Joshua."

"This is Deputy Collins, Mr. Carpenter. Sheriff Branham asked me to give you a heads-up. We're at the Eden County National Bank. There's been...an accident. Forest Erickson... well, sir, he's dead."

"I'll be right there."

Josh hung up the phone and rifled through the news desk for a pad and pencil. After writing a quick note for Angie, the part-time secretary who came in at ten, he grabbed the keys and headed toward his car. Barely nine o'clock and the day had already turned sour. What a week!

Coming to his car, Joshua grabbed his cell phone and pressed a number he'd had memorized for years.

"Hello?" a voice asked pleasantly. She must have had her coffee already.

"Katy?"

"I thought you would be sleeping by now," she replied. He could tell she was smiling.

"Can you meet me at Eden County National? Remember how last night we talked about some evil curse on the town? Well, we may have been right."

The scene at Eden County National had slowed to a chaotic crawl by the time Josh arrived. He'd stopped to pick up Katherine, reasoning that one car took up less space than two. Eden was a small town, and any excitement drew a crowd. The unexpected death of a prominent citizen like Erickson would draw a parade.

"Sheriff?" Josh asked as he and Katherine walked toward the police line. Yellow tape had cordoned off most of the sidewalk on the south side of the bank.

"Josh, I'm glad you could make it. Nice to see you again, Miss Adamson. Sorry for the reason though. Did George fill you in?"

"He said Erickson had died, that's about it."

Katy followed the two men underneath the yellow tape and into the crime scene. "Don't worry too much about destroying evidence. It's pretty clear what happened here. Splat. Sorry, Miss Adamson," he added, seeing her expression. "Over this way."

The sheriff led them to a knot of uniformed county men talking to three men in plain clothes. As they neared the group, Katherine took in the sobering sight before them. An ambulance sat four feet from the impact site, where a WNN photographer snapped digital images to upload via satellite. Eden would be in the national news again. A town cursed.

Near the photographer, Katherine thought she saw a woman she knew, or at least someone she had known in St. Louis.

"Sheila?" she asked, closing in on the blond woman, taking care to watch where she stepped. "Sheila Williams?"

The woman glanced up, motioning to the photographer, apparently giving orders for the next phase of the assignment.

"Sheila?" Katy asked again, walking up to her.

"I'm sorry, I don't believe I know you," she said to Katherine, her ice blue eyes perfectly dressed in rosy brown eye shadow.

"Well, I've lost a little weight in the last year. Katherine Adamson."

"Kathy Adamson? Oh my, you *have* lost weight! I apologize for not recognizing you. It's Van Williams now, by the way. A better anchor name."

Katy smiled. "That's right. I thought the woman from WNN looked familiar. I saw you on the news last night. Congratulations on moving into the big-time. But I thought you would still be in New York. You're here already?"

She sighed audibly, a practiced affectation. "The red-eye to Indianapolis then a puddle jumper to Eden Airport. I got here around six this morning. Brent is back in Washington. Did you see him?"

"I did, although I didn't spend much time chatting. With all that's been happening here, it didn't seem like a proper time for a reunion. Besides, I don't really know him all that well."

Joshua came up behind Katherine, touching her elbow. "Katy, Sheriff Branham needs to go meet with Mrs. Erickson. Did you want to speak to him first?"

Katy glanced at her watch. It was already after ten.

"I need to get home. I have a date, remember? I'll walk. It isn't that far. What if I give you a call later? I'm sure you have a story to write, and I have a movie to see. I'll probably make a stop by SuperMart, too. I'll get that answering machine."

He kissed her cheek.

Katy tried not to act surprised, although she was. "I'll call you," she muttered. Then, catching Sheila's catlike smile in her side vision, Katy turned back to Josh, returning his peck with a more prominent kiss on his cheek. "Thanks again for last night," she said, taking note of Sheila's response.

Gotcha, she thought, walking back toward the bank. As she walked, she could feel Joshua's eyes on her retreating back. This could get interesting.

———

Grace Alcorn had been sitting by the front door for nearly twenty minutes when Katherine pulled into the busy cul de sac. Waving good-bye to her mom, she ran out to the street, meeting Katy with a broad smile.

"Hi, Miss Adamson! Ready to see *The Two Towers?*"

Opening the door for her "date," Katherine nodded. "Absolutely! Sorry I'm a bit late."

"Oh, that's OK. The movie doesn't start until one o'clock."

"Yeah, I checked into that. Good thing I bought tickets online, huh?"

"Cool! Do we still have time for lunch? If not, we could just get some nachos or a pizza at the theater."

Who cares about a diet when you're with such a great kid? she thought. "Nachos are one of my favorite food groups. Chocolate's pretty important, too."

Grace laughed, her giggle as musical as tinkling wind chimes. "I wish Mr. Carpenter could have come along, too."

Thinking of the scene at the bank, Katherine shuddered. She didn't want to start that conversation. A man bursting headfirst into the pavement, then being all but obliterated by a passing truck doesn't make for a pleasant sight. "He had to stay at the paper and write a story for tomorrow's edition," she said honestly. "I'll tell him you asked about him."

They talked and giggled all the way to the theater. Katherine plopped down a ten for two plates of nachos and two Cokes, and they sat in a little bistro just outside the theaters.

"I have all the books," Grace said as she swirled a chip in cheese. "You have a jalapeño on your lower lip."

Katy wiped her mouth with a scratchy napkin. "Thanks. I have several copies of the books myself. In fact, Tolkien was one of my big inspirations to become a writer. Do you write?"

"Oh, I write stuff, but none of it is any good. It's mostly about animals and stuff. Have you ever read Brian Jacques? Stuff like that."

Katherine scrunched the napkin into a ball and dropped it onto her paper plate. "Brian Jacques is great. I met him at a writers' conference last year in Florida. He's pretty cool. If you like animals, you might try *The Chronicles of Narnia* by C. S. Lewis. You know, Lewis was a good friend of Tolkien's."

"I've heard of that. Good, huh?"

"Really good. And filled with adventures."

As they made their way into the theater, Grace put her hand into Katy's, squeezing it hard. "Thanks for noticing me, Miss Adamson."

"You're hard not to notice, Grace. You're bright, you're kind, and you are beautiful. And you promised to call me Katherine. But Katy's even better."

"Deal," the girl giggled. "Let's get a front seat, Katy. I like to see Frodo really close."

CHAPTER Twenty-One

WEDNESDAY EVENING

A s she walked through the back door into what had become her kitchen, Katherine heaved a monumental sigh. *The Two Towers* had proven as mesmerizing as ever, and Grace's company equally so, but Katy's nerves had begun to scream somewhere between dropping off Grace and shopping at SuperMart.

Back home now, with the time nearing six-thirty, she was hungry and growing steadily crabbier. The weight of the last three days, the grief of her aunt's passing, and the strain caused by poor sleep all pounded out a rhythm on her brain. She'd call Josh and see if he was OK with pizza. He could watch the movie she'd rented, and she could sleep. Not an exciting evening, but right now it was the most she felt she had to offer.

To her surprise, someone knocked on her front door.

Oh, not now, she thought, dropping her keys onto the table along with her shopping bags. It was still light outside, and she could see two shadows on the ivy-covered front portico. *Jehovah's Witnesses,* she thought as she switched on the porch light. *The perfect capper to my day.*

"Hi!" her neighbors said with bright smiles.

Bill and Helen Markham.

"Hi, yourselves," Katy answered, finding her own voice had genuine delight. They were, after all, very nice, likeable people. "Come in!"

Helen looked at Bill. "Oh no, you just got home. We just thought you'd want your packages."

Katy slapped her forehead. "The FedEx stuff! I'd forgotten! It's been a day and a half. I'll come over and get them, thanks!"

Bill lifted his long arms, revealing two white packages. "Got 'em here. Shall I bring them in?"

Katy nodded, opening the screen door wide enough for the pair to move inside.

"From Apple Computer?" Bill asked. "Not trying to be nosy, but I use Macs myself. I'm always looking for another Mac nut."

"Guilty," Katherine replied. "One of these boxes has an AirPort Extreme inside. I'm going wireless."

"Now you're talkin'!" Bill gushed. Helen gave him a sharp look. "Well, you're busy. But I'd love to talk Apple with you soon. Maybe this weekend?"

"Sure. Why don't we get together on Saturday?"

Helen nodded. "That would be really nice. We have a couple coming in Friday night, but we'll be free after breakfast. Why don't you come over for lunch?"

"Sounds good. Noon?"

"Noon will do fine," Helen said. "Bill, we should let Katy open her boxes in peace. Come on. Good-bye, Katy!"

Bill reluctantly followed his wife out the door, and Katy closed the screen behind them. She decided to leave the main door open for a bit. The evening was warm, and the gentle breeze and scent of flowers from the front garden soothed her soul.

Although the temptation of the white boxes was strong, Katherine's hunger was stronger. She decided to call Josh to see if he'd mind pizza. Extra large with lots of pepperoni and mushrooms.

She retrieved her bags from the kitchen and found the brand-new cordless phone she'd purchased on sale. Within ten minutes, she'd plugged it into an outlet she'd discovered behind the china hutch in the kitchen and had started the initial charging process. The handset required twelve full hours, but she could use the speakerphone anytime. Dialing the news office, she wasn't surprised when Joshua's voice answered.

"Chronicle."

"Don't you ever go home?" she asked from the sink, thinking, *This speakerphone is going to be very handy.*

"I wish." She could sense his weariness. Maybe she should cancel tonight. "But not before seeing you, I hope. Are we still on for this evening?"

"If you can stand a change in menu. I'm bushed, so how about a gigantic pizza from Leo's?"

"Sounds good. I'll pick it up if you like."

"I can call for delivery. They shouldn't be all that busy on a Wednesday. Come on by, and we'll fill our bellies and fall asleep in front of the television."

"Perfect. I'm on my way. Oh, no anchovies."

Katy pressed the off button then pressed on again. She called Leo's Perfect Pizza for their biggest pie, sans anchovies, and hung up once again. Forty-five minutes was the promised delivery time, which left her just enough time to unpack the Apple boxes and set up the AirPort.

The doorbell rang.

"Coming!" she called, wondering if the Markhams had returned. To her surprise, Gerald Anderson was waving to her through the closed screen door.

"Evenin', Kate. Sorry I'm a bit early."

She'd forgotten that he'd made an appointment to go through the paperwork!

"Mr. Anderson! I had forgotten! Please come in."

He looked disappointed. "Forgotten? Should we reschedule?"

"No, no. It's fine! Excuse the boxes. I just received some new computer equipment."

He glided past her, remarkably easy on his feet for someone so round. "Shall we work in the kitchen? Cissy always preferred it."

"That will be just fine," she replied, leading him toward the back of the house. "Would you like some coffee, Mr. Anderson? I'm making a fresh pot."

"It's Gerry, remember? And I'd love some."

Katherine removed the SuperMart bags from the table and ground some fresh hazelnut. "Sit down, Gerry. It'll only take a few minutes. Say, I found some of Cissy's peanut butter cookies in her freezer. Would you like some?"

"Oh, I love those cookies. I could eat a dozen at a time! Mind if I spread out?" he asked, lifting his briefcase.

"Go ahead. Are there a lot of papers?"

"A few," he replied, bringing out the fat file he'd shown her in the office. "You know, we're going to need a witness for some of these. Do you have a neighbor you can call?"

Joining him at the table, she nodded a yes. "Josh Carpenter will be here in a little while. Will he do?"

"Oh, yes! He's a good man. I didn't know you knew each other."

"We go way back."

As if on cue, Joshua appeared at the open French doors. "Yoo-hoo!"

"Perfect timing, Carpenter!" Katy laughed. "Come on in!"

"Hello, Gerry," Josh greeted. "Hi, Katy Celeste," he said, kissing the top of her head. "Legal stuff?"

"Lots of legal stuff," Gerry said with a belly laugh. "Aunt Cissy took good care of Miss Adamson. You're just in time to be our witness."

"If I can have some of these cookies, it's a deal."

Katy started to get up.

"Stay put," Josh told her. "Coffee, Gerry?"

"Sure. Black for me. Gotta watch my figure," he laughed, patting his ample belly.

"Katy? Three sugars and some of that vanilla creamer?"

"Perfect," she answered, content to let him serve. "The fridge is stocked with cold Big Red. Help yourself."

Once the snacks were distributed, Gerry began explaining the first of a dozen legal documents. "Simply put, this whole mess explains Cissy's finances and her disposition of those finances. Like I said in my office yesterday morning, Cissy left her house and all her real property to you as well as her other assets. There is only one thing she left to someone else. She left two letters. One's addressed to you and the other to Enoch Jones."

"Jones?" she asked, setting her coffee mug down. "Well, I suppose that makes some sense. He was her pastor."

"True. I haven't opened the letter, Kate. Although your aunt left one for each of you, you don't need to wait until Jones is present. So, here it is. You just need to sign here, showing receipt of the letter."

The meeting passed in that fashion, with the lawyer explaining fine legal points of Katherine's inheritance, Katy and Josh signing on a series of lines marked with red Xs, and Gerry stamping each document with a notary's seal.

By the time they finished, the delivery girl from Leo's had arrived, and Gerry begged off their invitation to join them.

"I have to get home," he told them, gathering up the paperwork. "Doris has a roast in the oven. I'll call Pastor Jones tomorrow morning about his letter. Should I suggest that he contact you?"

Katy followed the Kentucky lawyer to the door. "That'll be fine. I'd like to meet him anyway. Tell your wife I'm sorry to have made you later for dinner. Oh! Here's a bag of Cissy's cookies. I think there are two dozen in there."

Gerry took the zippered bag eagerly. "These are a true gift, Katy. I'll keep them in my office. Doris isn't much on letting me have sweets. Well, good night!"

He shouldered his heavy bag and turned toward the front door, but stopped suddenly as though he'd forgotten something. "Katy, there is one more thing, and it's something your aunt was real particular about."

"Yes?" she asked.

"Well, she told me you needed to find her diary. She was insistent that you find it and read it."

Katherine looked puzzled, and Josh stopped cutting the pizza. "Diary?" he asked.

"That's right," the lawyer continued. "She was supposed to give me the diary for safekeeping, but she must have forgotten. I assume it's here in the house somewhere. Maybe she mentions it in your letter. Anyway, I've done my job. That's all there is to it! I'm headin' home. You can call me anytime, if you have any more questions. Good night!"

"Good night, Gerry," Katy said with a smile. "And thanks for everything."

"Good night, Gerry," Josh called as they waved good-bye to the attorney.

Once he'd gone, Katherine returned to the kitchen and began serving up the pizza. As he had done the night before, Joshua insisted on saying a prayer of thanks for the food. Afterward, as they sat on the four-season porch, enjoying their food, Katherine began to talk about Cissy.

"What can you tell me about Cissy's death?" she asked him, her voice growing serious.

Josh wiped his mouth. "Well, she hadn't appeared sick at all. In fact, she headed up the ladies' circle that cooked for Ernie Pigman's eightieth birthday celebration at the church. Best fried chicken in town, that was Cissy's magic touch. That was only three days before she died."

"How did she die?" Katherine asked, looking into Joshua's honest eyes. "No one gave me a good answer to that. I assumed it was a heart attack or something."

"No one told you?"

"Gerry Anderson called me at ten o'clock Sunday night. He said I should come right away, but that Cissy's funeral had already taken place. So I got up at dawn, drove like a banshee, and arrived here late Monday morning. I'm still wondering why the hurry and why all the secrecy?"

Joshua swallowed his last bite of Leo's special recipe, dabbing his mouth before he answered. "Well, I honestly am not sure about Gerry's odd request that you come right away. I heard about Cissy when Enoch Jones called me. He asked if I could come over and identify her for the funeral home."

"Why is all this so complicated?" Katy asked, her voice rising in frustration. "Did she die of some terrible disease?"

159

"I don't think so. I drove to Eden Bible, and sure enough, Cissy's body lay in a little wooden coffin there in the vestibule. Doc Prosser and Toby Wilson from Wickert's Funeral Home were there. Pastor Jones said she was to be cremated right away. She looked really peaceful, Katy. I don't know if I've ever seen a more serene face."

"Thanks, Josh."

"You should read the letter, Katy. Maybe there are some answers in it."

With all the other legal papers, she'd forgotten about the letter. Clearing the plates to the kitchen sink, Katherine retrieved the slim, white envelope and returned to her chair on the TV porch. She opened it with her thumb, forming a jagged edge along the opening. "I never was much of a one for letter openers. Seems like they're handier for murder mysteries than day-to-day use."

"Yes. Well, you always did choose the hard way to do things, Katy girl."

"You should talk. OK, so here it is:

> *Dearest Little Katy,*
>
> *Soon, you will be reading this letter, and if I know you, you'll be mad at me for keeping such a secret. No doubt, Gerry Anderson has called you, and you've rushed to Eden to pay your last respects. First off, don't blame Gerry. He's doing my wishes, and he's a friend I can trust. You can trust him, too. That's the problem here, you see. Trust. This town's changed since you were last here ten years ago, darling Katy. Now, I'm not saying that because I'm trying to make you feel bad about not visiting much. Not a bit of it. Although you didn't call much, you were faithful about sending your little letters, and bless you, you always sent*

a check, too. Gerry will tell you what I've done with those checks. God has grown them into a nice little nest egg. You use that money to help fight the good fight.

What fight? Well, you'll figure that one out. Pastor Jones can help you. He sees things. He helped me to see them, and I've stood up to them when I could, but mostly I've fought from my knees. God watched over me, and He strengthened me, and He'll strengthen you as well, little one.

Remember how you gave your heart to Him when you were just ten? I wrote it down in my Bible. You look. It's there. It's to remind you of Whose you are.

Now, back to how you're mad at me. I didn't tell you I was sick, because I'm not. If I do get sick, I'll call you, and I'll rewrite this letter. But right now, I'm fit as a fiddle, waiting for the Good Lord's return to catch us up to His bosom. However, since you're reading this, I've gone on ahead. Ask Pastor Enoch about the why and the how of it. I can't see ahead, but I know right now I'm healthy, so my death may be natural or it may be through <u>their</u> unholy hands. If that is so, you promise me and God—no vengeance. That belongs to Him. He'll make them pay.

You, darling girl. You call on your old beau, Joshua Carpenter. He isn't married, because he's waiting for you. So, you get back with him. And you talk to Pastor Enoch. The three of you can trust Gerry Anderson and Doc Prosser. Use the little nest egg and the house I'm leaving to you.

Finally, read my diary. It's here, but I can't say exactly where, just in case this letter gets stolen. I'll try to remember to give it to Gerry, but I can't promise anything. I may not have time.

I love you so, Katy dear. Just like a daughter. Your poor parents did well by you by sending you to church, and I wish

*you could have had them with you always. That's not God's
way, hon. Oh, but what a gift He gave to me when you came
to my home! I have always been proud of you, Katy darling.
God gave you the heart and the brains to fight His fight.
Your books show that. I've read each one over and over.
They've helped me to see how brave you are.*

*I thank Jesus our Redeemer for His many gifts to you.
May His Holy Spirit protect you and instruct you and give
you the insights and discernment to test the spirits. We don't
wrestle against flesh and blood, Katy. The fight is a spiritual
one. And the evil is here in Eden.*

*I will see you soon, dearest one. I'll be waiting for you
on that Great Gettin' Up Mornin'! Until then, be vigilant.
Keep to your knees, Katy. And keep your eyes on Him.*

Love, Cissy

Katherine lowered the letter, her eyes filled with tears.
"She's gone, Josh. She's really gone!" she cried, burying her
face in her shaking hands.

Joshua moved to her, sitting on the arm of her chair. "She's
in the presence of God, Katy. And she's pain free and more
joyful than she had ever imagined."

Sobbing uncontrollably, Katherine was content to let him
hold her. The pain of losing the one anchor in her life had
only just become real to her. Cissy Adamson was gone. Eden
would never feel like the same town.

CHAPTER Twenty-two

THURSDAY MORNING

E noch Jones had chosen to walk that morning. Having risen early, before five, he'd donned a light jacket and an old pair of Adidas and taken to the hills surrounding Eden. The brisk morning air of mid-May stung his cheeks a bit, but the sensation helped to wake him.

He'd slept little the night before, yet Enoch felt alive and alert. His small parsonage sat on the same wooded lot as Eden Bible, nestled into the embrace of Paradise Hill, one of the four miniature mountains that fed into the valley of Eden. Jones loved these hills. To the east, the midnight blue sky had begun to lighten, and the faintest hint of pink brushed the crown of the hill beyond. Climbing to the highest point on Paradise Hill, a wide plateau he'd nicknamed Little Zion, Jones lifted up his hands toward the sky and began to talk to God.

"Good morning, Lord! What a blessed day this is! It is another day, handmade by You, and handpicked for our enjoyment. I thank You for it. And I pray for Your strength to lead me to and through whatever joys or sorrows this day may have in store. I ask this is Your Son's name—Praise Jesus! My blessed Redeemer! Amen! Amen!"

Then he began to sing an old spiritual his mother, Abigail Jones, had taught him as a young boy. He remembered how she would sing it while washing dishes in their tiny house, her soft, dark hands wrinkled with age and hard work. Her voice had filled the corners of the house and filled up the emptiness of his young heart. She sang like a nightingale, golden alto tones of rich warmth and love.

I am a poor wayfaring stranger, travelin' through this world below! There is no sickness, toil, nor danger in that bright world to which I go! I'm goin' there to see my mother—she said she'd meet me when I come! I am jes' goin' over Jordan! I am jes' goin' over home!

As he sang, Enoch wept. Not tears of sadness or regret, but of unspoken joy and anticipation. She waited for him there. Just as his father waited. Just as his dear wife waited. Enoch knew it as surely as he stood now upon this earth.

As he looked below, he saw Eden, the city named for a garden of eternal perfection. This Eden bore little resemblance to that glorious place, with one exception: This Eden, too, had a snake.

Closing his eyes, Enoch began to pray softly. Time grew shorter every day. *We wrestle not against flesh and blood.* Yet the enemy had begun to use the flesh as a harbor, and people as cattle. *Fight the good fight.* Looking eastward, the sun had begun to rise, and the skies brightened to proclaim God's victory.

Jesus Christ has won the war already, Enoch told himself. *All you need do is stand ready to proclaim it.*

Wishing he could linger here in this glorious place, Jones sighed and began the careful descent back to his home. *I am a poor wayfaring stranger,* he thought. *But the road still requires my earthly feet to trod upon its rocky pavement.* A sudden gust nearly blew him off the path. The northwestern wind chilled him to the bone, and he drew the light jacket closer to his throat. The last breath of winter nibbled at his unprotected ears, whispering hateful things.

Enoch ignored the whisperings and sang, his eyes filling with tears as he lifted his hands to heaven.

I know dark clouds will gather round me—I know my way is rough and steep. But golden fields lie out before me, where God's redeemed shall ever sleep. I'm going there to meet my Father; He said He'd meet me when I come! I am jes' goin' over Jordan. I am jes' goin' over home!

Home. How sweet a word that was! But before he could see that golden land and meet his heavenly Father face-to-face, Enoch Jones knew he must face the evil one. The fight had only just begun.

CHAPTER Twenty-three

Katherine had slept in, her weary body forcing her to catch up on days of restless nights. Although Heidi had begun her usual evening barking, she had stopped before eleven, leaving Katy a peaceful night for uninterrupted dreaming.

Joshua had left relatively early, sensing Katy's need for sleep, but promising lunch the next day. The kind newsman had been her rock all evening, listening to her as she reminisced and drying her tears with his strong hands. In only a few short days, Katherine had come to rely upon Joshua Carpenter. Either he had grown more reliable with age, or she had simply begun to see him with clearer eyes.

As she sipped her coffee, Katy realized suddenly that she hadn't needed or even thought about her anxiety pills for days. Was it this town? Surely not. She'd come here because of her surrogate mother's death, to resolve her estate, and now she'd even taken up residence in a house filled with memories.

But somehow, this was now Katy's home.

Wishing to stay home for the morning, but knowing she had errands to run, Katherine decided to call the Eden Home and Eden County National Bank to make appointments to go over Cissy's accounts. Then she realized that ECNB might be closed today. After all, the bank had just lost its president in the worst way possible.

What was going on in Eden? Two teens kidnapped or worse. The mysterious sightings over Miller's Farm. Professor Fields' weird allegations, and his even weirder abrupt departure and denial of those allegations. Then there was Aunt Cissy's sudden death, as of yet unexplained.

And poor Amy Horine was still missing.

No matter what his last denials might show, Fields knew something. Katherine had left three more messages for him, but either he hadn't picked them up or he was ignoring her calls.

"I'll find out why he's ducking me!" she said aloud, gulping down the last of the coffee. Despite Katy's wish to lounge about the house for a few hours, she decided to shower and dress. She'd relax tonight. For now, she owed it to Aunt Cissy to find out what was going on in Eden.

According to the school's published schedule, classes didn't end until Friday, so Fields should be in his office. Katy checked the campus website and discovered Fields had office hours of one to two-thirty. She had a little time until he'd be in the office, so that meeting could wait.

First stop for the day, then, would be Eden Bible Church, where she'd pay a call on Enoch Jones.

———

Thursday mornings at Eden Bible were fairly quiet. Wednesday nights, the church's prayer meeting and Bible study drew in a decent number, especially lately. The previous night, Jones had been delighted to greet nearly fifty eager parishioners, who had crowded into the front pews for a few old hymns and an hour-long lesson on Revelation, chapter three. The new study in prophecy, begun in March, had steadily drawn larger midweek crowds, and Jones considered it a privilege to open God's Word to his growing congregation.

Thursday night meant visitation, a chance to pay a call on shut-ins, new visitors from the previous Sunday's services, and a chance to share the Gospel with those who were ready to hear it. Enoch had learned that, like all things, there was a season for planting the seed of God's Word. The parable of the sower made it plain enough. The ground of a man's heart had to be ready to receive, so Enoch had learned to plow and till that ground first through genuine love and help with life's material needs.

Very often, he and whoever might accompany him on visitation night would carry groceries, medical supplies, or reading material to those with such needs. Usually, people were surprised but grateful. Sometimes, they listened as he read from the gospel of John. Eventually, some of them heard and believed, for the Spirit had given them the ears they needed. When the heart's ground is ready, God's seed takes deep root.

This Thursday morning found Jones sifting through the morning's mail. A few bills, advertisements from local businesses, a postcard from a church member on vacation in Hawaii, and a personal letter from a fellow he'd studied with back in Bible college. Just as he was about to open it, he heard a soft knocking at his study door.

"You have a visitor, Pastor Jones," his part-time secretary, Emmy Callahan said with her usual bright smile. "Are you expecting a Miss Adamson?"

"Miss Adamson? No, I wasn't—wait. Miss Katherine Adamson?"

"That's right," the young woman answered. "Do you have time to see her?"

Rising, Jones nodded his graying head. "Of course. Show her in, Miss Callahan. And could you bring in a pot of that wonderful coffee you make? And sugar and some creamer, too. I think this meeting could take a while."

"I brought in some lemon squares from home, Pastor. Want some?"

"Am I dead, Miss Callahan? Your lemon squares could revive me even if I were! Bring them in, and thank you for being so kind."

Emmy disappeared, her broad smile and slight blush evidence of her genuine, giving heart. Moments later, she reappeared with Katherine and a tray laden with goodies. "Miss Adamson, this is Pastor Jones. Here's some coffee and home-made lemon squares. I can make tea, if you prefer, Miss Adamson."

Katy helped the secretary with the tray. "No need. Coffee runs in my veins. And the lemon squares smell heavenly."

"I'll leave you to it then," she said, leaving the pair alone.

"Good morning, Miss Adamson. Won't you sit down?"

Katherine took a seat in an aging walnut chair opposite an equally battered old desk. The office couldn't be any larger than twelve by twelve. The cramped space was packed with three bookshelves, stuffed to bursting with commentaries, lexicons, dictionaries, study guides, and fifteen different translations of the Bible. Katy hadn't realized that preaching the Gospel required so much scholarship.

Looking at the man who read these many volumes, Katy found him to be amazingly charismatic. There was something special in the soft brown eyes, framed by salt and pepper eyebrows and a host of pleasant creases. *He wears his life on his face,* she thought. *A hard life is written there, as though God carved his noble character into each gentle line.* She had never seen a face with more dignity. No wonder Aunt Cissy admired and trusted this man.

"Good morning, Pastor Jones. My aunt spoke very well of you in a letter she left me. And Gerry Anderson told me how you took care of Cissy after her passing. Thank you for honoring her last wishes, although I confess I don't understand them."

"I can see why you wouldn't," he told her. "Cream and sugar?" he asked, pouring the coffee. "Your aunt shone like the sun, Miss Adamson. She's with our Lord now. You know that."

Katy took the cup. "Thank you. Yes, I know she is in heaven. If anyone could make it there, it's Cissy. She worked harder for God than anyone I've ever met."

Jones sat forward. "Hard work, no matter how much or how noble it may seem to us as human beings, is never going to buy a ticket to heaven, Miss Adamson. I'm sure you know that."

"You mean Jesus chose Cissy. I realize that. She loved to talk about Jesus, and she walked with Him, too."

"Jesus chose to die for Cissy, and she chose to accept that gift. And you? God has no grandchildren, Miss Adamson."

Katy began to feel a bit uncomfortable. "If you are asking me if I chose that gift, well, the truth is, Pastor Jones, I'm not sure. That's not why I'm here, though."

"Yes it is. You just don't realize it yet."

Sipping the strong coffee, Katherine fought the urge to squirm in the old chair. "You're certainly direct. How about if we talk about that later? I have several questions for you now. Then, I promise, you may ask me your pointed questions. Is that a deal?"

The preacher smiled, leaning back in his chair. Katherine relaxed, finding genuine warmth and reassurance in the broad smile. "Very well, Miss Adamson. Ask your questions. But don't presume to think I will forget to ask mine."

"Good enough. Pastor, can you tell me how my aunt died?"

"I thought that might be your first question. It certainly would be mine, had Celeste been my aunt. I'll tell you what I know. You said you received a letter from her. Did she mention anything about the recent changes in Eden?"

Katherine nodded. "She used that very phrase. By the way, she left you a letter as well. Gerry Anderson has it."

Jones appeared thoughtful for a moment. "That explains a lot. Mr. Anderson left a message for me at my home this morning, but I wasn't able to get back to him right away. I'll see about retrieving the letter from him this afternoon. But to answer your question, let me tell you just how Eden has changed.

"I've been pastor here for twenty-seven years. In that time, I've watched Eden go from bad to worse. According to my understanding of Eden's history, the town has never been a fortress of honor. It's ironic, is it not, that our little town should bear the name of God's perfect garden? Have you ever thought about it, Miss Adamson?"

Setting down her cup, Katy noticed a small finch that had landed on the window behind the pastor's head. The bird hung there, grasping at the peeling mullions as though trying to get their attention. His head feathers were etched with bright red. A house finch, Katy realized. A male. Behind him, swaying in the wind, perched upon the thin finger of the silver maple that sheltered the western section of the cemetery, was his mate, plump with the product of procreation.

171

"You'll need to find a place for your little finches," she said, not intentionally changing the subject, although it was making her a bit edgy.

Jones turned around. "Oh, so our Adam and Eve are back, are they? They're looking for the birdhouse we had out there last year. I'll have to put it out again this afternoon." Turning back to face her, he smiled again, not just with his mouth the way so many people do. He smiled with his eyes, too. He had a natural gift for putting people at ease. "Well, Miss Adamson? Do you think there even was an Adam and an Eve?"

She hadn't expected this question, although she should have. "I suppose so. I've never really thought about it. Does it matter much? I believe in Jesus. I've done that bit, you know, walked the aisle and all. Isn't that what you mean?"

Enoch Jones stood up, and she realized how tall and lean he was, elegantly lean like a wizened prophet of old. She could imagine him in ancient Israel, wrapped in billowing folds of muslin, his dark feet shod in well-worn sandals, his hands and face creased with the winds of many hard years. He seemed ageless. And she felt like a babe, awkward and answerless in the gaze of his piercing eyes.

"I'm pleased to hear that you walked the aisle, Miss Adamson."

"Call me Katy. My aunt always did."

"Katy then." That smile again, soft and filled with light.

Walking to one of the bookshelves, Enoch removed a large black volume. "This is the entire Bible in the original languages. I can't read it in all those original languages, not fluently, but I can read the translations. Do you read Hebrew, Katy?"

She shook her head. The question sounded rhetorical.

"Few can. Nor can most average folks read ancient Greek or, heaven help them, begin to understand Aramaic. Yet, those who can do so, inspired and led by God, have unlocked the language doors for us and provided each of us a free pass to the incredible truth that is in this book. Why even little children can understand it. I'll bet you were taught to memorize verses from it when you were young."

Katherine nodded. "Each Sunday morning, we had to recite a verse, and back then in Miss Ford's class at school on Monday, she'd expect us to say our Sunday morning verse. I tried to pass off 'Jesus wept' on her one Monday. I had to write an essay as my reward for being insolent."

"Would that schools today had such curricula!" Jones said, returning to his chair. "The point is that anyone can have access to this Book. It's God's Word, Spirit-breathed. And every word in it is true and important. That includes the bit about Adam and Eve at the beginning. If I were to read one of your books, which I have by the way—I enjoy your writing very much—but if I were to read one and tear out the first chapter, saying it didn't matter, would that disturb you? Would that affect my understanding of the remainder of the book?"

"I've never really thought of it that way, but yes. That would make understanding the book pretty much impossible."

"It's the same with God's Word, Katy. If you can't believe the beginning, then how can you expect to believe the rest? Adam and Eve were created in God's image, but they chose to believe Satan's lie over God's truth, and their sin is born into each one of us. Mankind—you and I—we were forever separated from God, because we were no longer perfect. But in His love for Adam and Eve, God provided a covering for them in the garden by slaying an animal. Why, it may even have been a lamb. That animal's blood covered the original sin, just as the skin covered their nakedness.

"But animal blood doesn't last. It would take the blood of another Adam to do that. That Adam—the last Adam—is Jesus Christ. You see, without believing in the garden, you cannot really know the Creator of that garden. You have to know why we need a Savior first."

Katherine had listened carefully, and she could see that his argument had merit. She didn't want to think about eternity, however. Not now. Maybe tomorrow.

"Pastor Jones, you have a lot passion, and it's clear you love God. I admire your gentle manner, and I suspect you are both a faithful friend and a formidable foe. Forgive the alliteration. It's my writer within, you know, but I would love—for now—to hear about Cissy. With the promise that we'll talk about this again, could you tell me about Cissy's last days?"

He laughed. "I'll hold you to that promise, Katy."

She felt lighter somehow. It was his easy manner. Perhaps here was a man who could be trusted. "Fair enough. Now, if you could tell me about Cissy?"

He handed her another cup of coffee, and then began to tell a tale stranger than even she had ever been told.

CHAPTER Twenty-four

By the time Katy left Eden Bible Church it was nearly noon. Her mind reeled with the stories—for stories and fables they must be!—that Pastor Jones had told her. As a writer of fiction based on life, she felt now that her life was based on fiction. The entire tale had sounded like one of the outrageous conspiracy theories Katherine used as fodder for her novels.

As a writer, Katy loved to scour the Internet for wild tales of paranoia, then twist them into the shape of something salable. She knew that many of her fans believed in her fantastic yarns of Masonic Masters and Jesuit Assassins. She had told her readers of alien advances and government cover-ups, that a heretic clique of blue bloods sought to rule the world and enslave the dull-witted masses, and that ghosts and goblins were nothing more than embodiments of dark forces seeking to eradicate humanity. She'd made several million in royalties by trading on man's inherent need to seek the sinister in life.

Now, she was being told that all these conspiracies had more than a grain of truth to them. Wickedness really did exist, and it had taken control of Eden.

As she fumbled for her car keys, she suddenly remembered her lunch date with Joshua. She was supposed to meet him at Little Tubby's near the college. Hopping into her car, Katherine drove back down to Main Street and took a right toward Eden College.

Established in 1822, Eden College overlooked the valley like a great stone sentry, perched upon a high impenetrable cliff. Below, the Ohio River snaked along the sandy shoreline of Eden, providing the connection to the east that the early settlements had required. Two centuries before, flatboats had glided lazily along the river, carrying supplies to the new frontier in exchange for warm beaver skins, so prized by the eastern elite, while curious natives, watching from the shores of Kentucky, looked upon the white strangers with suspicious eyes.

Katy remembered Eden College with mixed emotions. She'd gone to school here, earning a bachelor's degree in literature before moving on to dual master's degrees at IU in journalism and creative writing. Indiana University had seemed like a huge fishpond compared to the little mud puddle of Eden College, but Katy had loved it here. Maybe it was because she had been only moments away from town and Aunt Cissy. Maybe it was because of time spent with her friends—with Joshua.

Little Tubby's sat on the western edge of campus, squeezed in between a copy shop and a small bakery called Bread of Life. Katy parked in the tiny lot on the river side of Little Tubby's. Walking inside, the familiar, wonderful smell of prize-winning pizza hit her hungry nostrils. She'd spent many happy hours here, studying and laughing with Josh and Linda.

"One?" the young waitress asked. Her hair was bright blue, spiked into a rooster tail at the back of her head, and she wore a silver nose ring.

"I'm meeting someone. May I see if he's here?"

The girl shrugged, and left Katy to her own devices. The restaurant had a distinctive atmosphere. The main room's tables were square, topped with red-checkered vinyl, and the place looked very much like an old Italian restaurant. Each table was dressed with a trio of daisies in a vintage Coke bottle, and the air was filled with the music of Verdi's *La Traviata*.

Far to the back of the main room, Katherine spied a familiar face. Heading to the table, she put on her best smile. "Professor Fields?"

The man's head jerked up from the sheaf of papers where it had been buried. His nose seemed to twitch, and he looked for all the world like a rabbit caught in a trap.

"Miss Adamson! Well, uh, I'm in the middle of grading papers. I really don't have time to chat—I'd love to, you know, but..."

"Nonsense! You wouldn't want to spill wine on those papers anyway, Professor. And this saves me from meeting you later in your office. Why, it's serendipity!"

"Yes, so it is," he muttered, shifting the papers to his large and weather-beaten leather satchel.

She sat, deliberately not asking if he minded. "I understand classes are over tomorrow. You must have some exciting summer plans."

Swallowing, nearly choking, Fields dabbed his mouth. His smeared lenses made his eyes appear to swim. "Yes. Well, not exciting perhaps, but I will still be here. I teach a summer class, and I also plan on conducting some research into the mythology of southern Indiana's Melungeon legends."

"No UFO studies, Professor?"

"Miss Adamson! I know that my meeting with you on Tuesday may have given you the impression that I lean toward the salacious, but I assure you I do not. I would appreciate being taken seriously."

"Isn't Katy taking you seriously, Adrian? You're not giving her enough credit."

Both Katherine and Adrian Fields looked up. Joshua Carpenter's wide grin brightened the dim interior of the restaurant. "Sorry I'm late, Katy Celeste. I wasn't aware we were sharing lunch with the great professor. It's an unexpected delight!"

"Good afternoon, Joshua," the professor said meekly, his face beading with sweat. "Perhaps I should leave you two to your lunch."

"No, no!" Katy insisted. "Please, Professor Fields. I apologize for being so forward, but your sudden departure the other day got me thinking. It's clear you have insights into the recent UFO phenomena. I'd like to hear them. And I'd like to help you explain to the world."

She then took a pen from her purse and wrote a note on one of the napkins and handed the small note to the professor. When he had read it, his rounded shoulders sagged, and he buried his face into his hands. He shook like a child.

"Dear God, I don't know who to turn to anymore! Do you mean it? I can't talk here, I don't think. But I'll meet you at Miller's Farm. I trust Ben Miller. And I believe I can trust you."

"All right," Katy replied, ignoring Carpenter's puzzled expression. "Joshua and I will meet you there at four o'clock. Here's my cell phone number." She wrote the number on another napkin. "Don't worry, Professor Fields. You aren't in this alone."

He shook her hand, and she noticed how cold he was. "Four o'clock today? I can make that. Thank you. Thank you both." He rose, grabbed his satchel, and headed to the front to pay his bill.

After Fields' departure, Josh leaned forward and took Katy's note from its place near the professor's half-eaten spaghetti.

I know you've been threatened. We will help you.

"What's this all about?" the newsman asked her.

"It's a long story," she said. "But if you'll promise to buy, I'll fill you in."

Amy Horine had never enjoyed a shower more. It felt like ages since she'd been permitted to leave the isolated lab where she'd been held prisoner. Until this morning, she had been certain the shadows would kill her. Now she wasn't so sure. Though still frightened, Amy thought the woman who had helped her to this new room had appeared pleasant and very human.

The warm water streamed down Amy's small body in miniature rivers, and the fine, white soap cleaned away the stink left by her captors. Amy had no idea how long she'd been standing in the wonderful waterfall, but she knew she couldn't remain there. Soon the woman might come back, or worse, the *things*.

"Amy? Are you finished?" the woman's voice called from the other side of the door. "I have some towels for you."

Stepping out of the liquid warmth, Amy opened the door a bit. "Thanks," she said to the woman. "I'll put on the clothes you gave me."

"I'll be out here if you need me."

Amy dried her shivering body, toweled her hair, and put on the soft, white sleeping dress she'd been given. The bathroom appeared to be a normal one, the kind you'd find in any suburban home. Everything was white and sparkling.

Opening the door at last, the girl blinked at the brightness of the large bedroom. Why did her head hurt so? And her eyes felt small, contracted somehow. The room began to swim.

"Careful there!" the woman said, steadying Amy with smooth, white hands. "Come now, we'll take good care of you. You've been through quite an ordeal. Here, sit down on the bed. This will be your home for a while, Amy. I hope you like it."

"I want to go to my own home," she said for what felt like the millionth time. "My mother will be worried."

The woman wore white, and her long dark hair fell across her shoulders in gentle waves. Her pale, porcelain skin and bright blue eyes were a sharp contrast to the black waves of hair, and the woman's lyrical voice seemed almost otherworldly. "I know you want to see her, Amy. I promise, you will. Soon, she will be brought here. For now, we want you to make yourself at home. If this room isn't big enough, just let me know. We will see that you're pleased."

"Why? Where's Donny? I want to see Donny!" The knot that had formed at the back of her head tightened, and Amy's eyes instinctively closed to shut out the light. "It's too bright in here!"

The nurse stroked the girl's wet hair. "I'll turn down the lights. You need rest, dear. You mustn't get too excited. All will be explained in time. You'll see Donny and your mother, and you'll go home. But for now you must spend some time regaining your energies. I know you're full of questions, but you really must trust me. See the gorgeous view we've given you? After you've recovered completely, you can walk in that beautiful garden. Would you like that?"

Amy did feel tired, but she wasn't ready to sleep. Not yet. Too many questions were unanswered. "Why am I here?"

The woman took her pulse. "You're just overexcited, Amy. Remember how we found you in the woods outside? Do you remember anything that happened to you?"

Amy tried to recall, but it only made her headache worse. "Call my mother. I want to see my mother!" She pushed against the woman, making it to the door before soft arms enfolded her, and she felt a tiny prick at the back of her right arm.

"What was that?" she screamed.

The woman's hypnotic voice and soft hands surrounded her. "There, there, child. You're exhausted. You need rest. Here, come back to the bed, and Lilith will make the pain go away."

Near the bed, a floor-length picture window opened up onto an inner courtyard, lit in soft blues. Amy gazed out the window, her hair dripping onto the rich carpeting below her feet. The headache eased slightly, and she felt a wash of weariness overtake her.

"Is that a bird-of-paradise?" she asked the woman.

"It is," the dark-haired woman replied, turning down the temptingly soft comforter on the queen-size bed. "Here, come to bed for a rest. The harsh cold of what was is no more, little one. You can trust Lilith."

"Lilith? That's your name? It's so pretty."

"I am honored you think so. Now, rest. Close your eyes, dear one. I will put on soothing music for you."

Amy did as she was told, snuggling into the downy softness of the big bed. Somewhere, she could hear the gurgling of a brook. Lilith had put on a relaxation tape. Amy had heard them before in her mother's home. The soothing sounds took her to a natural space deep within her mind, and she drifted into a dreamless sleep.

CHAPTER Twenty-five

Miller's Farm lay seven miles east of Eden College, then a mile and a half south on Old Airport Road. Ben Miller had inherited the land from his father, who had inherited it from his father, and so on going back to Amos Miller in 1827.

Started as a truck farm to help support Amos's growing family, Miller's Farm had burgeoned into a local cornucopia of organic delights. Sweet corn, apples, pumpkins, sunflowers, and strawberries were raised on the seven-hundred-and-fifty acres, and a U-Pick-Em campaign had brought in big bucks with little effort.

Inside the pavilion, Ben Miller and his wife and three daughters sold jams, jellies, pies, breads, crafts, snack items, and toys for the kids. Depending on the season, the festive farm might draw as many as three hundred people per day. Lately however, it had begun to draw far more.

National attention for UFOs had never been in Ben's dreams. Since the sighting on Sunday night, his farm had become unwilling host to nearly a hundred hippies, yippies, and self-proclaimed moon goddesses. Tents sprang up like mushrooms, bonfires glowed at night, and Ben even considered sending his girls to their grandmother's in Seymour for their own safety.

He wished he'd never heard the word *alien*.

Barely sleeping at night due to the noise of late partiers and moaning chanters, Ben had been pleased to receive the phone call from Joshua Carpenter, who had promised to write an article debunking the landing if he found no evidence of aliens. Ben fairly jumped when he saw the lanky newsman walking toward the pavilion with an attractive lady.

"Mr. Carpenter!" he cried out, running to meet the pair. "Is this your wife?"

Josh blushed. "I wish. This is a good friend of mine, Katherine Adamson. She's a writer from St. Louis, and she's promised to demystify your aliens for you. Has Dr. Fields arrived here yet?"

"No, sir. He's supposed to meet you here, right? We haven't seen him. He'll be along, though. He's reliable, if a little kooky."

"Can you show us to the field then, Mr. Miller?"

"Ah, call me Ben, Mr. Carpenter. My dad was Mr. Miller. I'm just plain Ben."

"And I'm just plain Joshua, Ben. And this is Katy."

"Pleased to meet you, Miss Katy."

Katherine smiled. He was so wonderfully polite. She liked Ben Miller. No wonder Fields trusted him. "Nice to meet you, too, Ben. And it's just Katy."

Walking toward the back of the pavilion, Ben led them to a wide, freshly painted green gate. "The thing actually landed in a meadow where my cows graze. Like to scared the milk right out 'em! Really! I couldn't get any of them to give milk 'til this morning."

"You operate a dairy as well, Ben?" Katherine asked, suddenly glad that she'd gone back home to change into an old pair of jeans. She was doubly glad she'd put an old pair of sneakers that afternoon following lunch with Josh. Ben's cows had certainly made their marks in the world. Soft, circular, squishy marks.

"Good gracious no!" the farmer laughed. "We only have four milk cows, just for use in the goodies we make for selling. Of course, we use the homemade butter and the like ourselves. You should check out our store before you go."

"We'll make a point of it," she replied, following the two men through the gate and onto a heavily tracked dirt road. "How far is it?"

"The store? You just passed it. Oh, you mean the landing site! Sorry, I ain't sleepin' all that well of late. Brain's goin' soft. The site's not too far. It's just a few hundred yards over that little rise in front of us."

"You're not much of a country girl, are you Katy Celeste?" Joshua asked her, laughing.

"Yes, well, I don't see you volunteering to work the land there, Cowboy."

"Do they raise ham sandwiches, do you think?" he said as he helped her maneuver a rather large rut. "That lasagna I had at Tubby's is long gone."

"You and your metabolism! Just stay with it, and we can have an early supper, all right?"

"Wait!" a voice shouted from behind them. The group turned to see a frantic Adrian Fields, waving his thin arms wildly, his graying comb-over flying in the breeze.

"Wait for me!" he called again, doing his best to run.

"Hey, Professor!" the farmer called. "You're just in time. Come on!"

Katherine and Joshua helped the teacher over a mud puddle, and everyone shook hands. "Sorry I'm late," he said, fixing his hair as best he could. "A student showed up at the last minute wanting to know why she flunked the last exam."

"No problem," Miller said happily. "Well, let's go see this thing."

The trio followed Miller through several gates and into a field left fallow for the year. Guitar music and singing filled the air, and Katy saw what could only be described as a tent city. Miller hadn't been kidding when he'd said a hundred hippies had moved in. Katy estimated even more. As they walked past the circus of alien-watchers, hands reached out to touch the farmer. "Way to go, man!" and "Hey, dude, you're too cool!" and "Have they contacted you yet?" were heard as they passed through the crowd.

"It's only a little bit further," Miller muttered, embarrassed by the attention. "Up there, just over that rise." He led them past the last of the tents and helped Katherine climb the small hill that led to the site.

"Whoa!" Josh said suddenly. "Is that it?"

"That's it," Miller said, his voice strained. "That's the gosh-darned thing that's ruining my farm."

Ben Miller was one of the last of a rare breed. Taller than Joshua and stockily built, Miller's rough hands and gentle soul were the hallmarks of heartland farmers. As he stood next to the outer edge of the landing site, it struck Katherine just how strange this juxtaposition was. Before them stretched a gigantic scorched circular formation, a form that appeared to follow intelligent design. Had it been a simple ring, the phenomenon might have been more easily explained, but this ring's exterior showed an intricate chain pattern, while the interior rings—there were six concentric rings—were really a series of shapes that formed a circle. At 6'5" tall, even Miller seemed tiny compared to the gigantic imprint in the grass.

The farmer slapped his seed corn cap against one thigh. "Helluva thing!"

Joshua squatted, picking at the darkened grass. "You may be close, Ben."

"Ah, Joshua, you don't think it's real, do you? Tell me this was made by some big acetylene torch or somethin'!"

"Adrian, you came out within hours, didn't you? Has it changed since then?"

Fields caught up to the group and shaded his eyes against the sun. "Changed? I'm not sure what you mean, Joshua."

Carpenter pointed toward the hippie compound, raising an eyebrow. "These people would have a vested interest in making this appear to be extraterrestrial. Can you see anything new or different than when you first came out?"

The professor studied the blackened areas carefully. "It appears to be the same," he admitted. "Though I'd have to compare photographs to know for certain. You know, Miss Adamson, I've studied these phenomena all over the world for nearly twenty years. Most crop circles follow a general pattern. That is, they generally consist of a geometric shape formed by altering the orientation of grass, wheat, corn, or whatever vegetation exists in the field. But this one, well, it's different."

"Different?" she asked. "How? The burns, you mean?"

"The burns, as you call them, are something much more. Look carefully," he told them, bending toward the ground.

The grass, although clearly blackened, hadn't been burned or painted. Instead, it looked as if it had been redesigned from the inside.

"Touch it," the professor said, taking Katherine's hand and pulling it into the formation.

As her fingers touched the grass, Katherine's mind seemed to open. She heard voices, music, felt heat and cold, all at the same time. And behind her, she heard a clicking sound.

"Katy?" called a woman's voice.

Katherine looked up, still touching the ground. "Aunt Cissy?" she cried out softly like a child who's been lost. "Is that really you?"

The image shimmered in the sun, smiling just as Cissy always smiled. "It's me, dear," the image spoke, but the mouth continued to smile without forming words. "You should rest, child. Go home. Back to your own house in Kirkwood. You'll be happiest there."

"Cissy!" she cried out, trying to rise, but she was unable to remove her hand from the circle. "Cissy!"

"Katy!" came another voice from somewhere beyond space and time. "Katy Celeste!"

Someone pulled her up, jerking her back into reality.

"Katy!" Joshua called, spinning her to face him. "Honey, are you all right?"

Blinking, Katherine struggled to recall where she'd been. Had she seen her aunt?

"You see?" she heard another man ask. The professor? "You see? Now, tell me this isn't real!"

"Are you OK, Miss Katy?" Miller asked, his face filled with worry. "I'm sorry! We shouldn't have come out here. This thing is spooky! Come on, we'll go to the house. You'll feel better after you sit down."

Katherine shook her head. She had seen Cissy. Or had she? "I'm all right. I—I'm just a little bit tired, I suppose. Thanks, Ben. I'm fine. We should—we should get some pictures."

"We'll get pictures later," Joshua insisted. "Ben's right. We should go on home, Katy."

187

"Home?" she repeated. "Should I go home?"

"She looks real pale," Miller said. "Should I call Doc Prosser?"

Adrian Fields pranced alongside her like a puppy. "You felt it, didn't you? The same thing happened to me! It's harmonic, isn't it? Like being inside music!"

"That's enough for now, Adrian," Carpenter said flatly. "Why don't you take some photos for comparison, and I'll see that Katy gets home. We'll give you a call this evening."

Fields shrugged. "Very well, but you should experience it for yourself, Joshua. There's much more here than anyone can imagine!"

"Ben, you stay with Fields. Perhaps this thing is real, but we still need to find out why it's here. Can you get a sample of the grass for me? I'd like to send it to a molecular biologist friend of mine."

"Sure thing, Mr. Carpenter."

―――――

Once back at the car, Joshua settled Katherine into the passenger seat and started the motor.

"What happened?" she asked, her eyes clearing. "How did I get here?"

Joshua looked at her with worried eyes. "I'll explain it on the way home. Why don't you close your eyes, and try to get a little rest."

"Rest?" she echoed, sitting up straight. "I thought we were going to see the crop circle? Wait—we did. Isn't that Ben Miller? I did meet him, right?"

Joshua nodded, kissing her forehead. "I'll go see what he wants." He exited the car, leaving the engine running.

"Sorry to stop you, Mr. Carpenter, but I thought you might want to know we found another one."

"What?" Josh asked. "Another crop circle?"

Miller nodded. "Now those people will never leave."

"Ben, keep this quiet, OK? Tell no one. And make the professor promise the same thing. Try to take samples of both formations, and I'll call my friend about analyzing it. Here, you watch Miss Adamson for a moment while I make the call. We should probably get right on this."

"OK, Mr. Carpenter."

"You can call me Joshua, Ben. You know that."

"OK, Mr. Joshua."

"Thanks, Ben," he said, taking his cell phone out of his pocket. "Give me a minute." He walked away a few short paces, leaving Ben to talk to Katherine.

"You feelin' better, Miss Katy?"

Katherine smiled. "Much better. Thanks, Ben."

Ben touched her hand, and she could feel the rough calluses. "You and Josh just friends, Miss Katy?" he asked her suddenly.

Katherine blinked. "Are farmers always so direct, Ben?"

Removing his cap, Miller scratched at his head, further tousling the thick crop of sandy blond hair. "Time is short, Miss Katy. We may think we have years for makin' choices, for livin', but all we really have is today. You know what I mean? Don't waste the time you're given."

Katherine realized suddenly that her mouth was open. Few people surprised her anymore, but she would not have guessed that this man of the earth had the soul of a philosopher. "You're a very complex man, Ben Miller. Thank you for the advice. I promise to think about it."

"Think about what?" Josh asked, returning to the car. "My friend says he can't make it here today, but he will come out here tomorrow. He's from Bloomington, and he's a smart

189

cookie. His name is Alan Dylan. He'll call you, if that's all right. If his schedule eases up today, he may want to come out on his own this evening. Is that all right, Ben?"

"What's one more?" the farmer asked. "Will you two be coming back?"

"I'd like to," Katherine said. "I'd like to see this from the air, too."

"Great idea!" Joshua cried. "Ben, we'll call you and let you know just when we're coming back. Thanks so much for giving us your time."

"My pleasure," he answered with a tip of his cap. "Nice to meet you, Miss Katy. I hope you're feeling better. And you remember what I said now."

Katherine smiled. "I will. We'll see you soon, Ben."

Getting back into the car, Joshua kissed her hand. "Feel up to an adventure? Or should I take you home?"

"Adventure is my middle name," she answered, suddenly feeling much better. "Where are we going?"

"You'll see," he laughed, and pointed the car east.

CHAPTER Twenty-six

Digger Martin had been flying crop dusters for twenty-seven years. A Vietnam pilot, the eccentric Martin had floundered for years following his return to the States. Flying a chopper for the MASH units had meant flying a chopped meat wagon. Martin had seen more death and dying than any man should. After returning home to Indiana, he'd found the irritating normality of his former neighbors maddening. Martin no longer fit in.

Then he'd met Arnie Putnam. Putnam ran a small airport and needed topnotch pilots who could fly short hops to Indianapolis or Louisville, but who weren't so high fallutin' that they saw themselves as too good to fly a crop run. That had been twenty-seven years before. Since then, Arnie had gone on to his eternal reward, whatever that was, and Martin had bought out Arnie's widow.

Martin had met Joshua Carpenter during last summer's hydroplane races in Madison. Carpenter was there to cover the boat races, as well as the local festivities. Martin had gone as part of an air show. The two had hit it off instantly.

So, when Josh called to ask if Martin could help with an aerial surveillance project, he had jumped at the chance.

"So, what is it we're looking for, Josh old buddy?" the quirky pilot asked.

"You can't miss it, Digger. Just fly over Ben Miller's place, and you'll see it."

Martin gnawed the unlit cigar that always dangled from his mouth. Martin shaved once a week, only when necessary, and he wore the same clothes every day—not that he wore dirty clothes, he just had identical clothes in his closet. His therapist claimed it was his compulsion to remain in uniform. Martin just figured it was his need to keep it simple.

"You're lookin' for that UFO site, aren't you?"

"You could call it that. I want to get some photos from the air."

"You're gonna love it, buddy. I been over it seven or eight times the past two days. WNN paid me for it. You ever met Brent Snowman?"

"You mean Brent Snowden?" Katherine chimed in. She'd been making quiet observations from the back seat of the Piper Cub. She wasn't crazy about flying, and it was easier to worry about crashing if you kept nice and quiet.

"Snowden? Oh, yeah, I guess so. Anyway, and you'll like this one, Kate, he blew back to D.C.—he's a bigwig you know—so he's replaced by a blond Amazon woman! Oh man, she can fly with me anytime!"

"You've never been married, I take it, Digger?" Katherine asked, keeping her mind on anything other than flying.

"Oh, yeah, sure I have! Been married four times. But no one stays with me for long. Guess I'm a bad husband. Krystal, she was number three, she stayed with me for—uh, let's see—goin' on five years."

"You have children?" she asked.

"Seven. All girls. We all get together a couple of times a year. Their mothers don't hold grudges. I'm likeable enough. I'm just no account as a husband. You ever know a man like that, Kate?" He banked the plane heavily to the right, throwing both passengers askew.

Closing her eyes to regain her tenuous composure, Katherine took a deep breath. "I've known such men." She imagined David, who had claimed to be single, with his wife in California and three children.

"Well, I hope you dump them when they come along. My kind, Kate, we're no good. Now Josh here, he's all right. Why not clamp onto him? Josh, whatcha think?"

"I think Katy is a very discriminating woman, Digger. Isn't that Miller's Farm down there?"

Below them, a panorama of patchwork formed a natural quilt. Newly planted cornfields, green meadows, and rolling hills seemed stitched together by giant hands into a breathtaking artwork of the land. However, one portion of this landscape appeared grossly out of place. Close to Miller's barn, lay a large square of green centered with an angry brand of black circles.

"Yup. That's the place. I'll get in closer. Hang on, Katy girl!"

He dove forward, taking the plane into the heart of the meadow, straightening at the last moment to fly just a few hundred feet above the field. Joshua snapped wildly with his digital camera, then with a second film camera. "I make out three circles. How about you, Digger?"

"Three?" the pilot asked as he tapped on the altimeter. "I thought there were just the two."

"You saw two on every trip?" Josh asked, looking back at Katy to see if she was all right. She nodded, though her face had gone rather pale.

"Well, Josh, I can't really say. I figured my passengers were the ones looking at that stuff. I just fly the plane. I think Snowman..."

"Snowden," Katy corrected.

"Yeah, Snowden—thanks, Kate—well, he said something about two instead of one. You see three?"

"Three," Josh answered, using binoculars to examine the field more carefully. "Make that four."

"Four?" both Katy and Digger echoed. "That can't be!" Katherine added, leaning into the window. "That has to be impossible!"

"You'd think so," Joshua continued, exchanging his binoculars for the film camera, snapping additional shots of all four shapes.

"Can you take us over again?" he asked the pilot. Katherine moaned.

"Sure!"

The plane climbed then made an identical dive and flyover. After seven such maneuvers, Joshua tapped Martin on the shoulder. "Thanks, Digger. That should do it."

Once on the ground, Martin handed out complimentary Cokes to his passengers and offered a free ride to Katherine anytime. "I'm taking that beauty of a WNN gal out this evening. Who knows? Maybe she'll be number five!"

Josh nearly choked on his drink. "Digger, I'm beginning to see you're more than just a pretty face."

"Ain't it the truth, Josh, old man?" he replied, his unshaven face widening into a broad grin. "Ain't it the truth?"

CHAPTER Twenty-seven

I'm taking a quick shower," Katherine told Joshua once they'd returned to her home on Main and Broadway. "Are you staying for supper?"

"You did promise," he said, taking a seat in one of two overstuffed chairs on the TV porch. "I'm going to catch up on the national news while you wash off the, uh, mud, OK?"

"I'm not a city slicker," she said in her own defense. "I just don't want to get cow manure all over Cissy's furniture. You might want to go home and take a shower, too."

"I wore protection," he said with a laugh, pointing to the rubber overshoes he'd removed and placed near the back door. "An ounce of prevention, you know."

"Is worth a pound of manure," she finished, quoting a favorite movie. "OK, I'll be down in ten minutes. You can start the coffee."

Half an hour later, the two of them sat in front of the television, sipping Joshua's superstrong hazelnut cream while surfing through the cable news stations.

"Joshua, do you ever wish you'd followed your college dreams and headed off to some foreign land as a correspondent?"

The newsman stretched his long, lean legs across the coffee table and thought for a moment. "Maybe that's what I'll end up doing yet. I think I'm going to close the paper."

"What?" she gasped, nearly spilling her coffee. "You can't close the *Chronicle*! Who would report the truth around here?"

"I suppose the college paper could handle some of it. Then there's the *Daily News* that Eskel Kyne puts out. That's out of Seymour, but a lot of people subscribe to it. I'm just not sure anyone reads the *Chronicle* anymore."

"You're just tired," she said softly. "Say, didn't you once tell me that you have a cousin who wanted to run the paper? Why not bring him in on it? Share the burden, Josh."

Carpenter looked weary beyond all measure. "I'm not sure. You're right, at least partly. I actually have two cousins who'd love to take over. Dad nearly sold it to them a few years before he died. Maybe I could call them—see if they're still interested. That would give me a break at least."

"Then do it. No time like the present! You use this phone," she said, handing him the new cordless, "and call your cousins. I'll make a couple of sandwiches."

Just then the front doorbell rang.

"I'll see who that is while you call," she said.

She stayed just long enough to make sure he was dialing, and then headed to the front of the house to answer the bell. Darkness had started to fall outside, so she turned on the porch light before opening the door.

Before her stood a tall, lovely woman of about fifty, dressed in white slacks and top, and wearing a pale pink sweater knotted around her waist. The yellow gleam of the bug light Kate had put into the overhead fixture cast a gentle halo around the woman's strawberry blond hair.

As Katy opened the screen door, the woman offered a lovely, white smile. "I'm sorry to bother you. But are you by any chance related to Celeste Adamson?"

"I'm her niece. I'm Katherine Adamson. May I help you?"

The woman appeared to be perplexed. "This is going to sound odd, but I think I have a letter for you."

"Come in," Katherine said, opening the screen widely.

The woman entered the foyer, and Katy noticed her white, sensible shoes. "You're a nurse?"

"Yes, how did you know? Wait, let me guess. It's the clothes. My boss says I can wear whatever I want, but I don't feel right in anything but white. I'm old-school, I guess. At least I stopped wearing my cap."

"I like old school," Katherine replied. "Won't you come in?"

Katy led the woman into the parlor, where both women relaxed into the soft embroidered support of the turn-of-the-century furniture. "I'm Bridgette Elson. I work for Med-Care. It's a home care company that sends nurses and nursing assistants out to shut-ins who need special care. One of my clients asked me to mail a letter for him, but—well, it's not really addressed." She opened her tan leather handbag, which was extremely well organized from what Katy could tell, and removed a crinkled white envelope.

Another letter, Katherine thought.

"You can see from the envelope that I couldn't mail it. Besides, he insisted I hand-deliver it." She handed Katherine the letter.

"To Celeste A. or to her next of kin," Katherine read aloud.

"You're right. I doubt the post office would have delivered it. How did you figure out the A. stood for Adamson?"

Bridgette smiled. "I didn't. My grandson Andrew fancies himself a bit of a sleuth. He came up with the idea to look through the phonebook under the letter A and see if anyone had the first name Celeste. Fortunately, there was only one."

"You have a remarkable grandson," Katy told her. "May I ask who sent it?"

"Well, I guess I can tell you. He's one of my tougher cases. His name is John Thundercloud. He's a double amputee and suffers from emphysema. Too much smoking. I hope you don't smoke, Miss Adamson."

"Never have," she answered honestly. "Do you know why he wanted to get in touch with my aunt?"

"I've no idea, Miss," she answered, rising. "I need to get back home. My grandsons are alone right now, and I'm not comfortable leaving two kids under fourteen alone for too long these days. Andrew and Rick have been staying with us while my son and his wife are in Hawaii on a second honeymoon. It's gotten scary in Eden lately. Those poor high school kids, you know. They still haven't found the girl. You don't suppose the boy had anything to do with it, do you? I know some people are saying he killed her. Can you imagine that?"

"I hadn't heard that," Katy said. "I saw him on Tuesday. He looked shell-shocked. I really doubt the boy's involved."

"I'm glad," she said, heading to the door. "I know the girl's mother. She works for a doctor here in town, and she doesn't seem like the kind of mother who'd allow her child to go out with a homicidal maniac."

"You're probably right," Katy said. "Thank you for delivering the letter. And please tell Mr. Thundercloud that I'll answer, that is, if the letter requires it. Is he in the book?"

"Oh yes. He is. But he doesn't have his telephone plugged in. It's still active, but he likes his privacy. So, if you want to talk to him, you'll have to write or drive over there. He lives on Divine over in the west end. It's a cute neighborhood, but he hasn't kept his place in very good shape. A lot of my clients' homes are like that. Well, I'd better get home. Nice to meet you, Miss Adamson."

"And you as well, Mrs. Elson. Good night."

Returning to the TV porch, Katherine found Joshua scratching notes in a small spiral pad. "Well? Did you make the call?"

"Made it. I'm writing down Matt and Mark's addresses. They live in Charlestown near the old ammunition plant. They're identical twins, born a few years after me, and they've spent the better part of the last twenty years working with the military as civilians. Their trucking company runs long hauls for Uncle Sam.

"Anyway, Matt had asked Dad to notify them whenever he wanted to sell, so he was pretty happy to get the phone call. They said they'd drive in to Eden on Saturday to talk turkey, so to speak. Matt's words. Happy?"

"Who cares if I'm happy? Are you happy? That's the point."

Joshua stood up, moving close to Katherine. "I care if you're happy. Haven't you figured that one out yet?"

"Josh, I'm—well, I'm not sure if..." She stammered, wanting to avoid what promised to be a serious moment.

"Shh," he whispered, taking her into his long arms. "You and I talk too much. Sometimes, you just have to act." He pulled her close, lifting her chin gently. "I love you, Katherine Celeste. So deal with it."

She felt his kiss, his arms, his incredible presence. She loved him, too. No matter how she might deny it, she loved him. She guessed she always had.

"Shall I make supper?" she asked, wishing the kiss could last forever, but wanting to avoid the conversation that came with it.

"Tell me you love me," he whispered, running his hands through her short thatch of auburn hair. "Tell me how you feel, Katy."

"I...I...oh, it's hard to say. Give me time, Josh. Can you do that? I want to say it—it's just too soon. Please, can you give me a little time?"

He kissed her forehead. "I'll give you all the time you need, as long as you marry me. You don't have to answer that one yet, either. But give it some serious consideration. If I sell the paper, then we'd be free to live wherever you want. I have a comfortable savings, so we can make it for a while."

Katherine thought of her own bank account and of the million dollars Celeste had left her.

"I somehow doubt money is a problem."

Grace Alcorn finished making her twin bed, tossing on two flower-shaped pillows to complete the look. Her small bedroom, located upstairs toward the back of the split-level house, should have been her sanctuary, but the lavender walls trimmed in yellow daisies were meant to please her mother, not Grace.

Grace had never been a girly girl, no matter how much her mother pushed her to be so. Given her own choices, Grace would have decorated the room with hobbits and wizards and other fantastic images from the world of Tolkien. Grace loved to imagine, and she loved to write. The shelves of her pink and yellow bookcases were stacked with plaid journals she'd filled with her own drawings and biographical sketches for characters that lived inside her head.

"Grace! Finish up! We're going to be late!" her mother called from the first floor. Grace sighed, looking at herself in the daisy-trimmed, white mirror that decorated the left-hand door of her closet. Tonight was opening night of the high school play, *Don Juan*, and Grace had been blackmailed into attending. She'd begged for a night off, suggesting she could spend the night at her friend Kylie Kendall's house on Dover. Her parents had refused the overnighter, saying instead they'd trade a copy of the newest Zelda game for Grace's attendance without complaint.

Grace had jumped at the chance for the game. Now she was stuck going to the play.

Since Donny's return on Tuesday, their house had been a circus. Grace had survived by hiding most of the time, even begging her mother to let her return to school for the final days of classes. The Alcorns had pulled Grace out of school when Donny had disappeared. Grace's straight As since kindergarten assured she'd have no trouble, and the teachers had agreed to administer final exams early. She'd been promoted to the seventh grade without ever really finishing the sixth.

"Grace! Get a move on!"

The slight twelve-year-old donned a pair of sneakers to go with her black jeans and left her daydreams behind. *Don Juan* couldn't be all that bad, could it? Donny wasn't going, so that might be nice. Grace had grown fearful of her brother since his return. He was different, though no one else seemed to notice.

Grace noticed. Grace noticed many things about Eden.

Taking the steps slowly, she thought about her time with Katy Adamson. She'd so enjoyed her time with the lady writer that she'd begun to imagine baring her soul to Katherine. She had told Grace she could call her anytime. Maybe she should call. Maybe tomorrow. Maybe she'd mention Donny.

CHAPTER Twenty-eight

Don Juan, José Zorrilla's play about the legendary lover, had been an odd choice for the Eden High drama department. The school's principal, Daniel Cheatham, had suggested the unusually graphic play about a braggart who woos lusty women until he meets a just end at the hands of a demonic shadow.

Drama head Cassie Price had balked at first, but her students had overruled her, since they thought a play about a dude who gets all the girls he wants would mean lots of on-stage kissing. The casting call had taken seven hours. The long line of young men and women had included nearly every member of the senior and junior classes.

Two months of preparation had gone into the play. Two months of set design, costume fittings, endless tech rehearsals, and principal line coaching. Cassie Price, in only her third year of teaching after graduating with a BFA in theater and a BA in education, seemed pleased with the end result. Price had started work on her MFA the previous summer, so she had invited her student adviser to watch the play.

Professor Malinovsky had driven all the way down from Bloomington. Even he had shown surprise that such a young troupe of actors had chosen the complex *Don Juan* as their spring performance.

Traditionally, opening night fell on a Friday, but Price had felt a Thursday night opener would remove the pressure normally felt by actors, given that a Thursday audience should be light. She'd been right. Although Friday and Saturday had been sold out for weeks, tonight's performance might as well have been a dress rehearsal. The main floor of the newly renovated Eden High auditorium looked only half-full, and most of that consisted of parents.

There was one exception. The members of Miss Grimes' sophomore English class had been assigned the task of attending and then critiquing the play. Grimes was there to take attendance—showing up meant one hundred extra credit points. Not showing up, except for a very good reason, meant a deduction of twenty-five points for the total semester's grade. One hundred percent of the class had turned out.

The role of Don Juan, the hell-bound lover, had gone to Jared Buchanan, undeniably the best-looking senior at Eden High. Buchanan, last year's Curly in *Oklahoma!*, had received a full scholarship to the University of Nebraska-Lincoln, where he would be studying opera theater.

More pretty than handsome, the tall lyric tenor had cut a sharp swath through the female portion of Eden High's student population, beginning with his wooing of cheerleader Connie Breathitt. Connie's round with Buchanan had lasted the longest of his many romances, nearly a year, leading many to think she had been the love of his life. Connie had moved to Wellington during the last week of her sophomore year, and Buchanan became the school's prime catch. He soon began mending his broken heart in the arms of any willing blonde, brunette, or redhead.

Two years had passed since then, and Jared had continued to use women like tissue paper. Many snickered at the mention of the school's very real Don Juan. Typecasting, everyone had said. Oh, but those lucky girls in the play!

Trish Gabriotti could be counted among that lucky bunch. Cast as Doña Inez, she had spent many hours rehearsing their amorous scenes. Ironically, it was Trish's old boyfriend, Mitch Iverson, who had been cast as Don Gonzalo, the very man who would call the character of Don Juan to account for his sins against women.

Donny Alcorn had originally been cast in the part, but his recent disappearance had forced the school to recast it. Trish, who had a tremendous crush on Donny, had nearly suffered a nervous breakdown during his mysterious absence. Jared, however, had managed to soothe her nerves, and she now could be found hanging out with the tall tenor and had even asked her parents to send her to UNL rather than to Notre Dame as they had planned.

Grace and her parents had enjoyed the first act of the long play, or at least her parents had. Grace fidgeted now and then, wishing she had brought her Game Boy. All this kissing was beginning to wear thin. Deciding at the last minute to attend, Donny had accepted an invitation to watch the play from backstage. The decision had surprised Grace. Her brother had shown little interest in anything since his return, save his constant cravings for rich food, but he'd actually looked pleased when Ms. Price had phoned with the personal invitation.

Act II, scene ii opened to the strains of Mozart's *Don Giovanni* played haltingly by the school's student orchestra. Waiting for his moment to enter, Buchanan smiled at the music choice. It had been his suggestion to use the lush opera score, Mozart's perfect composition of the Don Juan legend.

Just before moving into position, Jared blew a kiss to the play's Doña Inez, who would make her entrance at the very end of the scene. When she had turned away to ask stage tech Annie Branham for assistance with her costume and wires, Jared turned to look for Ms. Price. She had moved around the backstage crossover to the upstage right wing, where she stood chatting with Donny Alcorn.

Jared had come to hate Alcorn. Unknown to everyone but Donny, Jared and Cassie Price had been having a torrid affair, conducted after rehearsal in the back of Price's sand-colored Toyota. Cassie, a nicely rounded brunette with big brown eyes and generous assets had fallen into his arms easily enough, and Buchanan had played her for all she was worth. She had been worth a lot.

Donny Alcorn had seen them together one night, a week before the prom. Jared had confronted the football player, warning him not to reveal their secret, but Donny had laughed. He outweighed Buchanan by seventy pounds of muscle, and his large hands had a reputation for finding punching bags in the oddest places. And on the oddest faces.

Jared's handsome looks could get him a ticket to Hollywood one day, so he took great care of his face. A broken nose might be useful to a character actor, but not to a lead. He'd have to avoid Alcorn if he wanted his dreams of stardom to come true.

Of course, if something were to happen to Donny, that would be different. Jared had secretly cheered when Donny had vanished. He had also cursed the day when the rugged football star had returned. He faked a cheerful wave as Donny and Cassie looked his way. Just a few more days, then Jared could blow this podunk town. He'd put in a few years studying

voice and theater in Nebraska, and then he'd head for Hollywood or New York.

The music swelled, and Jared knew the curtain was
about to open. In the audience, his parents watched, as did
the meager house. Jared didn't care. He'd pack them in one
day, and everyone here would say they saw his brilliant performance as Don Juan.

In the audience, Grace Alcorn watched the act open,
something in her mind twitching to life. She felt anxious, tight
inside. "Mom, can I go to the bathroom?" she asked, thinking
she could just hide in there until the play finished.

"After it's over," her mother replied, handing her daughter
a tissue. "Blow your nose."

Blow your nose. That was Meredith Alcorn's answer to
everything. "Thanks, Mom," Grace answered. Maybe she could
call Katherine tomorrow morning. She could tell Katy to avoid
this play. Boring!

The music grew soft and the lighting fell across the ominous statue of the Commendatore, who cried out, "Here I am
then, Don Juan! And here in the company of those who call on
God, you see, for your eternal punishment, as man!"

Grace sat up. This might get interesting. Apparently, Don
Juan was about to get his!

She watched the scene unfold, the parrying between the
fallen man Don Juan and the shadow of death in the figure
of the statue, mesmerized by the great theme of crime and
punishment.

"And that burial procession whose feet go by?" Don Juan
asked the statue.

"Is yours!" the shadowy figure screamed with delight.

Grace had read through some of the play when her brother
had been learning his part. She remembered that Don Juan,

who had lived only for himself, was to be lifted up from the very grasp of hell by the woman who had so loved him, the now dead Doña Inez.

Grace giggled. Wouldn't it be funny if the dear Lady Inez didn't show up?

Just then, she heard a blood-curdling scream. *The demons must have come for the old lover,* she thought. Everyone's eyes were glued to the stage, waiting for hell's minions to begin dragging the repentant Don Juan toward hell, only to be out-done by the divine love of a woman.

No one could have expected what happened next.

The stage had grown dark and smoky, and fires from somewhere beneath the stage burned red and amber through the stage floor. Flames literally licked the actor's shoes and legs. Panic began to fill the auditorium, as thick smoke filtered into every corner.

Grace knew this was not part of the play.

As the smoke rose into the fly space, the wings began to glow orange, and dark figures could be seen writhing onstage, shadows even blacker than the darkness that had already descended there.

Grace's jaw dropped and she huddled close to her mother. More screaming, screams from the stage, screams from the wings, screams from the panic-stricken audience. Something huge and black had descended from the fly space, and it hovered over Jared Buchanan like a great cloud of doom. The thing held a whip in its right claw, for it had no real human hands, and with its left it yanked Jared from his feet so quickly, his boots were left behind. The enormous shadow cried out victoriously, its shrill scream sending shivers down Grace's small spine, and then it vanished.

And with it, so did Jared Buchanan.

CHAPTER Twenty-nine

John Thundercloud snorted a quick, deep shot of oxygen before removing his nosepiece.

"Want a candy bar?" he asked his guests. "Clark Bars are the world's best nutrition. Go ahead, I have plenty."

Katherine and Joshua exchanged glances. "Thanks," she said, taking one. "Can we get you a glass of water or anything?"

Thundercloud shook his head. His hair had been recently shaved to barely visible, a manageable length for a man who couldn't shower or bathe on his own. The old man's face looked like a map of the moon. Pockmarks from a teenage battle with acne, deep grooves from two different knife fights, and a web of creases from dozens of years in the sun, all combined to give him both a hideous and a compelling presence.

"No water. I had some already today. Water'll kill you. Don't you know that? They lace it with fluoride that's suppose to keep us from losing our teeth, but you know people have more fillings now than ever? Dentists are in on it. Candy bar, Josh?"

Carpenter smiled. "Sure, why not. How long have you lived here, Mr. Thundercloud?"

"John," he said, tossing his empty wrapper onto the rolling tray. "You don't care how long I've lived here. You just want to know why I sent that letter to your girlfriend."

"I'm not his girlfriend," Katy mumbled, chewing the chocolate bar. "Sorry. I mean, we're just friends."

"She's my girlfriend," Josh said, winking at Thundercloud. "She just doesn't want to admit it yet."

"Gotcha. You keep after her. She's all right. I know these things. I see a lot. So, Katherine, you want to know about this letter. Why I sent it, right?"

Katy held up the note with its singular sentence in John Thundercloud's shaky script. "'They're here. Come see me,'" Katherine read aloud from the page. "What is that supposed to mean? Why would you send a note like that to my aunt?"

Thundercloud spit into a paper cup. He didn't chew tobacco or even bubblegum, but he had a habit of spitting. It seemed to John that old men should spit. "How well did you even know your aunt, Katherine? How can you ask me why, when you don't know it yourself?"

"Huh? Listen, Mr. Thundercloud, you seem like a nice enough man, but..."

"John. Call me John. And I'm not a nice man. I'm an honest man. There's no time now for being nice. Phonies are nice, saying, 'hi there' and 'yes, ma'am' and 'what a fine day.' Phooey! People should be asking each other the real questions, not all that phony crap! Excuse my language." He spit again.

"All right, John. You're right. I didn't know my aunt well. At least not from the viewpoint of an adult. I lived with her through my years at college, then I left and hardly looked back. Celeste Adamson lived and died, and I let it happen. I let it all happen, and I scarcely noticed. Happy now?"

"You're an excitable girl, aren't you, Katherine? Why don't you two sit?"

Josh took Katy's hand and led her to an old nylon couch covered in copies of both the *Watcher* and the *Chronicle*. Moving them to one side, he helped Katherine to sit, then joined her. "You're a complicated man, John. These newspapers are all from this week. Have you read them?"

"I read everything," he said, reaching for a cigarette. "Mind if I smoke?"

"I'd rather you didn't," Katy said, staring wide-eyed at the oxygen tank.

"A response from the heart!" he cried, laughing so much he had to gasp a bit of oxygen. "Oh, I'm OK," he told them, seeing their worried faces. "I'll live until my work is done. Part of that is to bring you up to speed, Katherine. Now that you're here, I can do that."

She started to stand, but Joshua pulled her back. "Mr. Thundercloud, I mean, John, just why did you want to bring me here? Did you have some sort of relationship with my aunt?"

"Ah!" he cried, pointing toward them both with a tobacco-stained forefinger. "That's the question! Your aunt and I did have a relationship. But not the kind you might imagine. We both work for the same side. That's it. And now that's she's gone on ahead of me, you have to take her place. So, let's get to work."

Katherine closed her eyes tightly, drumming her fists against her thighs. This old man was making no sense, and Joshua seemed determined to egg him on. "Just what sort of work do you mean, Mr. Thun...John?"

"The Lord's work, Katy. The work of our Savior and King. I may smoke, and I may not have more than a lick of breath left in my scarred lungs, but I have been made whole in Him, made clean through His blood. And He allows me to see the truth of our time."

Katherine stared at the old man; her jaw dropped. He was a nutcase. He probably didn't even know her aunt, and he'd gotten Katherine's name off a book jacket or out of the paper, and he'd sent the note to tease her into coming to hear his rants. She'd come across his kind before. They lined up at book signings like crooked lemmings on a greased slide, heaving with joy at throwing themselves into eternal nuthood. Next he'd start talking conspiracy, and she'd have to beat it out of here.

"Have you heard of fallen angels?" the old man asked her, cracking two walnuts open and letting the meat fall into his left hand. "I mean the whole story? About how the sons of God came unto the daughters of men to destroy the gene pool?"

Katherine stood, pushing at Joshua's hands. "Next you'll tell me the UFO seen on Ben Miller's farm was a demon. That's it. I'm out of here."

"Then prepare to leave, young lady," the old man said soberly. "If by demon you mean fallen angel, then you've spoken the truth. UFOs are merely a manifestation of these evil creatures. They are also called the Watchers, for some believe they were sent to Earth to observe and teach mankind. But they do more than watch—they interfere, and they are trying to foil God's plans by destroying man."

"Joshua, I'm leaving! Are you coming?" she crossed over his long legs, nearly falling, and headed toward the door. "Mr. Thundercloud, I am certain you never knew my aunt. She was a God-fearing woman who went to church every Sunday and who never saw a demon in her life. I'll thank you to leave me alone!" She pushed open the neatly carved Arts and Crafts door, heading for the porch.

"You saw her, didn't you? At the circle. You saw your aunt," he said.

Katherine stopped, turning on her heels to glare at him. How could he have known that? She hadn't even told Joshua about that.

"Who are you, Mr. Thundercloud? Really?"

The old man laughed. "Someone who knows things, Miss Adamson. And I know a scared woman when I see one. Ah, well, you don't care, do you? Let those creatures have the town—have the world. What does it matter to you as long as you can get a good book out of it? Did you know your aunt left a diary? Have you found it yet?"

Katherine held her breath. She could feel Joshua staring at her behind her back.

"You know she left it," he continued. "You find it, wherever it is she hid it, because I know she kept it safe. She was that kind of woman, a true lady. You find it, and you read it, and then you'll be back here."

"Not likely," Katherine said, trying her best not to slam the door as she left.

Joshua rose, not sure of how to respond. "I'm sorry, John. She's excitable, as you said. And she's had a rough time lately. When you get to know her, you'll see what I mean. How did you know about the diary?"

Thundercloud opened another Clark Bar, unwrapping the slick, red paper with care. "Cissy told me. We all kept them. Mine are rather prolific, 'cause I write down everything and anything. I figure you never can tell when something that seems small now will grow to be big later. Cissy made notes about what she called the proper things, the important things. She had a rare insight, that Cissy. I miss her. You tell your girl-friend that. I like her, too. She's got spunk."

"She does at that," Josh said, smiling. "We'll see you again, I imagine."

"You will. Meantime, you watch after her. Don't let her be alone too much. She's under attack, just as you will be. Well, see you Saturday."

"Saturday?"

"Trust me, you'll see me. Bring some Clark Bars when you come, OK?"

"OK."

All the way home, Katherine remained quiet. Josh wanted to break the weighty silence, but he knew she needed time to think. Once home, he suggested he remain there with her, but she refused. Making Katy promise to call if she needed him, he left her at the door, kissing her good night on the cheek. He was about to leave her there when his cell phone rang.

"It's probably Chuck Manion. I asked him to call me about working for the *Chronicle*. I guess he'll be working for my cousins, huh?" he said. "Hello?"

The voice on the other end sounded excited from what Katherine could hear. The man's voice was strident and loud, but Katy couldn't make out the words. Joshua's face blanched as he listened. Hanging up, he clicked the phone closed.

"That was Chuck Manion all right, but he wasn't calling back to arrange for a job interview. He was at the high school tonight with his wife and son, watching a play that his daughter was involved in. She was playing in the orchestra."

"Did she mess up or something? He sounded pretty upset."

"Hardly. But he was most definitely upset. In fact, he was in an old-fashioned panic. It seems the final act of *Don Juan* had a surprise that no one expected."

"Yes?"

"According to several hundred eyewitnesses, the lead actor, a kid named Jared Buchanan, was snatched right in front of them."

"Snatched? What do you mean by snatched?"

"Snatched. You know, taken, as in he vanished from sight."

Katherine blinked. "Oh my Lord! Like Donny and Amy? Did anyone see the one who took him?"

Joshua nodded. "Everyone saw it."

"It? What do you mean it?"

"I mean it. Everyone appears to have described the same thing—and Chuck saw it as well. Jared Buchanan was taken by something huge—something that everyone there is calling a demon."

CHAPTER Thirty

The scene at Eden High School could only be described as orderly pandemonium. Several hundred people, who had been in the audience, had been told to remain by the police, and the cast and crew along with members of the orchestra were each being questioned while the unlucky theatergoers waited their turns.

While a few waited quietly in their seats, most chose to chatter on and on to anyone who would listen about how the enormous beast had not only taken poor Jared Buchanan, but had also loomed nastily toward the audience, threatening them with eternal fire. Occasional screams punctuated the low muttering, startling even the screamer.

Joshua and Katherine met up with Chuck Manion, who retold his tale while hanging on to his sixteen-year-old daughter as if he expected her to disappear next. "It was horrible! Like something out of a nightmare! I know a demon was here, Joshua! I saw it! God help me, we all saw it! Blast it all, I *felt* it!"

Sheriff Branham and half a dozen deputies manned the stage, trying to make some orderly sense out of disorderly nonsense, and Branham waved to Josh. "Hey, Carpenter! You want to come up here?"

The newsman waved back. "Coming?" he asked Katherine, who was about to answer yes when she heard the plaintive cry of a familiar young voice.

"Katy!"

It was Grace Alcorn. Upon seeing Katherine, the girl pried herself away from her mother's smothering chokehold and ran to embrace Katherine. "Oh, Katy! It was awful! It was really, really awful! It looked like the Balrog! Just like it!"

Katherine held the trembling girl close, her mind struggling to recall what a Balrog was. Something from Tolkien. Something truly evil.

"You mean like that thing from, uh, from *The Fellowship of the Ring*? Like that?"

She nodded furiously, her small head bobbing like a crazed bird's. "It was real, Katy! Real! It filled the stage, and it had a whip, too! It grabbed that guy—the actor. It grabbed him, and they both disappeared!"

Katherine glanced up. Grace's mother had come up to the pair. She looked dazed and a little bit angry. "Good evening, Mrs. Alcorn. Grace is understandably upset. Did you see this—this thing?"

Meredith Alcorn looked around as though not wishing to make any statements that could be overheard. "I think I saw something, but I'm not ready to say what. The stage was dark, and I suppose part of it could have been a special effect. Donny is the one to ask. He was in the wings when it happened. He's still up there, and no one will allow me on the stage!"

Katy could see the woman was near hysterics.

"Perhaps I can help. How about if I take Grace and..."

"Grace stays with me! Come here now, Grace. You mustn't make a pest out of yourself. Miss Adamson has things to do."

"Grace is never a bother, Mrs. Alcorn. However, both you and Grace have been through a terrible shock. Perhaps Joshua and I should take you and Grace home."

Meredith appeared nonplussed. "My daughter is a strong girl, and I am fine! Donny's the one I'm worried about. After all he's been through, good heavens! His father is up there with him now, just as I should be."

Grace lowered her head, and Katherine knew the brave girl was trying not to cry.

"Grace is very strong, but I think I'd be a basket case if I'd witnessed what you two did tonight. Shall I try to find your husband and Donny?"

The woman's shoulders drooped, and Katy could see anger give way to exhaustion.

"Do you need a ride home, Mrs. Alcorn?" she asked, gently touching the frightened woman's left shoulder.

"Thank you," Meredith Alcorn whispered tightly. "I'll be fine. But my husband should take Grace home. If you want to help, then please ask Harold to come down here as soon as possible. He can drive Gracie home while I stay with Donny. I'm sure the police are going to interrogate him again. Maybe I should call our lawyer."

"I'll do that, Mrs. Alcorn," Katherine said, bending to give Grace a hug. "It's OK, Gracie. No matter what it is you saw, I promise you don't have to worry. Even Balrogs can be beaten. Remember, Gandalf killed it."

She nodded, but it was clear that she remained unconvinced. "He beat it, but he didn't kill it, Katy. And it nearly killed him. Be careful, OK. Deal?"

"Deal," she replied, patting the girl's coppery curls. "I'll call you tomorrow. Maybe we can catch another movie."

"All right." Grace took her mother's hand, but her eyes followed Katherine's movements until she'd disappeared behind the stage curtain.

Once onstage, Katy looked around for Joshua. Kate had done a bit of theater work while at Indiana University. Although not a part of the music department, she had a close friend who was an opera major, so Katherine had managed to snag a job as a techie during one summer's production of *Don Giovanni*. Funny that Eden High had been presenting the very play Mozart had based his famous opera upon.

Kate recalled the horrific final scene when Giovanni is dragged into hell by the demons summoned by the Commendatore's living statue. Mozart's dark opera had not included the more satisfying happy ending that Zorrilla's play had. There was no final salvation for Don Giovanni as there had been for his non-singing counterpart, Don Juan. Don Giovanni had received the final punishment meant for all sinners.

Had the school merely fashioned a spectacular effect that completely fooled its terrified audience? Had the monstrous demon that Grace had called a Balrog simply been made of light and shadow or even papier-mâché?

Curving into the upstage wings, Katherine caught sight of Joshua and the sheriff sitting with several high school kids. The students looked pale and tired. Their faces were motionless and their eyes large with fright. They looked as though they had seen hell come to life before them.

"Good evening, Miss Adamson," the sheriff said with a tip of his tan and green hat. "Seems like we're always meeting lately. Following Josh Carpenter around will do that for a person. You often find yourself in some nasty spots."

"Hello again, Sheriff. Have you been able to elicit a coherent testimony from any of the students or staff? Is there any evidence that might show this to be nothing more than a parlor trick?"

Branham motioned for her and Josh to come aside, away from the knot of terrified thespians. "This isn't going into the paper is it, Josh?"

Joshua stopped taking notes for a moment. "Not if you don't want it to it doesn't. But I can't promise not to print it eventually."

"OK," the sheriff sighed. "This sure has been some week. Guess I'm just tired. These past few days have been the most hellish of my entire career. And I've seen a lot of bad stuff. That train wreck five years back, you remember that, Josh? More dead than alive, bodies twisted into pretzels, and babies crying everywhere. Gosh, that was a night. But this stuff. Man, I'm stumped if I know what to make out of demons! That's what they're sayin', you know. A big old demon appeared on the stage and grabbed the boy right out of his boots! Right out of his boots!" He looked at the floor, his eyes genuinely filled with regret. "Sorry for raising my voice, Miss Adamson. It's just awful."

"That's all right, Sheriff. It's been a bad week, as you say. Were you able to interview Donny Alcorn? I'm told he was in the wings when this thing appeared."

"Alcorn? He was here? Nobody told me that! Willie! Get over here!" he called to one of the deputies.

A round man who looked a lot like a human tribble appeared. His face was flushed, and his full beard and thick curly hair reminded Katherine of a hobbit or, even better, a dwarf. Maybe there really was a Tolkien theme going on. She'd have to remember to mention it to Grace. The poor girl could use a laugh.

"Willie, did you see Donny Alcorn here tonight?" the sheriff asked the rotund deputy.

"No, sir. I been talkin' to the technical people. They said nothin' about Donny."

"Well, his mother says he was here. Onstage or backstage or something. I want you and Thompson there to go through this building with a fine-tooth comb and find me that kid!"

Willie, which stood for Wilson—Bradley Wilson—saluted. "Yes, sir! We're on it!"

The sheriff turned back to face Katherine and Joshua. "He's a good man, that Willie. He's been my deputy for going on eleven months, and I've yet to see him out of uniform in any way, shape, or form. He's strictly by the book, but I'm afraid in his case, that book lacks a few pages if you know what I mean. Good man, though. Joshua, how is it you heard about this?"

Before Josh could explain, George Collins, who had missed Willie as they crossed the chaotic stage, ran up. "Sheriff! We found him!"

"Who? Donny Alcorn?"

Collins looked puzzled. "Uh, no, Sheriff! The boy from the play! That Buchanan boy! He's outside in the parking lot."

Branham paled. "Alive?"

The deputy shook his head. "You'll need to take a look at him, Sheriff. I may not be a medical expert, but I'm guessin' he's not alive. In the shape he's in, he's better off."

Joshua, who was closer to the side exit, led the group to the hallway that fed into the south exits of the auditorium, where all but the faculty parked their cars during school activities. A fine rain had begun to fall, and the tall black lampposts that illuminated the parking lots stared with their single yellow eyes into the shimmering night. The lot was barely half-full, including the many police and media vehicles that had assembled for the investigation. Most of the cars had been parked close to the entrances, but a few were scattered into the far southern fringe of the lot. It was there, in a brightly lit area, that Katherine saw a dark form.

"Back there!" the deputy directed, leading them to the shadowy shape. "I've already called for an ambulance."

Following Collins, she and the others ran until they stopped just short of a pitiful pile of burnt flesh. The smell reached them first, that sickening smell of hair and bone, deeply charred. Kate swayed for a moment, leaning on Joshua for support. She'd seen some bad deaths in her day, but this horrifying heap had to be the worst. It had to be. How many people are killed by demons?

"He's a mess, Sheriff," the deputy said, as both men looked down upon the smoldering remains.

"Dear God in heaven," Branham moaned, his eyes filling with tears.

Katherine joined them, walking slowly next to Joshua. The pile of black and red flesh still twitched off and on—nothing more than residual muscular contraction, she reminded herself. She hated looking at it, but she found it hard to look away.

Then she noticed it.

Shoes.

The lump of twisted flesh wore shoes.

"Sheriff, I'm not sure, but wasn't Jared Buchanan lifted right out of his boots?"

"Right out of 'em," Branham answered. "Why?"

"Look at this poor soul," she said, pointing to what had once been feet. "Look. Shoes. Black sneakers, from the look of it."

"Well, what the...they are!" Branham gasped. Kneeling, he searched for other identifying clothes or marks. The face and body had nearly melted with the severe heat to which they'd been exposed. The clothes had fused with the body. "Here now, Collins. What do you make of this?"

The fair-headed Collins knelt down, peering carefully at the area where the sheriff had pointed. "It's a watch, sir. Or what's left of one. Looks like a Rolex."

Branham straightened. "Yeah. A Rolex. That's what I thought, too. I remember seeing a watch just like that not all that long ago. You recall, Deputy?"

Collins scratched his head, nearly knocking off his hat. "Well, sir, I don't believe I do. Wait a minute! You mentioned it, didn't you? After we found him at the SuperMart. Dang, Sheriff! This ain't the Buchanan boy! It's Donny Alcorn!"

CHAPTER Thirty-one

A ll Katherine could do was stare into space. After he'd driven her home, she'd sent Joshua away, partly so he could get the sleep he needed, but mostly so she could be alone. Too much had happened. Too much heartache. Too much death.

And in the midst of it all, she had finally begun to grieve.

How could Cissy leave her all this mess? Why didn't she ever mention John Thundercloud? What on earth was going on around here, and what did Katy's sweet, maiden aunt have to do with it?

Katherine had only a cloudy memory of her vision back on Miller's farm. She faintly recalled seeing her aunt, but alone now and with a clear mind, she wondered what she had really seen—and what it was that had seen her.

Katy poured a cup of coffee to help stay awake and decided to catch up on the news. Sitting in Aunt Celeste's favorite chair on the moonlit TV porch, Katherine turned on WNN but kept the sound muted. Images of Tony Blair's bid for presidency of the EU flashed across the screen. Footage of President Shepherd speaking at a rally for Senate candidate Marilyn Maxwell of Tennessee. The search and rescue efforts in Turkey to recover anyone still alive after the 7.4 earthquake

SHARON K. Gilbert

there on Sunday. The lined brown face of a father in Somalia, squinting into the camera, no doubt begging the cameraman for a morsel of food. The gleaming teeth of a picture perfect model, brushing her teeth with the latest craze in toothpaste.

What a mixed-up world. Didn't anyone understand the real questions that needed answering? Politics, publicity, and power were the triumvirate that drove cable news, but none of that mattered in the trenches of real life.

Katy thought of her own corner of the public eye, her novels. What good did they do? Was anyone changed or made better through her words? Had she improved that Somali man's lot in life? Had her small thoughts effected any change whatsoever for the common good?

No matter how many lines she wrote, no matter how many books she signed, Aunt Cissy would remain dead. Donny Alcorn—dead. Forest Erickson—dead. And Amy Horine? What of that sweet child? She was probably dead.

She thought of the strange, disturbing conversation with John Thundercloud. She had dismissed him as nothing more than a kook, but even now she couldn't dismiss him completely. She'd seen insane eyes before, back in 1998, when she'd interviewed Thomas Allen Stroud, the convicted serial killer who had claimed the lives of eleven teenage boys, saying he had merely helped them cross into an eternal playground. Stroud's pale green eyes had held every dark emotion that existed. He had looked right at her during their interviews, glaring into her inner thoughts, picking at them and dissecting them. Dissecting her.

Stroud was dead now. In hell, Katy supposed. And now the demons of that pit must be dissecting him.

Demons. Fallen angels. Just what had Thundercloud meant? That old man may be shaky and his body dying, but his brain is

224

alive and kicking. He knows many things, Katy Celeste. If madness can masquerade as wisdom, perhaps wisdom masquerades as madness.

Katherine clutched a throw pillow to her chest, squeezing it tightly. How would she feel right now if she were Donny Alcorn's mother? How must Grace feel? Terrified, that's what.

Next door, she heard the nightly barking begin.

Why did that dog bark and howl at night?

She wished she hadn't sent Joshua home, wished she'd had the courage to confess her true feelings to him. Wished she could be honest with herself—no, with God—just once.

She picked up the phone, dialing without thinking about it. She was sure she had dialed Josh's number, but the phone rang twice, and the man who answered was not Joshua.

"Hello?" he asked. She knew that voice. Why had she dialed him?

"Pastor Jones?"

"Yes, it is. Who is this...is this Miss Adamson?"

"Yes, Pastor, it is. I know it's late, but do you have a few minutes to talk?"

His voice grew soft, and she knew his eyes must look as gentle as a lamb's. Maybe she wasn't meant to call Joshua. Not yet, at least.

"I'd be happy to talk with you, Miss Adamson. I have all night if you need it."

She gripped the phone. She hadn't expected tears to start, but start they did, opening a floodgate that she'd barred ages ago. This would be a long night.

As Katherine poured out her heart to the comforting words of a man she'd only just met, Amy Horine prepared for what she prayed would be her first good sleep in weeks. Clad in white satin pajamas, Amy had been reading a romance novel when she'd overheard a commotion coming from somewhere else in the complex.

Not that she knew what the complex really was. Since her arrival here—since what seemed like years ago—Amy had spent most of those endless moments unconscious. Major gaps in her memory plagued the girl. She had a vague recollection of shadows, but little else. She thought Donny had been with her, but Lilith had reassured her that he was fine. He'd come see her in the hospital as soon as she was up to visitors.

Thank God she had Lilith!

The soft-spoken woman with the beautiful ice-blue eyes had kept Amy sane in all this confusion. Lilith must be a special kind of nurse or something like that, she reasoned. Really, she didn't care. Lilith had been a sister and a mother to Amy, and that was all that mattered.

Mother?

Amy thought of the long, thin hands that had smoothed her curls as a child, dried her tears, and mended her clothes. She thought of the songs her mother had sung to her, of the white rocking chair that creaked with each hypnotic movement. She thought of the many selfless acts of love Maria Horine had offered up, sacrifices only a mother could make.

What had Lilith said? She would see her mother soon.

Amy had to be good. Her head began to ache again.

A bell sounded delicately, indicating the last medications of the day. On cue, Amy heard the opening of her bedroom door, followed by the soft padding of Lilith's footsteps.

"Bedtime already?" she asked the woman in white.

"Another night's sleep, another's day's healing," she whispered, her voice like the sound of a waterfall. "Tomorrow, we have a surprise for you. Your mother will be here."

"Mother?" Amy asked, thinking how strange the word sounded.

"She will be here, and if she likes, she may remain with you while you complete your recovery. Would you like that?"

"I think so," Amy said sleepily.

"Yes, it's difficult to choose sometimes, isn't it? Sleep now, little one. Sleep and heal. Heal and sleep." Removing a syringe from her white pocket, the dark-haired woman gently injected the clear liquid into Amy's arm. "That should help that awful headache."

"Thank you, Lilith," Amy answered wearily.

Lilith began to sing, and she stroked Amy's hair tenderly. As the young girl drifted into a dreamless sleep, she imagined her mother Maria. But somehow her features had altered. They swam in a pool of forgetfulness, blending into an image of a highborn mother from beyond the stars. Lilith.

CHAPTER Thirty-two

FRIDAY MORNING

All of Eden woke to the sounds of helicopters. Choppers from all the major networks and every local station in Indiana, Kentucky, and Ohio, and a black chopper with no markings had begun to circle the southern Indiana town, videotaping background footage and searching for an appropriate place to land.

Katy jumped to her feet as one chopper hovered directly over her house. She'd finally drifted into a weeping sleep sometime around three in the morning. Pastor Jones had patiently and lovingly listened to her moanings and groanings for two hours, promising he would pray for her and visit her the next day. She'd only been asleep for five hours, but she felt remarkably well rested.

Running to her window, the morning's bright sun revealed the source of the noise. She'd seen unmarked helicopters before. She'd written about them in two of her novels, *The Eye of Horus Is upon You* and *America's Phoenix*. Conspiracy theorists loved black helicopters. Katy just wished they weren't in her backyard.

Donning the chenille robe and scuffs, Katherine made a beeline for the kitchen and a welcome cup of java. What had she said to Pastor Jones last night? He'd been a rock for her, and he hardly knew who she was. He'd done it as a gift to Aunt Cissy. Everyone loved Cissy.

Had he said something about coming by this morning?

Through the east window over the sink, she could see the Markhams waving to the chopper while Heidi barked furiously. Helen was already dressed and no doubt getting her home ready for tonight's guests. The Apple Tree Inn would welcome them with open arms. We're delighted to have you visit us. We hope you don't mind an occasional demon with your morning paper.

Stirring three sugars and a nice splash of hazelnut creamer into her Kenya AA, Katherine decided to take the coffee out onto the veranda that overlooked the rose garden out back. She grabbed her cup, the morning paper, the new cordless, and a pair of reading glasses and headed out the French doors.

Sitting at the glass table, she opened the paper to a huge headline:

HAS THE DEVIL COME TO EDEN?

It didn't seem like Joshua's kind of journalism. Skipping down to the byline, she discovered the reason. Joshua hadn't written the article. Someone named Cheryl Steinhardt had. She'd never heard Josh mention anyone by that name. In fact, Katy had been under the impression most of Josh's reporters had deserted for either *The Sun* or the college paper, *The Watcher*. *The Sun* was actually a Kentucky paper, but many of the locals read it. Eden sat right on the Ohio River, so residents spent nearly as much time on the south side of the river as they did on the north.

So who was this Cheryl Steinhardt?

Stop it, Katy. You're feeling a little bit green, girlfriend. He's a grown boy, and he can hire any woman he wants.

Skip it, she was jealous.

"Good morning!" Helen Markham called from the picket gate that bordered Broadway. "Busy?"

Katy waved her on over. "Hi, Helen. Welcome to Eden Airport."

Helen laughed, joining Katherine at the table. "I don't suppose you have another cup like that?"

"I'll wave my magic wand!" Katherine answered. "Give me a minute to find it in the mess."

After a moment, Katy returned with a yellow carafe of Kenya, a Winnie the Pooh mug, sugar, and creamer atop one of Cissy's antique Coca-Cola trays. "Help yourself, neighbor."

Helen took hers black, sipping it gratefully. "You heard about last night at the high school, I take it?"

Katherine shifted to avoid the glare of the morning sun. "I'm sorry to say I witnessed part of it."

"You were there? Is it true? Was there...a...a demon?"

Helen looked like a sensible woman. She wore cute denim overalls, had intelligent blue eyes, seemed to like sunflowers and daisies (based on Katherine's observations of the younger woman's wardrobe), and wore comfortable leather shoes. Helen might well represent every normal American woman of the heartland—all heart and close to the land.

"I'm not the one to say if there was a demon or not," Katherine admitted honestly. "Joshua Carpenter and I were called over there after the—well, after the thing appeared onstage. We did, however, see what was left of Donny Alcorn."

Helen's soft eyes moistened. "His poor parents. Here they thought he was home, safe and sound, and he's stolen from them again—this time forever."

Overhead, the helicopter grew louder.

"Which channel do you think that is?" Helen asked, cupping her eyes with her hands as she looked up. "I can't see any marks."

Katy sipped the last of her cup. "I'd say that it's the IAO."

"What? I've never heard of that one," Helen said.

"Information Awareness Office. A little part of your government and mine."

Helen looked puzzled. "Our government has a news station?"

Katherine chose to drop it. Helen was better off in her sunflower world. "It's not very well-known. So, you have guests coming this evening?"

Helen brightened. "We do! They're coming down from Michigan, and we're a little nervous about it. We haven't had very many guests yet. I suppose it's not really the season. I'm told summer and fall are best for our area. Anyway, that's why I'm here. I wanted to talk to you about Heidi."

"Heidi? Oh, I'm getting used to her."

"Well, so are we to be perfectly honest, but you see there's a problem."

Katherine liked Helen Markham. She had an endearing manner and a habit of biting her lower lip when she was nervous. She was practically devouring it now.

"Problem? Is there anything I can do to help?"

"Oh, I wish you would!" Helen said, leaning forward anxiously. "You see, my sister called last night about picking up Heidi. Remember, I told you they had moved to Seattle, but they're in an apartment now until they close on their house.

231

Well, my niece, remember she named the dog and she really loves her, anyway she just had a round of doctor visits to find out the cause of her allergies. I'll bet you can see where this is leading."

Katherine smiled. "Your niece is allergic to dogs."

Helen nodded, stirring her black coffee absentmindedly. "She is. Hannah has been sneezing a lot ever since they got Heidi as a puppy. Since Brenda and Doug used to live in Alaska, it followed that Hannah might simply have had a series of colds. Nothing so simple. When they drove down here in March for Easter, they left the dog here as a test as much as anything else. Doug was being transferred to Seattle, and Hannah would be starting preschool in the fall, so it seemed like a good time to see if Hannah could manage without Heidi."

"That makes sense," Katherine said, thinking she should offer her neighbor something more than coffee. "I have donuts inside. Cream-filled. Would you like some?".

Helen shook her head. "Oh, no. We ate a big breakfast about an hour ago. Thanks, though. You go ahead. Don't mind me!"

Katy excused herself for a minute, returning with several donuts on a china plate. "Sorry. My blood sugar was dropping. Go on. Hannah was missing her dog."

"Right. She wasn't sneezing anymore. In fact, she has been in the peak of health ever since they moved out there. So, Brenda took her to the doctor, and he ran allergy tests. She had hits on certain pollens, dust mites, and pet hair, especially dog hair. They can't take Heidi back."

Helen looked as though she would cry. "I'm sorry to dump this on you, Katherine. I mean, we just met you, although you do seem like a very nice person. We just don't want to ruin our friendship before it even gets started!" She was crying now.

"Helen, honey. It's not the end of the world. So you need to find a home for Heidi, that's all. I'm sure anyone would be happy to have her as a pet. She's a great dog."

"You think so? Really? She likes you a lot, you know."

Katherine began to see where this was headed. "Yes...well, I guess we got along all right. But I'm sure she's friendly with most people."

"No, she isn't! She barks at almost everyone! You're the only person we've ever seen her take to. We can't keep her, Katherine. What if one of our guests has allergies? We can't take that chance. Besides, Bill wouldn't want me to tell you this, but Heidi gets on his nerves."

She had that crying look again, and Katy was beginning to feel cornered. She liked dogs well enough, but she didn't know how long she'd even be living in Eden. And her place back in Missouri wasn't all that big.

Still, Heidi was a nice dog. And she might prove to be a great protector.

"OK, you don't need to worry, Helen. I'll be happy to take Heidi, at least for now."

"Oh, Katherine! You don't know what a relief this is! Bill didn't know what we were going to do. These people coming down tonight might hate dogs, and if they do, what would we do, and oh! Thank you so much! I'll be over in a little while with her food and leash and things. You'll love her!"

Katy watched helplessly as Helen jumped to her feet and dashed toward the other side of Main, bounding all the way.

Pouring a second cup of coffee, Katherine grabbed another donut, filled to bursting with rich vanilla cream, and took a satisfying bite of the sugary confection. This was going to be a very interesting day.

Joshua had been answering the phone since five that morning. Seven cups of coffee and a bag of cookies later, he felt no further along than he had the night before. After leaving Katy's, he'd gone straight to the *Chronicle* and started sorting through the photographs he'd taken of the high school and of the crop circles. That had been around midnight. It was now after eleven, and his story lacked focus. Worse yet, it smacked of something the grocery store rags would pay big bucks for.

It stank on ice. It reeked of the kind of exaggeration one gets when asking a street corner drunk to describe how he won't use your kind donation to buy a drink.

He'd been surprised and secretly relieved when Cheryl Steinhardt had called to ask if he'd like to use her version of the Don Juan Demon, as it had come to be called. Josh had met Cheryl several years earlier at a local writer's guild meeting, and she'd written small pieces for him on and off. He'd never appreciated her contributions more than he did this morning.

To top it all off, his cousins Mark and Matthew Benjamin had called around ten, saying they were in town, and would he be able to show them the *Chronicle* and meet with a local attorney about the sale.

When it rains, it pours. Noah, start building the ark.

"Mr. Carpenter?" a woman's voice asked.

Josh jerked his head up. He'd been so involved in looking through the photos that he hadn't even heard the doors open. "Yes? Don't I know you?"

The tall blond woman smiled. "I'm pleased you remember me. Sheila Van Williams, WNN. I know you must be swamped right now. Your town's had to deal with a lot the last few weeks, but I could really use your input on some features of my report. Do you have some time for collaboration?"

Something in the back of Joshua's mind screamed no. There was something about the woman's beguiling smile that smacked of deceit. "I'm pretty busy right now. Could it wait until after lunch?"

Sheila moved further into the newsroom. She swayed slightly when she walked. Men often followed her walk as though hypnotized, thinking her gait a naturally sexy one. Sheila would never admit her sensual saunter was merely the result of sawing down her right high heel by a quarter of an inch. If it was good enough for Marilyn Monroe, it was good enough for Sheila.

"I'm afraid that will be too late. I have a live spot in just over an hour. I suppose I could give the basic facts for now and then add some color later. How about dinner?"

She was coming on to him! Joshua wasn't usually a target for women like Sheila. He couldn't decide whether to feel flattered or frightened.

"I'm afraid I'm busy for supper...I mean, dinner. We usually call it supper around here. I'm meeting Katherine Adamson. You could join us if you like. Katy grew up around here, too. I'm sure she'd be happy to help you out."

Van Williams' smile disappeared then suddenly reappeared as though willed to do so by the reporter's internal programming. "All right. It's a date. Where shall I meet you two?"

Surprised, Josh had to think fast. "Sandy's, I guess. That's close to your hotel. Say, seven o'clock?"

"Seven'll work just fine. Mind if I bring a buddy along?"

This was not going as Josh had expected. "Sure, why not?"

"Great! We'll meet you two then. Thanks, Josh. You're terrific!" she kissed him on the cheek, her warm breath lingering over his left ear momentarily.

She turned and sauntered back toward the door, leaving Josh blinking in confusion. *I'll never figure women out*, he thought, returning to his photos. *Then again, there's only one I'm really interested in knowing.*

He picked up the phone to call Katherine.

The phone rang seven, eight times. Where was the answering machine she'd promised to connect? Nine times. Ten.

Josh hung up. He'd have to go over there.

"Hey, cousin!" Matt Benjamin called from the doors.

"Matt! Mark! Man, I didn't see either one of you come in. I'm going to have to see Doc Gondry about my eyes."

"I'll tell you, cousin, if you didn't notice that gorgeous woman who just came out of here, then you're right! Does she come with the deal?"

"Huh?"

"You know," Mark said nudging his brother, "Is she one of the perks?"

Joshua laughed. "That's the kind of perk that'd skin you alive and have you on toast. She works for WNN."

Mark sighed. "Oh, well. I doubt Margie'd let me have her anyway. She frowns on me bringing home strays."

Joshua led them into the main room, spreading his hands to show off the bare-bones look of the *Chronicle*. "Here it is. Dad's dream and my nightmare. Are you two sure you want to run a newspaper? You'll have to move to Eden, unless you want to pay someone else run it for you."

The twins exchanged glances. "We have someone in mind," Matt said, removing his cap. "You know me and Mark. We like to put our fingers into the pie, but we don't want to wash the dishes. Besides, running the trucking company keeps us pretty busy. You got a lawyer we can talk with?"

236

Josh nodded. "I asked Gerry Anderson to meet me for lunch today so we could work through the legalities. You guys like Mexican food?"

"Does a pig squeal?" Mark asked with a broad grin.

"Margarita's has Mex-American food that will make any pig squeal," Josh smiled in return. "Let me give Gerry a quick call to confirm, and we'll be on our way."

Margarita's had become a culinary Mecca for many of the weirder visitors who'd come to frequent Eden since Sunday night's alien encounter on Ben Miller's farm. Gomez and Angelina Ramirez had even risen to local celebrity status. Josh and his cousins arrived around eleven forty-five, but the place was already packed with newspeople, gawkers, and several dozen hippies from the fast-growing commune on Miller's Farm.

Seeing one of her favorite customers, Angelina left the kitchen to help them find a table. "Señor Joshua, I could have delivered to the paper like usual. Oh, you are three? Let me see if I can find a table. If not, we'll make room in the kitchen. OK?"

Josh smiled at her honest face. "Wherever you want us, Angelina. The kitchen's fine. Just make sure Gerry Anderson knows how to find us."

"You be four, OK. I seat Señor Anderson when he come in. This be all right?"

She had led them to a four-topper right next to the kitchen. "This is fine."

Pleased with their approval, Angelina took their orders— chicken tamales for Josh, beef burritos and salad for Matt, and beef tamales with a side of home fries for Mark.

Gerry Anderson sidled up, squeezing his wide girth past several men sporting shaved heads and multicolored beads.

"Afternoon," he said as he met up with Joshua and his cousins. "Or morning. I've lost track of the time. Interesting crowd. Most of these folks aren't local, huh?"

Josh pulled out a chair for the lawyer. "It's going on noon, so you're safe either way. This is the last table Angelina had. We've already ordered, Gerry. We figured we'd better get the order in before the cook's overloaded."

"Not a problem," Anderson said, waving to Angelina. "Angie knows what I always eat."

"Hola, Señor Gerry. Beans and cornbread?" asked Angelina Ramirez as she passed by their table. "We have some really fine habañeras in today."

"Bring it on, Angie. I can eat all you can cook!"

She smiled, placing four glasses filled with ice water on the table along with tableware. "Your orders have been placed in line first, Señors. While you wait my husband will bring you some tortillas and picanté. You like some Big Red, Señor Josh?"

"Love some, Angelina. Matt? Mark?"

"You got Mexican beer, little lady?" Mark asked as a brightly attired waitress nudged past.

Angelina pointed to a sign in the corner. "See that, Señor? It say we sell no alcohol here. Sorry. I can bring you root beer if you like."

"Root beer will be fine," Mark said happily. "You're a lovely lady, Angie. We promise to behave."

Matt laughed. "We're just a couple of kidders, Angie. Thanks for bein' so nice to us."

She left the table, calling out orders in Spanish to her sons in the kitchen. Gerry opened his briefcase and removed a legal pad. "I'm Gerry Anderson," he said to the twins. Handshakes were exchanged and Gerry settled down to business. "So, tell me, Josh. You and your cousins here want to have a nice legal change of hands of the *Chronicle*, am I right?"

"Right," the twins said simultaneously.

"That's right, Gerry," Josh added. "We talked price on the way over here, and we've settled on that. Now we just need to know about the fine print that needs to go into it."

Anderson interlaced his fat fingers and pushed them outward with a loud crack. Then, taking hold of a black ballpoint pen, he began to take notes.

CHAPTER Thirty-three

FRIDAY AFTERNOON

Enoch Jones pulled in to the side drive of 777 Main Street, reminiscing about all his many visits to this prestigious address. He'd first met Celeste Adamson when she'd called on him at the church office back in July of 1995. The stately home she'd left Katherine had been lovingly cared for through the years and through generations of Adamsons. It felt good to come here again.

After parking on Broadway, Jones stepped out onto the sidewalk and happily took in the fragrance of Cissy's prize-winning roses in the north garden. He knew Cissy had planted most of those bushes with her own arthritic hands. Fifty rose bushes in a wide array of reds and pinks and one singular yellow stood proudly, a beautiful testament to Cissy's unfailing green thumb. She'd never complained about work. This house told of her dedication to her family, just as the many lives she'd changed through her testimony told of her dedication to the Lord.

"Good afternoon!" he called as he locked up his green station wagon. "Beautiful day!"

240

Katy was sitting on the veranda, perpetual coffee cup in one hand and her cordless phone in the other. She waved to the pastor. "Good afternoon to you! Come on up and join us. I'll be off the phone in a minute!"

"Us?" he asked, looking around for another person.

He pushed through the gate, passed by Katherine's sedan, and walked slowly up the five steps that led to a wide, brightly tiled outdoor room, roofed in slate and supported by vine-covered columns. He was glad to see Katherine looking so well.

"I'll see what I can find out for you," Katherine was saying into the phone. A pause. "All right. And please let Grace know how sorry I am for all she's gone through. And you, too, Mrs. Alcorn. I'm very sorry for the loss your whole family has suffered." Another pause. "Monday? Of course I'll be there. I'm sure Josh will be there, too. Good-bye, Mrs. Alcorn." She pushed the button to end the call.

"That was Meredith Alcorn," she said to Jones as he joined her on the veranda. "Donny Alcorn's funeral is Monday at two. Does this town ever stop dying?"

Before he could answer, something that looked for all the world like a wolf came bounding out of the kitchen and onto the veranda. "Woof!" the dog barked softly.

"Great wonderful Lord!" Jones cried out, certain he was under attack.

"Heidi, kisses!" Katy commanded, and the dog bounded into Jones' arms and began happily licking his face.

"Good heavens!" he cried out, beginning to laugh. "Is she going to eat me?"

"She likes you," Katy said with a wry grin. "Heidi, sit."

The dog sat.

"Is that what I think it is?" Enoch asked, trying to recover his cool, collected demeanor. "Is that a...a wolf?"

241

"Half wolf," she said. "Heidi, shake."

The dog raised her right paw for Jones to shake.

Shaking the paw obediently, Jones removed his hat and sat opposite Katherine.

"Half wolf? What's the other half? Wolf?"

Katherine laughed. "Husky. She's from a mixed litter up in Alaska. She was going to lose her home, so I've been elected foster mom for a while. For some reason she took a shine to me. Outside of that, she's pretty darn smart."

Enoch wiped his forehead. The day was going to be hot. "Oh, yes, she's smart. I can see that. She has had all her shots, I suppose."

Katy nodded. "Every one of them. I don't suppose you need a dog?"

"Looks to me like this dog has made her own choice. You teach her those tricks?"

Katy nodded. "Two hours ago. She learned them like a whip. Now, if I could just teach her to chase off helicopters."

Jones looked upward. "Yeah. They're something, aren't they? I can tell most of them are news helicopters, but a couple of them are unmarked. They hung out over the church off and on all morning."

"They like it here, too. I'm teaching Heidi to bark three times for unmarked, twice for WNN, and once for local. Of course, she'll have to learn to howl whenever she sees anything from PBS. Everyone knows they're on the government payroll."

Jones laughed. "Yeah, that Big Bird is pretty suspicious."

"Coffee?" she asked.

"I'd take some iced tea if you have it. How old is this dog?"

She pattered into the kitchen to make the tea, talking through the open French doors all the while. "Three years old, I think. She's really a pussycat. No offense, Heidi!"

The dog wagged her tail, nudging Jones with her nose for a scratch behind the ear. "She's very friendly. Her appearance is alarming though. I guess that's a good combination for a guard dog."

Katherine emerged with a tall, clear glass of tea with a slice of lemon. "This is Cissy's recipe, so I hope I made it right."

Jones took a long sip, letting the crisp, sweet taste revive him. "Perfect! Your aunt would be very proud of you, Katherine. Are you feeling better today?"

"I am. I can't thank you enough, Pastor Jones, for letting me go on and on last night. It's horrible that I was feeling more sorry for myself than I was for the Alcorns. Thanks."

"It's my job, and it's my pleasure. You're a remarkable woman, Katherine. And I know you're going to find your way."

Heidi bounded toward the pin oak at the back of the rose garden. Two squirrels, chasing each other up and down the tree, had caught her attention.

"Let's just say you're helping me to read the map. What do you think about the incident at the high school last night?" she asked.

Jones shrugged. "I'm not in a position to judge, since I wasn't there, but I can tell you that such things can happen. We live in a world that is on the brink, Katherine. There is an unseen world battling all around us. And sometimes those supernatural beings, be they good or evil, cross over into our own."

"So you think the audience may have seen a real demon last night?" she asked, her dark eyes wide.

"You saw what it did. Can you honestly tell me that a man could have done that to Donny in such a short time? And what about that other boy, the one the demon kidnapped? He must be found, too. And he may well be in just as poor a condition as the deceased Mr. Alcorn."

"What sort of world is this then? You mentioned something yesterday about not fighting flesh and blood."

Leaning forward, Jones' eyes centered on hers. "Wrestle. *'For we wrestle not against flesh and blood but against powers and principalities.'* It's from Ephesians chapter six, verse twelve. The apostle Paul was warning the believers in the city of Ephesus of the fight against Satan and his minions. I know in this day and age that sounds almost laughable."

"No one was laughing last night."

"Nor will they when the truth of how the world has sold out to Satan hits home. And it will, Katherine. One day, Christ will return to this earth to judge unbelievers, and the realization of how they've blown it will be the greatest devastation anyone could ever know. Now is when our eyes must open. Not then, when it's too late."

Katherine ran a finger around the edge of her coffee mug. "And these people—in Ephesus was it?—these people fought against Satan?"

"We all must fight the good fight."

"How?" she asked, her eyes growing deadly serious. "How can anyone fight against the kind of thing that was described to me? That demon was as big as the stage was high. Grace Alcorn said it actually had to crouch to fit! Do you know the hospital is filled with people from last night who claim they've lost their hearing or their sight or their minds? If that is a sample of what Satan can throw at us, how can we hope to fight?"

"You've hit on it, Katherine. We can't. Only God can defeat the Enemy. But He will give us His courage, if we rely upon Him."

"I don't know, Pastor Jones. I'd like to have that sort of faith, but I just can't. That little girl who went forward in church years ago has grown up. I don't see the world as black and white anymore."

Jones smiled. "Neither do I. The visible world is complicated enough, but there is so much that is invisible. Stuff we can't see, but we have to realize is there. Even science believes there's more to life than what we can sense. But if what you mean when you say 'black and white' is that there is truth and then there is the rest, then you're right. God is Truth. Simple. Satan is Lies. Simple. God's truth is inside you, Katherine. He put it there when you sought Him out as a young girl. You've just forgotten where it's filed, that's all. You pray about it. I know God is trying to talk to you, or you wouldn't have called me last night."

She shook her head. "Heidi! Come!" she called, figuring the squirrels had suffered enough for one day. "She's been digging out there all morning. Probably trying to sniff out a chipmunk or beat some squirrel to its cache of nuts!"

"You see?" he continued. "Those squirrels are like us. There they are, playing around that tree, taking no notice of the mortal danger that watches them from just a few feet away, that is until Heidi jumps at them. But once Heidi attacks, it may be too late for those defenseless squirrels. They aren't equipped to fight that dog, but you are. That dog knows you are in control. Well, Satan and his army of fallen angels and demons may like to watch us, and they may even jump at us, but God is in control. Simple as that."

"I'll think about it, all right? Part of me hears you, but there's another part that's still pretty mixed up. I hope you understand."

"Listen, Katherine. Listen to God's voice. That's where the truth lies."

She stood up as he rose to leave. Heidi ran up onto the veranda, her bushy tail swishing in circles. "She's a good dog, she is. I'm glad you have her, Katherine. Animals often see things we can't. You pay attention to Heidi. Good girl!" he added, leaning down to scratch Heidi's ears again. "By the way, have you found Cissy's diary yet?"

"Oh, you know in all that's happened, I forgot to look! Josh is coming over tonight after supper. We'll go through the house to see if we can locate it. I'll call you."

"I'd like that. Well, I need to get over to Wilson's Funeral Home. Mrs. Erickson and her family are having a viewing for Forest. That tragedy has sort of gotten lost in all the hubbub about last night."

"I know. I'll have to send her a card. Cissy had a couple of accounts there."

"Well, call me!" he said, heading toward his car. "Bye, Heidi!"

The green station wagon pulled out onto Broadway, and Katherine sat back into her chair. "What do you say we get our laptop, Heidi? I'll look up how to take care of a Husky, and you can take a nap. How do you like that?"

The dog sat, her blue eyes filled with understanding. Above them, a black helicopter circled again. Heidi barked three times.

"Pastor Jones is right, Heidi. You are a good dog. Who knows? Maybe he's right about everything. I'll have to think about that demon stuff. And I guess I'll pray about it, too."

CHAPTER Thirty-four

FRIDAY AFTERNOON—4:30 PM

Maria Horine shuddered as two men led her into a brightly painted waiting room. Her dark, sleepless eyes searched the high ceilings and fashionably decorated walls for any sign of why she might have been brought here.

She recalled the events of the day, hoping to make some sense of it all. After sleeping little the night before, she'd been awakened by the first of over thirty phone calls. Reporters had camped on her front lawn again, and then the Buchanans had called begging Maria to help them find their son, Jared. Maria had very few words of hope for the terrified couple, but she had promised to pray for them.

A Miss Van Williams from WNN had called, pressing Maria for an exclusive interview regarding her opinion about the high school horror. Maria hadn't known what the woman was talking about. Van Williams had then come to her home along with a dozen or more of her kind, dressed in expensive handmade suits, coifed with the utmost care, their microphones ready, and their shoes like mirrors.

247

Maria had watched them from behind her curtains, terrified. She didn't dare call anyone for help. The Voice had told her to say nothing. Van Williams had told Maria all about the terrifying apparition at the school, that it was being reported that a demon had kidnapped another boy and killed Donny Alcorn.

What if the Voice was the demon? What if this giant had her baby? Was Amy still alive?

Maria had spent most of the morning in prayer, counting the beads as she wept great tears to the Madonna. "Ave Maria," she said over and over. "Hail Mary, Queen of Heaven!" The words felt empty, but she prayed them again and again, desperately trying to put into them the emotion they required. She scrubbed her kitchen floor in penance, then scrubbed it again, hoping for some sign that her prayers had been heard.

Then the men had arrived. A helicopter had landed in the wide meadow that ran behind the Horine home just as the hour struck three o'clock. Maria knew that three was the holy number of the trinity, and she began to pray that this was her answer.

The helicopter's wide blades swung at the air like a scythe, cutting into the heart of Maria's ill winds. Divine help had arrived! As she watched two men in black emerge from the equally dark helicopter, she knew this was the answer to her prayers. Once outside, the reporters parted, just like the Red Sea had parted before Moses and the Hebrew children, and Maria and the two men—Maria's angels—had passed through unimpeded.

Then Maria had boarded the helicopter from heaven. She had waved to the clamoring caucus below, watching them turn into chittering ants as the mighty blades, like four cherubic wings, carried her to see her baby girl.

But now she sat in an ordinary room built with ordinary, mortal hands. She was confused and weary, and she had begun to doubt her earlier trust in the men in black.

"Mrs. Horine? Maria?" a man called from a doorway that had opened without her notice.

"I am Maria Horine," she answered.

"I am Dr. Apollo Bell. I have been looking after your daughter since she was brought here."

Maria fell to her knees. "Holy Mother of God! Blessed Virgin! Can it be true? Is my Amy here? Alive?"

Bell smiled, and his entire face glowed with a calming light. "Mrs. Horine, she is more than alive. Amy is whole."

"Praise our Lady! Oh, oh!" she cried, her eyes rolling into her head. With a sudden thump, she hit the hard, tiled floor.

"She's fainted," he said softly, knowing Lilith stood behind him without the need to turn to see her. Lilith was never more than a few steps or a whisper from Bell's side. "Take her to Amy's suite and settle her in. She'll be staying with us."

"Yes, Dr. Bell. And the explanation to the press?"

"That has already been taken care of," he answered. "Once mother and daughter are reunited, we will begin the next phase of their orientation. Oh, and send for Daniel Cheatham. We'll need to discuss the unfortunate appearance at the high school last night. Our plans require a slow release of information to the public, and that means using our contacts, even if it means using them up."

"Yes, Dr. Bell. I will see to it at once."

Lilith clapped her hands, and the two men in black appeared. "See that the mother is taken to Amy's quarters. We have already prepared a room for her there. And then bring the car around. I'll be going into town."

Joshua had spent most of the afternoon with his cousins and Gerry Anderson. Although the price Matt and Mark had agreed to exceeded the price Josh felt the *Chronicle* was actually worth, the twins had insisted, so Josh had at last given in. Pending the resolution of a few minor legal issues, the afternoon had ended with Joshua's signature on the dotted line. *The Eden Chronicle* now belonged to his cousins.

Josh had offered to remain on as editor, but the twins had insisted on putting in their own person right away. Josh hadn't questioned it. The Benjamin boys had been waiting for sixteen years to get their hands on the *Chronicle*, so Josh had good reason to believe they had been keeping their ducks lined up.

It was now six-fifteen, and he considered going home first to his apartment, but then reconsidered. He should just go by Katherine's to see if she still wanted to join him for supper. He'd not been able to reach her all day, and he had begun to worry about her. She'd been quite upset the night before.

Parking on Broadway and stepping onto the veranda, Joshua jumped back at the sudden howling of a dog.

"Sorry!" he heard Katy call. He could see her, hair still wet, padding toward the door in a robe and slippers.

"Hi," she said simply as she opened the door wide.

Joshua didn't move. He couldn't. A wolf stood between him and Katherine.

"Heidi, this is Joshua Carpenter, and he's a nice man. Sit, Heidi!"

The dog sat, her ice blue eyes fixed on Joshua.

"Will she bite?" he asked.

"Only if you do. Heidi, kisses!"

The dog instantly sprang against Josh's chest and began to lick his face. Josh hugged the animal for a moment, eventually breaking into laughter. "Call her off! I give in!"

"Heidi, sit!"

The dog sat in front of Joshua, her tail continuing to wag furiously enough to dust the floor.

"She's certainly obedient. Where'd she come from?"

"After last night, I figured I'd keep a guardian here," Katy said, still drying her short hair with a thick, yellow towel. "You're early. Did we say seven?"

"We did. I tried to call you, but no machine and no answer."

"Really? I've been here all day. I even had the phone with me most of the time. I'm sure I would have heard it. Are you sure you dialed it right?"

"I dialed it the same way I've been dialing it since we first met. I know this number better than I know my own. Which reminds me, my number may be changing. At least the work number."

Kate stopped. "Heidi, lie down, girl."

The dog went to a corduroy dog bed on the TV porch. She watched the pair for a few minutes, then, apparently convinced Josh could be trusted, fell asleep.

"Did she come that way? Geez! I've never seen a dog like that! What is she anyway?" he asked, sitting at the table.

"Husky mix. And yes, she's half wolf. Isn't she a dear? She already knew most of the stuff, but I taught her to kiss and shake. She learns very fast. So, what's this about your work number?"

Josh savored the moment, stretching his legs out in front of him and enjoying Katherine's expectant stare.

"Well?" she asked again, her tone indicating she'd better not have to ask a third time.

"You're looking at a man who's out of a job, my dear. I am completely unfettered. A man on the loose."

"Your cousins! They came early? Did they buy it?"

"They bought it, lock, stock, and the whole barrel of monkeys. They even have their own editor coming in tonight to put together tomorrow's edition. I imagine it will be a small one, probably letting the readership know about the new owners and all. But for me...Katy Celeste, I am a free man!"

"Hallelujah!" she cried out, falling into his arms. "This calls for a celebration!"

He hadn't expected to catch her as she fell into his waiting arms. He hadn't expected to be kissing her at that moment, but he was. And this time, she kissed back.

On the brown corduroy bed a few feet away, Heidi's tail began to wag again, but neither human noticed.

———

Sandy's had never been so packed. With the advent of the weekend, hundreds of strange tourists had descended upon Eden. Every parking lot, every restaurant, and every motel and hotel teemed with newcomers. A remarkable array of VW buses, some painted in flowers and swirls reminiscent of the '60s, lined the side streets of Eden, and locals were treated to a parade of poster-perfect saucer groupies, many wearing tin foil on their heads, others simply preaching the coming dawn of earth's rebirth.

"The nuts are gathering," Katherine remarked as she and Joshua wove through a line of illegal street vendors, hawking tin foil hats and other assorted anti-alien devices. "I'm trying to figure out if we're the squirrels or not."

Josh laughed, keeping her close as they maneuvered to Sandy's main entrance. The standing-room-only crowd appeared orderly, but Josh despaired of finding a table. "Maybe we should have called!" he shouted to Katy, trying to be heard above the din.

"Isn't that Sheila Van Williams over there?" she shouted in return, leaning in close to Josh's ear. "She's waving to you."

Josh felt a blush rising and did his best to beat it down. "I forgot to tell you she's meeting us."

Katherine shot back a look that read part anger, part question.

Josh hoped the questioning part of Kate would win out.

As they met up with Sheila, the tall blonde kissed Joshua's cheek and smiled a toothy hello to Katherine. "We got here early!" she shouted. "Come on! We have a private room!"

Following her hypnotic swaying, Josh and Katy were led into one of several rooms of varying sizes that Sandy's offered locals for meetings, parties, and the like. The plum room Sheila had snagged was situated on the riverside of the old warehouse with a gorgeous view of the Ohio.

"Will this do?" she asked the pair as they closed the door to the clamoring crowd.

"Very nice," Josh said. "Thanks for being so thorough."

"I'm always thorough," she replied with a wink to intimate subtler meanings to her words. "How are you doing, Kathy? Expecting rain?"

Katherine handed her light raincoat to Josh, who cheerfully hung it on the rack in the corner. "Just being prepared," she answered, smiling into the blonde's chilling blue eyes.

The intimate private room had one table, large enough to seat six comfortably, but Sheila and her mystery date were the only other guests. "There will be four of us tonight," she said to the young waiter who appeared from a side door that must have led to the kitchen. "How about a pitcher of margaritas to get us started?"

"I'll have regular old iced tea with lemon and sugar," Josh said.

"Same for me," Katherine added, noting the disapproval on Sheila's heavily made-up face.

"Not drinking any more, Kathy? That's a surprise."

Katherine forced a smile, but relaxed when Joshua squeezed her hand supportively. "Things change, Sheila. People change—or at least some do. Hello, I'm Katherine Adamson," she said to the fourth person in the room, an aristocratic man who had been standing quietly in the far corner of the room.

"You needn't introduce yourself, Miss Adamson," he replied. "I am a great fan of your work. *Mysteries of the Dove* is my personal favorite. Where on earth do you find your information? Is it true there is a shadow government that plans to enslave the human race through a message of false peace?"

"Don't answer that, Kate," Sheila interrupted. "Apollo likes to entrap people with their own words. He's done it to me often enough. Kate Adamson, Joshua Carpenter, meet Dr. Apollo Bell."

"It's a pleasure to meet you both," the man said, extending his hand to Josh. "Miss Adamson, I meant what I said. I'd love to discuss your writing sometime."

Katherine shook his hand, and then sat as Josh extended a chair for her opposite Bell. Josh sat next to Katherine after seating Sheila next to Bell. Bell sat last but made no move to assist his date with her chair.

As the waiter brought the drinks, Katherine watched Bell from over top of her menu. She'd heard the name once or twice even before her return to Eden on Monday. Some distant bit of information lingered in some corner of her brain, and she made a mental note to conduct a LexisNexis search as soon as she got home.

254

"You are with the Mt. Hermon Institute?" Katy asked Bell after the waiter's departure with their orders. "I've been meaning to take a tour. I don't suppose you could arrange one?"

Bell sipped his water. "I could arrange one anytime you wish, Miss Adamson. And yes, I am fortunate to run the Institute. I succeeded Dr. Browning after his untimely passing. Sheila tells me you have recently suffered the loss of your aunt. I am so sorry."

"Thank you. She passed away a week ago today in fact."

"Death is such a temporary state, don't you agree, Miss Adamson? Some may say it is the end, but I disagree. I believe it is just the beginning. What do you think, Mr. Carpenter?"

Josh had been very quiet. He cleared his throat and gazed directly into Bell's chameleon eyes.

"I believe our world is but a part of what exists. Man, in his present state, can't see the truth of all that surrounds us. It's like looking into a mirror in the dark."

"Gazing into a glass darkly," Bell rephrased. "You are well read, Carpenter."

"As are you, Dr. Bell. Tell me, your field is what? Genetics?"

Bell paled slightly. "My no! I'm a biochemist. I'll admit that I do hold a degree in human genetics, but it is a discipline I no longer practice. At the Institute, we seek to find organic cures for the diseases of our time—Alzheimer's, depression, schizophrenia, panic disorders, even a cure for Evil."

Sheila laughed. "Evil, Apollo? There's no such thing!"

"Ah, but there is. Isn't there, Miss Adamson?"

Katherine looked at the man, carefully considering her answer. The waiter returned, bearing a large tray laden with steaming plates, so she had a moment to think. Bell wore a white suit, probably an Armani, over a pink silk shirt. His height was close to Josh's, so Kate guessed him to be around 6'2". The doctor had bronze skin and dark wavy hair, worn slicked back from a broad forehead. He had a strong jaw and an interesting mouth that reminded Katherine of a man she'd met in Morocco some years before.

Bell was a very handsome man, and Katherine imagined Sheila must think herself lucky to be with him, yet something in Bell's eyes disturbed Katherine. She had been trying to fix their color, yet no matter how the light danced upon them, she could not. One moment they appeared to be dark, perhaps deep brown, but the next they seemed bright blue, another hazel or pale green.

Most of all, his manner bothered the seasoned writer. Katherine had spoken to several murderers, including the chilling interview with Thomas Allen Stroud, so she had a good notion of criminal demeanor. Bell slickly surpassed even Stroud's cool detachment.

Bell represented something far more sinister.

"Well, Miss Adamson? Is there Evil in our world?" Bell repeated.

Katy placed her napkin into her lap and smiled directly into Bell's elusively shaded eyes. "Oh yes, Dr. Bell. Evil exists. As does Good. I believe they're called Satan and Jesus Christ."

Bell flinched.

Joshua squeezed Katherine's hand once again. "Problem, Dr. Bell?" he asked, raising an eyebrow.

Bell patted his mouth with the linen napkin. "No, no, I'm fine. Something just went down the wrong way."

"I'll bet it did," Katy muttered. "Sheila, aren't you doing remotes for WNN these days?"

Van Williams checked the time. "I have over an hour. I can eat, then broadcast from that lovely little park area by the river. I've noticed it's become a hangout for many of the loons that are about. They'll add color to the background."

"Always thinking, aren't you?" Katherine noted, wryly.

"Yes, I am," Sheila answered. "So, Josh, have you given any more thought to our discussion today?"

Joshua swallowed a bite of his cheeseburger with everything. "Well," he said, gulping the last of it. "If you want to liaison with the paper, that's doable. You'll have to take it up with the owner, though."

Sheila looked puzzled. "I thought you were the owner."

"Not any more. I sold it today. The new owners took over as of five-seventeen this afternoon. In fact, I think they're burning the midnight oil tonight, putting together the first issue with all the details of the sale. You can catch them after your remote."

"Tough break, Sheila," Katy said with a wink.

Their meal continued in relative silence. Bell occasionally asked a polite question about Eden or Katherine's work. Sheila, who had begun to sulk, poked at her salad with rising anger.

An hour or so after the arrival of their food, the mixed quartet left their tips and parted company. As they exited the building, Bell turned to Joshua and Katherine.

"The Institute is a fascinating place, Miss Adamson. As a writer, I'm sure you'd find that it stimulates the creative part of the brain. We are currently conducting some miraculous research into those diseases that cripple the soul and make mankind weak."

"The soul?" Joshua repeated.

Bell offered a half smile, his eyes boring into Carpenter's. "The mind, I mean, of course. The mind." Then turning to Katherine, Bell added. "I would be delighted to arrange a private tour for you, Miss Adamson. Anytime."

257

"I'll call you, Dr. Bell," she replied coolly. Bell was playing cat and mouse games, and Katherine suddenly felt like the mouse.

Both Bell and Van Williams turned toward the river, leaving Joshua and Katherine standing in the midst of several brightly attired moon men.

"Home?" he asked, taking her arm.

"Home. That has a nice sound. Take me home, and I'll let you keep Heidi company while I do a bit of online sleuthing regarding our new friend, Dr. Bell."

"Better yet," he said with a broad smile, his hazel eyes twinkling in the lamplight. "I'll bring in my TiBook, use your wireless network, and we'll both be sleuths. Deal?"

"Deal," she laughed. "Race you to the car!"

CHAPTER Thirty-five

Maria Horine snuggled in close to her daughter. Amy had fallen asleep in her mother's warm, comforting arms over an hour before. Sleep, little one, she thought. You are safe now.

After meeting with both Amy and several of her daughter's doctors, Maria felt satisfied that both she and Amy were safe at the Institute. Maria had shown surprise when she'd learned of her daughter's discovery in the woods northwest of the research hospital. Thankfully, the hospital's security system had alerted a brave guard to Amy's presence in a secure zone.

Amy had suffered mild exposure to the elements, but otherwise, she appeared unharmed. However, the girl's memory had been spotty and she'd carried no identification, so the Institute had charted her as a Jane Doe until she had regained her senses and given them her name.

Thank you for saving my little girl, she thought as she watched the tropical plants sway in the light wind that blew through the garden outside her daughter's magnificent windows. Very soon, she would take her child home, and they would return to a normal life. They would leave Eden and all its evil. They would run from the Voice and escape to freedom beyond the Voice's reach.

FRIDAY—MIDNIGHT

Josh woke with a start. It took a moment for him to remember he was at Katherine's home, and that they had spent hours searching the Internet and LexisNexis for information about Eden's mysterious Dr. Bell. Somewhere amongst the hours of online searching, munching on Fritos, drinking Big Red, and scratching Heidi, the pair had finally fallen asleep together on the overstuffed couch that dominated the TV porch.

"Katy?" he called out, but she wasn't there.

"Katy!"

Heidi jumped up, her gray and cream tail waving like a bushy flag. "Woof!"

"You need to go outside?" Katy's voice called from the kitchen.

The dog ran to her mistress, sharp nails clattering on the kitchen tiles. Josh heard the French doors open, and he stretched himself awake.

"Sorry," he muttered, standing up. "I should go."

Katherine appeared bearing two cups of hot cocoa topped with cream.

"Sprinkles?" she asked with a laugh.

"You know me so well. But no, no sprinkles this time. Although you might want to save them for a hot fudge sundae with all the trimmings. I make some very excellent ice cream, and I think I remember seeing an ice cream maker in Cissy's cupboard."

She sat into a wicker chair, setting down the cups and licking whipped cream from her fingers. "While that sounds really good, I think it's a bit late for that. How about tomorrow? And regarding your suggestion that you go home, that's up to you."

Josh thought for a moment, his handsome face growing serious. "Are you suggesting what I think you are?"

She gave him a little smile and tilted her head. "Well? Would it be all that bad?"

He walked to the chair and pulled her up, into his arms. "I can think of nothing more inviting. However, I want to do this right. I meant what I said yesterday, Katy. I am in love with you. I always have been. I suppose I've waited all these years to get married because, in my heart, you're the only one for me. I've been waiting for you. You're my soul mate, Katherine Celeste," he told her honestly.

She wanted to blurt out that she was in love with him, too, but the ringing of the telephone offered her a way out. "Sorry, I'd better get that. It can't be anything good this late."

Katy left him there, while she took the cordless into the front parlor. "Hello?"

Dead air.

"Hello? Who is this?"

"Kathy?"

Katherine gasped. It couldn't be.

"Kathy? It's David. Please, let's talk."

She nearly dropped the receiver, her hand shook so much. How could she talk to him? Why had he called?

"Kathy, I need to talk to you. After nearly ten years together, I think you could give me two minutes. Please."

Forcing herself to calm, Katy sat, wondering if her heartbeat clanged as loudly into the phone as it did in her ears. "Two minutes."

"Thanks," he said softly. "I've tried your cell phone, but you either didn't get the messages, or you just didn't want to call me. I had to call George McMahon to get this number. Don't blame him. I told him it was an emergency."

261

She'd kill George tomorrow. "You still get what you want with lies, don't you?"

A moment's silence. "You're right. Old habits die hard. I'm sorry for that. I'm sorry I hurt you so much. Listen, Kathy, if I could just see you, then I could explain all of this. Believe me, there's more to it than you know. My wife..."

"Your wife is your wife, David. That's all I need to know about it. Now don't call here again. Your time is up."

She hung up, but she knew he'd call back. And now that he had the number, he would call every day.

"Are you OK?" came a concerned voice over her shoulder.

She turned to see Josh, his hazel eyes filled with concern.

Impulsively, she ran into his arms, and the dam broke, releasing a flood of tears. He held her like that for a long time, while she cried the poison out. Katy wanted to tell him everything, but she didn't have the right words. Joshua was so perfect, so unstained, and she had done practically nothing right. She did love him, but she couldn't tell him. He deserved better than her.

For now, she needed him, needed his kindness and his perfect heart next to her rotten one. Just for now.

"I'm sorry!" she blubbered between sobs.

"It's OK, Katy. You cry all you want. Cry out all the hurt and all the disappointments of the past. I'm here, honey. And I will always be here. No matter what."

CHAPTER Thirty-six

SATURDAY MORNING

Katy slept until almost eleven, waking only when she heard Heidi barking outside. Jumping up, she rubbed her eyes and pulled on a robe. Barefooted, she dashed down the stairs and toward the kitchen.

"Good morning!" called a man's voice from the kitchen.

There stood Joshua Carpenter, his clothes a mass of wrinkles from sleeping in them, but his wide smile as bright as ever. "What would you like for breakfast, my dear?"

Tying the robe securely, Katy scratched her head and took the coffee he offered her. "Thanks, Chief. You must be head of security here. Where's your pal?"

"Heidi? She's chasing a squirrel in the back. Eggs and bacon?"

Sitting, Katherine sipped the coffee. *Perfect,* she thought. "Do you do windows?"

"Nah, I'm a Mac guy."

Both laughed, and the tension broke. "I'm sorry, Josh. I should have explained everything before. I can tell you all about it—about him, if you like."

He raised his hand to stop her. "Sweetheart, you tell me when it's comfortable, when it's right for you. Or you can never tell me. It's all the same to me, so long as you're happy. Clearly this guy..."

"David."

"David. Clearly he didn't make you happy. You have nothing to be sorry for, Katy. In fact, if anyone should apologize, it's me!"

"You?" she gasped. "Joshua, you've been nothing but wonderful! Why should you have to apologize?"

"For hounding you about marriage. Oh, I'm not backing down, so learn to live with that," he flashed a smile. "But I shouldn't have pushed so hard so quickly. You need to think about it in your own time."

She considered kissing him, but Heidi's bark sharpened, and Katy's radar went up. "Someone's outside," she said, rising and peeking out the French doors.

There stood Helen Markham, scratching Heidi behind the ears.

"Good morning!" she sang as Katherine opened the door. "I was wondering what time you wanted to have lunch. Is noon still all right?"

Katherine ran through a mental calendar, sheepishly recalling a promised lunch date for today. Seeing her neighbor's puzzled expression and taking note of Joshua's wrinkled clothes, Helen laughed nervously. "You know, I'm just butting in where I don't belong. You have company, and well...I'll be going!"

"Wait!" Josh called, bringing Helen into the kitchen. "You're not interrupting anything, Helen. I fell asleep on the couch last night, so I have to be getting home so I can get a change of clothes."

Suddenly, Katy broke into peals of laughter. Within seconds, Joshua too began to laugh, and even Helen found a smile in her pocket—finally breaking into joyful laughter with the others.

"What are we laughing about?" she asked, wiping her eyes. Heidi snuggled up close, glad to see her former owner.

Waving her arms, Katherine nearly choked. "You just looked so uncomfortable, Helen!"

Helen laughed again. "Sorry, Josh! I know you're always a perfect gentleman."

Josh bowed and kissed Helen's hand. "Don't give it another thought, dear Helen. Now, what were you saying about lunch? Ladies, what do you say we go to Annie's Attic? I haven't been there in months, and I hear they have a new recipe for lemon chicken that's fantastic."

"Annie's Attic?" Helen asked, dumbfounded. "That's a New Age tearoom! You want to go there, Josh?"

"I'm an open-minded guy—at least when it comes to food."

Helen laughed again. "All right. I'll tell Bill. We'll meet you two there at, say twelve?"

"How about twelve-thirty?" Katherine asked, pointing to her bathrobe.

"Twelve-thirty," Helen answered, heading for the door. "See you there!"

After she'd left, Katy looked fondly at Joshua and smiled. "Annie's Attic?" she asked, shaking her head. "Boy, you are trying to impress me! OK, boy, go home and put on some clothes that don't smell like yesterday, then pick me up at noon."

Josh kissed her hand then headed out the door. Heidi wagged her tail, jumping up and leaning against the doors to watch Joshua leave.

"You like him, don't you, girl?"

Heidi barked, nuzzling in for a scratch.

"So do I, Heidi girl. So do I."

Annie's Attic was established in 1991, just after the Gulf War, by two sisters from Indianapolis. Considered a bit trendy by many of the locals, Annie's had become the preferred eatery of Eden's arts community. Mae and Jennifer Preston, who had originally owned a similar restaurant in Speedway on Indy's west side, had decided to retire in Eden, so they bought the top floor of the old Scott's five-and-dime and turned it into an artsy world of food and bohemian fun. After naming it Annie's Attic in honor of their grandmother, the Preston sisters had fashioned the space into a swank restaurant that turned a profit its very first year.

Joshua and Katherine had run a bit late, arriving at the restaurant at twelve forty-five. Bill waved to them as they were ushered into the main tearoom.

"I believe that's our table," Josh told the young hostess, pointing toward Bill's towering figure.

"Very good," the hostess said, leading them to the back. "Your server will be with you in a few moments. Enjoy your meal!"

Josh led Katherine to the table, feeling only slightly out of place amongst the cliques of college students and hippies. He'd been here before, more than a year earlier with Linda Kemp, but he'd tell Katherine about that some other time.

"Some place you picked, Carpenter," Bill Markham laughed as they sat down. "I'm glad we could get together, but next time, I'll pick the place."

All four laughed, and the waitress came round for tea orders. The young girl, dressed in black from head to toe, was tall and slim with green hair in a stylish topknot.

266

"I'm your server, Summer. What kind of tea may I bring you?"

The four suppressed snickers, which went unnoticed by Summer. "Our specialty today is raspberry tea with honey and lemon. And we also have a new flavor, which we just added," she continued, pointing to the insert in the menu, "watermelon blueberry tea."

Josh pursed his lips, while Bill simply closed the menu. "Do you have any beer?" Bill asked plainly.

"We don't serve beer, but we have a fermented tea that is really wonderful! It's made from lemon grass and..."

Bill held up his hands. "I'll just have a cheeseburger and fries and regular old iced tea."

Summer made a slight face but wrote down the order. "And for the lady?" she asked, looking to Helen.

"I'll have the lemon chicken salad and a raspberry tea."

Katherine was next, ordering a chicken salad sandwich and ginger tea, and Josh rounded out the order with a club sandwich and a Big Red.

Summer danced away. Her black sandals were decorated with miniature black bells that tinkled as she walked.

"This is some place," Bill laughed. "So, you two are an item, huh?"

Katy nearly choked on her water.

"Bill!" Helen scolded, tapping his arm. "You are so bad sometimes! Be nice."

Katherine was about to answer when she noticed an unusual woman on the other side of the room. Average height and willowy, the woman wore a gauzy white dress that made her raven hair seem even darker. The woman walked past the hostess, who seemed to take no notice of her, and wound her way throughout the room as though looking for someone. As she followed the woman's path, Katherine had the strange feeling she'd met this lady in white before.

"...so we offered her the dog, and, praise the Lord, she said yes! Isn't that right, Katy? Katy?" Helen Markham's voice filtered into Katherine's mind amidst dark visions of a world without time.

"What?" Katherine asked, turning away from the woman. "I'm sorry, Helen. I just couldn't take my eyes off that woman over there."

The other three craned their necks, following Katherine's nod to the other side of the room. "What woman?" Bill asked. "The one in the beret?"

Katy blinked. The woman had disappeared! "No! There was a woman with dark hair and..." she began, but seeing Bill's face, she waved it off. "Yeah, the one in the beret. Sorry. I guess I'm not great company yet."

Helen patted Katherine's hand. "You're still grieving, that's all. You just need a good meal and some rest. We won't keep you long today. We need to get back to the inn pretty soon. Maybe we can do this again next week."

Their food arrived and they ate mostly in silence. Bill told a joke or two, and Helen laughed nervously, keeping an eye on Katherine to make sure she laughed, too. Josh slipped his hand into hers occasionally, doing his best to keep the conversation going.

Suddenly, Katherine jumped up, begged everyone's pardon, and left the restaurant. Josh wiped his mouth quickly, offered apologies, left some cash for their lunch then dashed after Katy.

Outside, in the bright glare of the afternoon, Josh had to run to catch up with her.

"Hey, hey! Wait up!" he called, finally reaching her at the corner of Tulip and Main. "Is it something I said?"

Katherine looked tearful again, but she bit it back. "No. You're perfect. But I did see a woman in there. No one else saw her, but I did. Am I losing my mind, Josh?"

He kissed her forehead and touched her hair. "Not in the least. If you say a woman was there, I believe you."

"Don't patronize me!" she shouted back, the tears catching in her throat.

Just then, a tall woman waved from across the street. "Yoo-hoo! Miss Adamson!"

Joshua looked up, pointing to the waver. "Is that the woman?"

Katy sighed. "No. I don't know...wait a minute. That's the girl that works for Jean Davis. What does she want?"

"Miss Adamson!" the girl called, rushing against the light to cross to their side. The girl panted, pushing her cat glasses up on her thin nose. "I'm so glad I caught you!"

"It's Nancy, right?"

"Yes! Nancy Cheatham. Sorry to interrupt your walk, but I have a message for you. I tried to call your house, but, well Miss Davis had to leave town, and she wanted you to know. She tried to call you. Anyway, that's the message."

Katherine couldn't believe it. When she last spoke with Jean Davis, she'd said nothing about leaving town. "Where did she go?" Katy asked.

Nancy was busy smiling at Joshua. "Oh, sorry. She went to visit family in Atlanta. She said she'd be there for a week or so. Anyway, I'd better get back to the store. It was good to see you again. Come by the store and we can talk shop! And, uh, bring your friend."

"Nancy, this is Joshua Carpenter. Josh, Nancy," Katy hurriedly introduced them. Nancy gave Josh a slow, sweeping look.

Josh felt a blush rise, and stuttered, "I'm with her," putting his arm around Katy's shoulders briefly.

Nancy giggled. "Well, anyway. You come along, too, Joshua. Say! Are you going to be at the graduation ceremony tomorrow afternoon?"

Josh started to say no, but Katherine suddenly answered for them both. "We wouldn't miss it. Will you be there?" Katy asked, her entire attitude changing.

"Oh, yeah. My dad's the principal of the high school. He always makes me go to those things," Nancy replied. "Guess I'll see you tomorrow then. Bye, Miss Adamson. Bye, Joshua."

She turned, giggled, and headed back across the street.

"That was interesting," he said at last. "So, where to now, Milady?"

"John Thundercloud's place," she said flatly as they reached his car.

Josh helped her into his Chevette and started the engine. *See you on Saturday.* That's what Thundercloud had said.

How had he known?

CHAPTER Thirty-seven

pollo Bell closed the door to his office. "Come in, Mrs. Horine. We can speak more privately in here. Miss Prynne, would you please hold my calls?"

Maria felt incredibly small in Bell's immense office space. The walls were lined with expensive Honduran mahogany, and the lighting looked like it could be made of precious gems. Even the floor shone like polished gold. Bell's mahogany and glass desk stretched before her like a giant sentry, keeping her from approaching Bell directly.

"What is it you wanted to speak to me about, Mrs. Horine? Something to do with Amy?"

"Dr. Bell, you've been so kind to her—to both of us. I almost hate to ask, but I'd like to take her home."

Bell's elusive eyes snapped toward hers. "That is impossible."

Maria closed her eyes and prayed silently. "Please, Dr. Bell. Amy misses her home. And her friends need to know she is safe."

Bell thought for a moment. "Mrs. Horine, until now we have, to be quite honest, kept certain truths from you. Yes, I can see by your face that you know that. But can you imagine why we have been less than forward?"

Maria shook her dark head. She'd had little sleep, and her mind had grown numb. Bell seemed to be going somewhere with this, but Maria failed to see where. All she wanted was freedom for her and for her child.

"I thought not," Bell continued. "Amy is very special. Did you know that? She has a unique and honored place in the very essence of history. Has Amy asked to leave?"

In fact, Amy didn't want to leave. Bell must have known that. Maria had assumed her desire as a mother would be enough. "She isn't herself," she answered bravely.

"No, she is more than she ever was," he replied, his eyes glittering in the artificial light. "My dear, Maria. May I call you Maria?"

She nodded. "Yes. That is all right." Where was this going?

"Maria, your child, Amy, will change the world if she remains with us. You are welcome to remain here with her, and we encourage that. But if she leaves, her life will mean nothing. Nothing. Am I clear?"

Maria shuddered. She knew what he meant. Even in her brain-weary state, she knew. Both she and Amy were prisoners here. And Bell had no intention of telling the authorities that he had them.

"Excellent! I can see you finally understand our relationship. Well, that's all for now. You may return to your room, if you like. I understand there is an interesting play being put on in the theater. Perhaps you would enjoy passing the time there."

He rose, and Maria knew the meeting had ended.

"Miss Prynne," he called, and the dutiful assistant hobbled into the room as if by magic. "Ah, Miss Prynne, would you please escort Mrs. Horine to her room? She's chosen to remain here with us."

"Jean Davis?" asked Thundercloud, motioning for Joshua and Katherine to sit. "Yeah, sure I know her. Friend of Cissy's. She sometimes came here with Cissy. She even helped me out a few times with some research. What about her?"

Katy took a deep breath. If someone had asked her a week ago if she'd be in a run-down house asking help from a crabby old Indian with no legs, she'd have said he'd been reading too many novels. Yet, here she was, and she knew only John Thundercloud held the answers she needed.

"She's supposed to have left town," she replied. "Mr. Thundercloud, Jean told me on Tuesday that she would come over that evening with Cissy's urn. That's a pretty important errand, yet she didn't show up and she didn't call. Now, her store assistant tells me she's left town for Atlanta."

Thundercloud sucked up a bit of oxygen, breathing hard. Josh got up to help, but the old Indian waved him back. "I'm OK. Lungs gave out 'cause of asbestos back in the military. Secret work. One day you'll read my notebooks, and you'll become a smart cookie. Jean didn't show? That is odd. She doesn't like to travel. I remember that, because I once asked her to drive to Indianapolis for me to get a book from this fellow I know. But she doesn't like to travel far from town because she gets heart palpitations, and she's afraid to be away from her doctor."

Katherine clenched her fists. She had known it. Somehow she'd known it was all a lie!

Thundercloud gazed at his guests, his old eyes growing soft and warm. "Kids, you're only just now beginning to understand things. Katy, honey, you're seeing things, and it scares you. But you have to trust in the Lord. Listen to me."

She sat still, her face as white as death.

"Listen up now!" he said again, slapping his hand on the table. "This is about truth and lies. You have to discern the spirits—tell the truth from the lies! Now, buck up! Katherine Celeste Adamson, you can do this. Joshua is here to help, and I'll do what I can for now. Joshua, your path will become more clear as time passes. But, trust me, you're both in this up to your necks."

Joshua started to answer, but again Thundercloud stopped him. "Look, kid. Asking me to explain what I mean now won't solve your problem. You wouldn't believe me if I laid it all out on a platter. Look at your girlfriend there. She thought I was a grade-A kook with a bullet, but where did she come today? Here. Yeah, just like I said she would. But that's only a beginning. You go to Eden Bible in the morning, Missy. Yeah, Josh, I know you go. But you both go. And when it's all over tomorrow—when the impossible happens—you come back. Then our work will begin."

John Thundercloud opened a Clark Bar and began to write again. "Go away now. I have work to do."

Joshua looked to Katherine, but she simply rose to go. "You heard him, Joshua. He has work to do. And we need to find Cissy's diary."

"Now you're talkin', kid. Say hi to Jones for me. Now get out."

Rising to leave, Katy turned suddenly and rushed to the old Indian. "Thanks," she said, kissing him on his nearly hairless head. The Indian didn't even look up but kept on writing.

"Come on, Katy," said Joshua, opening the door. Katherine followed, looking one last time at the ancient man with no legs, scribbling in a notebook as if the entire world depended on it.

Once they had gone, Thundercloud glanced up, his old eyes brimming with tears. "You're welcome," he whispered, choking with emotion. "God be with you both."

Then picking up the pencil again, he returned to the half-written page, the heavy tears nearly blinding him and staining the page with the old man's pain.

CHAPTER Thirty-eight

SUNDAY MORNING

Eden Bible Church services began on Sunday mornings at nine o'clock with Sunday school, followed by praise and worship at ten-thirty. The small clapboard building had been erected in 1827 by a small group of settlers led by a Baptist minister from Virginia named Ethan Bailey. Since that first day, very little had changed inside the building, with two exceptions: The original hand-pumped organ had been replaced in 1946 by an electric one, and the bell that had been donated by Harlan Earlman in 1829 had cracked and been replaced by a newer one.

The original bell had been rung continuously for nearly twenty-four hours during Morgan's Raid in July of 1863, leading to a four-inch crack. Retired in 1869, the Earlman bell, as it had come to be known, now graced the cramped fellowship hall in a custom-designed glass case. The new bell sang out each Sunday morning at eight-forty-five and ten-fifteen, beckoning all of Eden to come and worship the Lord.

Katy had nearly overslept that Sunday morning, long and angry dreams of David and demons having haunted her night.

Joshua had picked her up at ten, so they had actually arrived a few minutes early.

Coming into the humble sanctuary, Katherine was struck by how sparse the interior was. Thirty solid oak pews, each with the capacity to hold ten adults, dominated the interior, standing fifteen to a side. At the end of the long room, a shallow stage had been constructed of native oak. Three wide steps led up to this platform, on which stood a simple wooden pulpit. The white walls were bare, except for a large copy of the famous painting of Christ by Warner Sallman, flanked by two handmade wooden racks that displayed the hymns for the morning and offering amounts from the previous week.

"This place is anything but pretentious," she whispered to Joshua as they found an open seat in the third pew on the right. "Talk about your bare-bones décor."

Josh tapped her hand lightly. "Now, now. Be nice. The people here put their money into missions rather than into fancy trappings. Believe me, you'll like the heart of this church."

The echoes of the morning worship bell had long ago died out, and Katherine noticed a small woman of advanced years, wearing a flowered shirtwaist dress and a blue straw hat, crossing the front toward a small electric organ.

"Is she strong enough to play, do you think?" Katy asked, only half teasing.

"That's Mavis Amburgey, one of your aunt's distant cousins. She's played the organ here for nearly forty years."

Katy rolled her eyes. "I can believe that. Now, who is that?" she asked, indicating a tall man with a cane who had just taken up residence in the front pew.

Leaning in to whisper, Josh replied, "Edgar Andrews. He's been blind since Normandy. His platoon was among the first to land at Omaha Beach. He took shrapnel in the face. There's a story waiting to be told!"

Katherine's face grew more serious. "I'll bet there are a lot of stories here this morning."

Several minutes passed, while Mrs. Amburgey played through several hymns. Just before ten-thirty, a man of medium height, wearing a dark blue suit and a hearing aid, stepped up to the podium.

"Good morning, worshipers! Welcome to Eden Bible Church! We're glad to see several new faces with us this morning. If you're happy to be in the house of the Lord, please stand, and greet your neighbor!"

Katherine stood along with Joshua, surprised to find the Markhams had just sat in the pew behind them.

"Good morning, neighbor!" Helen gushed, giving Katherine a hug. Katy accepted the embrace as best she could. She'd never felt comfortable with such displays, but she knew Helen meant it sincerely. "Isn't this a lovely day?"

Bill shook Josh's hand in a manly fashion, while several others around them walked over and welcomed Katy.

"Hey, Kate!" came a familiar baritone from Katy's right. She turned to see Gerry Anderson, his wide girth clothed in a dark gray suit and yellow shirt and tie. "This here's my better half, Kate. My wife, Doris."

Doris Anderson could have been a fashion model once, save for her diminutive stature. Although she must have been fifty or more, her face had few lines and her large blue eyes reminded Kate of Grace Kelly. In fact, she looked a great deal like the film star. "It's a pleasure," the small woman said with genuine affection. "Gerry's talked about you a lot this week. We were just saying how we'd like to have you over for dinner. Will you be staying for a while? In Eden, I mean?"

Katy nodded and started to reply, but the man with the hearing aid had taken to the podium again, and Mrs. Amburgey's organ strains had grown louder.

"There now!" the man began again. "Let's all worship the Lord by turning to hymn number one-eighty-eight, 'Amazing Grace'!"

And so the morning went, several more hymns were sung: "Rock of Ages," "Poor Wayfaring Stranger" (a special request from the pastor), and "Fairest Lord Jesus." After the announcements and the offering, Yvonne Wilson, Deputy Wilson's oldest daughter, sang a solo called "The King Is Coming." As she sang the final high note, the congregation broke into applause, and a few "Amens!" erupted from some of the older gentlemen. Edgar Andrews amened with the best of them, adding a few poundings of his cane for good measure.

As the girl left the podium, Enoch Jones rose to replace her there. Katherine smiled as the graceful, tall man took to the platform, Bible in one hand and a bundle of notes in the other.

"Good morning, my dear, dear friends," he began. "This is the day that the Lord hath made. And we shall rejoice and be glad in it!"

Andrews pounded his cane once and gave out a sharp "Amen!" to which Jones nodded a thank-you.

"Before I begin this morning's message, I'd like to make a short announcement. Please remember that several of our young people will be graduating today from Eden High, including Miss Wilson. Thank you, Yvonne. That song was lovely, and, as always, your voice reached to the highest heaven!"

Yvonne giggled softly, doing her best to maintain composure. Graduation for her meant going directly to Bloomington to work for the summer while she began taking private lessons from Antonio Vargas at the School of Music. Vargas had retired from his position with the Chicago Lyric, and the school had snapped him up immediately. Wilson's acceptance to the prestigious music school could mean a career in opera, and she couldn't wait to get started.

Jones continued. "We're delighted to have here this morning Miss Katherine Adamson, the niece of our dear, departed sister, Celeste Adamson. Welcome, Miss Adamson. I'm sure everyone here misses your dear aunt just as much as you. Please remember, too, the families of Forest Erickson, Donny Alcorn, and Jared Buchanan. We must keep them in our prayers. And for Amy Horine, we must not cease seeking God's intervention in bringing her home safely.

"Please turn in your Bibles to the book of Revelation, chapter three, beginning in verse seven. This morning, I want to tell you the story of two groups of people. One group serves the Lord and does their best to love Him while the other group has no love for the Lord but only mediocre self-appreciation and prideful works. But first, let's seek God's guidance so we may hear what the Spirit has to say to the churches. Father in heaven, we look to You as the Author of all that is good, seeking to know You better. We pray You'll open our minds and our hearts to the truth that is in Your Word. And if anyone here this morning does not yet know You as King and Savior, we pray, dear Lord, that You will open up that spirit to hear and obey. In Jesus' precious name, in His strong name, we pray. Amen and amen.

"Philadelphia and Laodicea. These were two literal churches that existed during the time of John, the beloved disciple of Jesus. One church, Philadelphia, or the city of brotherly love, received great praise from Christ in His letter, written down for us here by John. But the other church,

Laodicea, which means 'people's rights,' loved only themselves! Let's look at the Scripture to see what this means for us today."

And so it went. Jones spoke of the two churches, and Katherine became more and more uneasy. Something in her heart began to churn, indicting her for her own self-absorbed nature. Having come to Christ at a young age, she'd thought that was enough. She had a ticket to heaven, so not to worry! For now, she could live as she pleased, and nobody would be the wiser.

She'd been wrong. As she listened, she realized that her attitude was more like that of Laodicea than Philadelphia. She'd been so very blind! She squeezed Joshua's hand as great tears began to slide down her hot cheeks. How could she have been so centered on her own problems when loving others is so much more important?

Somewhere in the background, she heard the organ start up again, and she felt Joshua's gentle touch on her face, wiping the tears. "Katy, honey," he whispered.

She looked up, Jones had finished the sermon and was now speaking of coming to Jesus for forgiveness.

"Are you struggling with guilt? Are you blind like the Laodiceans? Is your treasure here on earth or in heaven? Are your works for yourself or for God? You can know the truth, friend. You can know you have eternal life! Jesus Christ died for you, beloved! All you have to do to receive it is to accept it! This gift is free! Just come to the cross, beloved. Come!"

Suddenly, Katherine was on her feet, moving toward the tall, welcoming figure of Enoch Jones, but her eyes were on the portrait that hung behind the pulpit. *Jesus*, she thought, weeping openly. *Jesus, I come!*

Jones took her hand. She felt Joshua behind her, his strong arms around her, and all three knelt at the altar.

"Katherine, do you know that your sins have been washed away?" he asked plainly as the organ continued to play.

"Yes," she whispered.

"Do you want to rededicate your life? Is that it?"

She began to weep into her hands, great heaving sobs of torment and grief. "Yes!" she cried out. "Yes! If God will let me."

Jones took her hands and began to pray, while Joshua closed his eyes and touched her back comfortingly. As Jones prayed, Katherine began to feel the weight of years of self-direction and fear leave her. She felt lighter, and for the first time since she'd first come to Christ, she felt clean.

Jones rose, and Joshua lifted Katherine to her feet. Jones smiled at her and then spoke to the standing congregation. "Many of you may already know Katherine Adamson, a dear hometown girl who has made it big in the world of books. But Katherine has realized that fame and fortune are temporal, that only those things done for Jesus Christ will last through-out eternity. And so, she has come this morning, rededicating her life to the Lord. Please welcome Katherine before you leave this morning. Let her know you will be praying for her as she stands up for Jesus in a world filled with Laodiceans. Show her the Philadelphian love that you have always shown to each other and to me. And, remember, the high school graduation ceremony is at one o'clock this afternoon! God bless you all!"

CHAPTER Thirty-nine

The Eden Bible morning worship had certainly been a time of change. Katherine began her life anew, and the good people of Eden Bible joyously welcomed her into their fold. After nearly half an hour of hugs, best wishes, warm handshakes, and loving words from many honest hearts, Joshua had taken Katherine to a short lunch at Grandy's Oven on Olive, where fried chicken and roast beef awaited along with apple pie and peach cobbler.

And the day had more surprises in store.

As they enjoyed their dinners, Joshua leaned toward Katy and kissed her suddenly.

"I just want you to know how proud I was of you today. God brought you back here for a reason, Katy Celeste. I know you're not here just for me, but I love you. I always have."

Katherine smiled, barely able to keep her joy inside, and whispered back, "I love you, too." She knew now that God loved her and that all the pain of the past was truly past and forgiven.

Joshua squeezed her hand tightly. "I know it's sudden. But we were meant to be together. I don't see why we should wait any longer. Marry me, Katy."

Katherine took a deep breath, looked at their entwined fingers and then into his face, her own shining like the sun. "I will."

The two lovers would have lingered over the cobbler had it not been closing in on one o'clock. Hastily paying the check and heading across town in Josh's Chevette, the pair arrived at the high school nearly twenty minutes past one.

"We're late," Katy said as they found their way to the gymnasium. "Let's hope this time there are no demons, right?"

Josh, who didn't laugh, scoured the sea of folding chairs for two open seats. "There!" he said at last, pointing to a row near the back. "Better than nothing."

Katy followed his lead and soon settled into the coolness of a beige metal chair stenciled EHS. The gymnasium, rather large by many high school standards, held five thousand when full, and gleamed from a fresh coat of wax. The center of the floor had been covered with several gray tarps to keep it from being damaged by the chairs, and the basketball hoops had been temporarily lifted into vertical storage.

"Remember when you played center here, way back in the Stone Age?" she whispered to Josh, nudging him playfully. "You looked pretty cool in those trunks, Carpenter!"

Josh laughed uneasily. Something had begun to nag at him ever since their arrival. He couldn't put his finger on it, but something felt wrong.

"What's up?" she asked at last, needing to make conversation. Katy, too, felt ill at ease in the confines of the school. Memories of demonic visits and of the many people still in the hospital, some who had even been transferred to the state mental hospital in Madison, pressed into Katy's brain, and she wondered what might happen today.

Josh started to answer, but the crisp echoes of sudden applause stopped him. On the makeshift stage ahead of them, Principal Daniel Cheatham had taken to the podium and was clearing his throat.

"Welcome to the 144th graduation ceremony here at Eden High School. It's been my pleasure to work with the young people whom we honor today for these past four years, and it's both joyful and sad to bid them farewell. I'm sure many of you parents feel the same way. Now that your student is off to college, you're delighted to see him grow up, but the cost of college is, well, saddening to say the least."

Light snickers sounded, and one father cried out, "You know it!" causing everyone else to laugh heartily.

"The class members who are seated before me, all three hundred and nine, have weathered many storms since they first walked these halls. Some will take with them memories of academic success, some athletic achievement, some musical and artistic creation, but all leave here changed."

Typical graduation stuff, Katy thought as Joshua took her hand. She was beginning to like his attention to detail, his gentlemanly ways. David's phone call, which had so devastated her the night before, now seemed like only a mild annoyance. She was finally over him. She felt strong now, and she loved having Joshua near. This one would be forever.

"...like to introduce this afternoon's keynote speaker, someone whom many of you will know from a class he taught here at the high school last semester on Eastern philosophy, the head of the Mt. Hermon Institute, Dr. Apollo Bell!"

There was light applause as Bell rose. Katherine shuddered slightly. Something about Bell didn't sit well with her. Looking up toward the right of the podium, she saw cameras rolling. WNN was here along with all the regional stations. Sheila Van Williams lurked near the WNN cameraman, dressed in a shimmering satin pantsuit, and she waved to Bell as he began to speak.

"This is an auspicious day," the Syrian began in clipped English, "and an equally sad one. When Principal Cheatham called and asked me if I would speak today, I nearly declined. My ties to these fine young people are slender at best, yet my fondness for each one overcame my natural reticence. And so, here I am."

Katherine began to wish she'd brought her camera. The gym, filled to capacity on the floor and crammed nearly to the rafters in the bleachers, seemed to have become a smaller version of Eden itself. Nearly everyone was here. Mayor Ned Sturgill and his wife, Tricia, who had been conspicuously absent on an unannounced trip to Mexico during the past few weeks, sat just behind the speaker's podium. Nancy Cheatham was there of course, sitting next to her father and mother. The Markhams had decided to come for a short while, although they had mentioned a need to get home early to check out their weekend guests. The Alcorns, including a very pale Grace, were seated in a place of honor near the front, along with the Buchanans and even Stan Horine and his wife, who'd come down from Indianapolis to work the press. Katherine also noticed the Andersons, Linda Kemp, and the Ramirez family, whose son Anthony was graduating today. Ben Miller with his wife and daughters filled out five chairs near the back on the other side, and Joshua's cousins had shown up to cover the event for the paper and hobnob with their readers. Standing off to one side, she noticed Enoch Jones, smiling as he caught her eye. Nearly everyone Katy had met or seen had come here today to pay homage to the hometown grads.

"There's that woman with the realty company," she whispered to Joshua and pointed to a tall blonde a few feet from Jones. "Rhonda Coleman."

Josh glanced Coleman's way. "Oh, yeah. I know her. She came by the paper a couple of times asking about you."

Katy started to reply, but Bell's speech caught her ear.

"...Amy Horine, who should be making this speech. Amy was one of the students in my Eastern philosophy class last year, and she made a great impression on me at the time. Seldom does a student come along who so embodies the soul of learning. I would like to honor her this morning, even as we all hope that she will still be found. Unfortunately, I understand her dear mother could not be here this morning because of illness. For those who may not know it, Mrs. Horine was airlifted to a hospital in Indianapolis. The strain of the press was too much, and she is staying under a pseudonym to avoid attracting attention. She couldn't be here with us today, but I hope that she is encouraged by the town's strength as we hold graduation today, even under such tragic circumstances."

"I'll bet Van Williams hates not being able to get her on TV," Josh said as he squeezed Katherine's hand.

"Shh!" she answered back, suddenly feeling happier than she had for years.

Bell continued. "Amy's absence is felt keenly by us all, and it is my hope that her memory will never die. I know many of you have shed tears for Donny Alcorn and Jared Buchanan, and for Amy. The three empty chairs in the front row only make it more difficult. But Amy and her fallen companions must never be forgotten. And so, it is my delight to announce the Amy Horine scholarship, which will be awarded each year to any student, male or female, who plans to study veterinary science in college. This award will be in the amount of fifty thousand dollars, and will, I hope, help the deserving student to pay for the high cost of veterinary school."

There was tremendous applause, and several students rose in honor of their fallen classmates. Soon, the entire gymnasium had risen to their feet, and the rafters rung with shouts of praise for Bell.

Suddenly, from the back of the gymnasium, shouts of amazement surged through the room like a wave. Bell, still in the middle of his speech, appeared nonplussed. WNN's cameraman, taking note of the commotion, turned his camera in hopes of catching something that would put them in the lead for the night's ratings.

He wasn't disappointed.

As Joshua and Katherine turned to the noise, the crowd parted like the Red Sea, and a figure emerged, battered, clothes torn, and face bloody.

"What is it?" she asked, not able to see past a tall man. "Joshua, can you see what it is?"

Carpenter's voice sounded hollow. "It's...dear Lord! It can't be," he muttered, amazed by what he'd seen.

Katherine had to see for herself. Standing up on her chair, she peered over the tall man in front of her, who had begun to murmur something about a miracle. The reaction of the crowd had changed from loud whispers of confusion to an awed hush, and she could finally see what had made everyone mute.

In the middle of the gymnasium, bruised and barely able to put one foot in front of another, walked Jared Buchanan.

Alive.

"Hallelujah!" cried out several in the crowd.

"It's a miracle!" cried others as all three cameras now pointed toward the prodigal son, returned from the very jaws of death. Rose and Eli Buchanan rushed toward their son as did Sheriff Branham and Dr. Prosser.

Jared stared at them all, pale as death. "Come forth," he whispered, then fell to the floor unconscious.

CHAPTER Forty

SUNDAY EVENING

The town of Eden would never be the same. That night, many of the town's residents fell into an uneasy sleep. Maria Horine prayed that someone might find her and Amy and help them to escape. The Buchanan family huddled around the hospital bedside of a son they had thought dead. Grace Alcorn wrote in her diary about the miracle she'd seen at the high school and of demons with whips. Grace's parents turned away from each other in cold silence. An old man with no legs wrote small scribbles in a green notebook. A neighbor knocked on Jean Davis's door to see why she'd not picked up her mail or collected her newspapers. Ben Miller made arrangements for his wife and daughters to visit family. Digger Martin sat by himself in a hangar drinking Cokes and looking at his children's photos with weeping eyes. Enoch Jones fell to his knees. As all this happened, in the north garden of the nicest house in Eden, a dog pawed furiously at the base of a singular, yellow rose bush.

Katherine, the dog's new human, had warned her off the digging several times that evening, but Heidi knew she had to dig. She could see the shadows that walked the perimeter of the white wooden fence that surrounded the yard of her new home. She'd been watching these shadows for days now.

She wouldn't howl tonight, she decided. The shadows appeared blocked by some unseen barrier. Heidi knew they couldn't invade the yard.

She dug further, her feet beginning to bleed. She was almost there.

Gradually, her keen nose and sharp vision told her she had found it. A dark, metallic box lay in the hole beneath the rose's base. She struggled with how to retrieve it, finally managing to grasp the thin handle with her sharp teeth.

Had Heidi been able to read, she would have known the box said Personal Papers of Celeste Adamson. She did know the box smelled like the house, human and loving. That's why she'd wanted to find the box—she knew Katherine would be pleased.

The shadows advanced closer to the fence, and Heidi raised her tail, and her hackles rose high, making her appear larger and sending the message that she would defend her humans to the death. The shadows retreated, moaning in an unearthly voice that only Heidi could hear.

Turning, the dog headed back toward the house, her tail wagging proudly. Her humans, Katherine and now Joshua, would be so pleased to know she'd found the box.

A box that held the secrets of Eden.

To be continued in *Signs and Wonders: Book Two of the Laodicea Chronicles*

MythArc
"THE GREAT MYTHARC OF MANKIND"

Warning: Once you've connected the dots, your concept of our world will change forever. Are you sure you want to continue? Or would you rather remain asleep?

The real war began long ago—long before mankind began to fashion killing machines, long before human generals plotted campaigns over the bodies of bloodied men, long before the lust for power became the greatest of all human sins. Before the births of Socrates, Solomon, or Shakespeare, Evil struck the first blow in the war for control of men's souls.

Throughout the millennia since, the Shadow has altered his form again and again to fool mankind into trusting his insidious lies. A snake, a dragon, a mythological god, a politician, a bashful poet. Or more cunningly, he infiltrates God's camp in the guise of a priest or preacher, spewing forth doctrinal lies. This consummate conniver has but one plan: to defeat God at every turn. But God strikes back, sometimes with His eternal hand, sometimes through His mighty angels, and sometimes through the creation made slightly lesser than the angels, Man himself.

291

SHARON K. Gilbert

It is these lost tales of God's human warriors that we hope to present. Tales such as that of a beggar named Simeon, befriended by an antediluvian preacher named Enoch who walked with God and was no more. Or that of Denko, a sixth century shipwrecked sailor who stumbled across a tribe of giants in the days just before a megalithic asteroid crashed into Earth and plunged mankind into an age of darkness. Then there's the story of Elizabeth Branham, a wealthy English heiress who uncovered a nineteenth century plot to unseat God and crown Satan as Prince of the World. And the battle fought by a gentle doctor who strove to convince a small Kentucky town that the 1918 flu epidemic killing their loved ones is not the secret rapture, even though a man who claims to be a preacher twists God's own word and proclaims it to be the season of sheep and goats.

Follow the path forged by John Thundercloud, a Winnebago Indian in the 1950s, who can see into the realm of the Shadow. He must prevent the Enemy's followers from opening the Seven Gates of Hell that will unleash those kept in chains, even if it means the loss of his own life. Experience the battle through the lives of Light Warriors, Katherine Adamson, Joe Unes, Matt McGlone, Maggie Taylor, and Daniel Tohe, who know all too well of the terrifyingly thin line that separates night from day, slavery from freedom, and Shadow from Light.

Husband and wife authors, Sharon K. Gilbert and Derek P. Gilbert weave a complex pattern of literary threads that rip through that thin line to reveal the spiritual warfare that surrounds us. Sharing characters, timelines, and events, the Gilberts will take you on a thrill ride unlike any you've ever experienced – because what you read is real. The battle is real. The Enemy is real.

And he has set his sights on you.

Are you ready for the Truth? Do you have the courage to read these tales—tales that will shake you from your happy slumber? Are you ready to become a Light Warrior?

Then prepare your heart and your soul and join us. Welcome to the battlefield, dear reader. You are about to become a part of the great MythArc of Mankind.

Current Mytharc Titles include:
The Armageddon Strain:
Book One of The Countdown

Winds of Evil:
Book One of the Laodicea Chronicles

Visit www.mytharc.com for more information! Join the MythArc forum to discuss the books and keep up with the ongoing battle!

ABOUT THE AUTHOR
Sharon K. Gilbert

Born in the rolling hills of southern Indiana to Appalachian parents, Sharon brings a rich heritage to her writing. A childhood spent meandering crooked streams and dancing meadows coupled with a degree in molecular biology and a short career in opera have created a patchwork personality that feels at home with many genres.

Sharon has lived here, there, and everywhere, preferring her native Indiana to all other lands. While living in Indianapolis, Sharon, whose name was then Sharon Ferguson, sang jingles with the likes of Sandi Patty and Steve Green, through whom she met David Clydesdale, then of Singspiration Music. As a born-again Christian, Sharon happily said yes to a one-year commitment as a featured vocalist with Clydesdale's CCM group, Life Unlimited, touring the continental US, Canada, and the UK.

Later, as an older student at both the University of Nebraska and Indiana University, Sharon studied human genetics, music, literature, and history, giving her a well-rounded approach to learning and a full quiver for writing.

A lifelong interest in the supernatural and how it might be portrayed in fiction and on film has led Sharon to her current career as a writer of supernatural thrillers. Married to fellow writer Derek P. Gilbert, Sharon is stepmother to a precocious and very gifted teen named Nicole, in addition to acting as assistant keeper to the Gilbert Zoo (three rag-tag rescue dogs named Murphy, Belle, and Gretel). The Gilberts live in Manchester, Missouri.

Learn more about Sharon at her website www.sharonkgilbert.com, and keep track of her projects and releases at the deepercalling website www.deepercalling.com.

Discover more about the MythArc fiction series at the MythArc website: www.mytharc.com.

EXCERPTS FROM
Signs & Wonders
BOOK TWO OF THE
LAODICEA CHRONICLES

Beatrice Van Horn looked like she'd enjoyed the financial fruits of her formerly miserable life. Looking at her attire, Jamie recognized prominent labels from her own shopping trips. Bea looked quite at home in a delicate, beaded necklace and tan day dress. Her long, slender, tan feet were expensively shod in supple, brown sandals that allowed the plum polish on her manicured toes to glimmer now and then. Her chin-length, Christophe cut made her silver hair shine in the lights of the chandeliers, and her richly tanned skin appeared remarkably smooth for her age, which Jamie guessed to be around sixty.

"When will you be leaving the Institute?" Jamie asked as the lights went down.

"Leave? Good heavens, child! No one leaves! What a silly thing to say!"

No one leaves?

"Surely, you've seen someone go home, be released?" she persisted.

Bea put a perfectly manicured finger to her lips. "Shh. Miss Stratos is about to sing."

No one goes home? Jamie thought with rising panic. "Surely people are released, Bea! Dr. Bell cures them, then they go home, right?"

Bea gave no reply, for she was lost now in the music. The soprano Stratos had begun to sing a beautiful aria from Gounod's *Faust* called *Il était un roi de Thulé*, where Marguerite sits by her spinning wheel and sings of the King of Thule, as yet unaware that she is about to be drawn into a fierce battle between Good and Evil.

"Stratos can melt your heart," Bea said as the aria ended with polite applause from the audience of twenty or so guests. She waved to a handsome man who sat third seat in on the next aisle to their right. "That's Harvey Angstrom. He's from Sweden, I think. Or maybe his parents came from there. Anyway, he's the president of...oh, I can't think of the name. It's a company out west that makes jets for the government."

Jamie looked at the man. He seemed nice enough, fair-haired, muscular, and tan like so many of the Hollywood producers she'd met and learned to hate. He looked as though he'd be on a first-name basis with most of the country club caddies across the country. She waved halfheartedly, hoping the man wouldn't recognize her, for her mind was still on Bea's earlier comment. "Bea, how long has Mr. Angstrom been here?"

Bea thought for a moment, adjusted her necklace, then coughed lightly. "I think he told me two years. Or is it three?"

"Three years!" she exclaimed, sitting forward. Several opera lovers shushed her, and Jamie shut her eyes tightly, trying to think. "Bea," she whispered at last, "you didn't mean years, did you?"

Bea smiled, her plum nails clacking against the necklace. "Oh yes. Now relax and listen to Stratos. You'll get used to it here, and you'll forget all about the outside world."

———

Grace Alcorn stared at the board on her lap, fighting a strong urge to run.

"Go on," her friend Marcie Cox said, tapping a pink gel pen against her green and white braces. "It's not going to bite you! Geez!"

Grace bit her lower lip and heaved a big sigh. "Marcie, I'm not sure this is right."

Marcie rolled her eyes and flopped onto her twin bed, kicking her feet into the air toward the ceiling. "Gracie, you're a scared little kid. I invite you over here, get you out of that mausoleum you call a home, and give you a chance to expand your mind, and what do you do? You sit there like a fried lump, too afraid of your own shadow to find out what's really out there! You know, like who we are!"

"I'm just not sure if using a Ouija board is a good idea, Marcie. Does your mom know you have it?"

"She bought it for me, silly. Last Christmas. It's just a game, Grace. All you have to do is put your hand on that triangle thing, close your eyes, and ask it a question."

Grace pushed the board away, and jumped off the bed. "I should go home. Mom's probably back from Columbus by now, so I should see if she needs help putting up the new drapes."

"Chicken!"

"I'm not a chicken, Marcie. I...I just don't think this is a good idea. I'll see you tomorrow, OK?" She opened the door that led into the upstairs hallway.

Marcie kicked off her yellow Chuck Taylors and waved without turning to see her guest. "Sure. Whatever."

Grace closed the door behind her and left. She was growing used to being alone.

———

Dr. Robert Prosser, who'd been on duty as part of a new rotation, now sat with Kate and Josh as he explained George McMahon's coma. "It's not uncommon with diabetics. Your friend must have overdosed his insulin. I'm guessing he's newly diagnosed, since there's no evidence of repeated injections. We're sending for his medical records, so we should have a better picture in a few hours. For now, we'll keep him on a glucose drip for a while. I expect he'll be fine in the morning."

"Diabetic?" Katy repeated. "I don't think so. George would have told me."

Prosser tapped McMahon's chart. "All our tests show a severe insulin reaction. Why would a man inject himself with insulin unless he's a diabetic? There's a clear injection mark on his right thigh. He's still learning how to use the syringe, is my guess. The site's bruising already."

Katy leaned into Josh's strong arms. "All right. May we stay? I don't want him to wake up all alone."

Prosser held her hand for a moment. "You're a good friend, Katherine. But Mr. McMahon will likely be out of it for a while. I'd drop by tomorrow morning after breakfast. We'll call you if there's any change, all right? Go on home now. You're a bit pale."

He left them alone, and Katy peered through the glass window into George's private room. A tall metal pole was his company now, with a sagging clear bag that fed his sleeping body, drop by drop. "Why didn't I see that he was sick, Josh?

Stupid me! I thought it was just nicotine cravings! Couldn't I tell?"

"No, you couldn't, and neither could I. God is caring for him now, honey. He'll be much better tomorrow. You need to stop blaming yourself and think about contacting his family so they can come out here. Is George married?"

Katherine shook her head. "Not married, no. I don't think he has any brothers or sisters either. His parents are both dead, I do know that. I remember, when his dad passed away a few years ago, that he said he was alone. Dr. Prosser said something about getting his medical records from Kansas. They should have next of kin listed somewhere in his file."

"You're right. Do you want to call anyone? Maybe we should call Pastor Jones."

She fell into his arms, small tears gathering at the corners of her eyes. "Yes, I think I'd like to talk with him. Oh, we missed church tonight."

"Maybe I should call Helen, too. I'll go do that, and I'll get us both some coffee."

Katy nodded, wiping the tears. "You go do all that. I'm gonna look in on him one more time before we go."

"Good idea." He kissed her forehead and headed toward the exit to find a phone.

Inside McMahon's room, a small heart monitor beeped steadily. The room smelled of disinfectant, and Katy noticed a small white bible on the nightstand.

Katy slumped into the plastic seat of a silver metal chair. She had to sit a moment to gather her thoughts. Maybe George had been on insulin. If so, he'd have to carry it with him. Seeing the agent's briefcase on the floor of the small closet, Katy decided it was a good time to go through it. Thank heaven, Josh had told her to grab it when the ambulance had arrived. He'd said even then that George might have meds in there that he'd need.

The bag was well-worn with a leather-covered handle at the top. Stamped on the front in gold were the initials GAM. George Alan MacMahon. Katy opened the case. She nearly cried when she saw the thick stack of white pages George had flown all the way to Indiana to give her. Pages filled with information from his secret government contact.

George could have died so easily. Katherine couldn't have taken another death—not this soon. So many had already died in Eden: Aunt Cissy, Donny Alcorn, Forest Erickson, and more than likely Amy Horine as well. Somewhere there must be a reason for all the death, something to elevate their sacrifice to a level Katherine could comprehend.

Cissy's diary.

Katherine thought about the mysterious metal box Heidi had recovered last month and of the small book with the floral cover they'd found inside. Cissy had been keeping careful notes about something, but all of her entries had been in some sort of code. Josh and Katy had spent weeks trying to decipher the writing, but so far they'd been unable to find the key. They'd considered talking with John Thundercloud about the code, but the enigmatic Winnebago Indian had apparently gone to Indianapolis to visit his son and grandchild. Bridgette Elson, Thundercloud's home nurse, had left Katy a letter, written in the old man's spidery scrawl. He'd be back in a few days, and she could talk to him then. For now, she'd have to rely on her own wits, and Joshua's support.

George's arrival had brought more papers to decipher. Lots of secret papers. And he lay in a coma.

Cissy wrote a diary about Eden. And she was dead.

Could the two be connected?

An icy chill swept through Katy's bones, and she snapped the bag shut. She'd seen no sign of medications there, and she had no desire to let anyone else see her with George's papers. She'd keep the case close to her. And tomorrow, she could begin investigating the truth behind George McMahon's sudden illness.

John Thundercloud wished he had legs so he could kick the so-called news people on that stupid Indianapolis station right square in their collective anchors. He'd been watching what passed for morning news, and some red-haired woman with silicone assets and lips puffy enough to hang your hat on had joined the la-dee-dah morning show. Where was the real news? The hard news?

Instead the trio went on and on about some hush-hush Hollywood wedding. It made you mad enough to spit. Was this what his son paid good money to a satellite company for?

Ever since Cissy Adamson's passing the month before, John had sensed a growing tension in his heart, a need to wrap things up. Something big was about to break back in Eden, and he knew his writings would be needed. That Cissy's niece, little Katherine, she had the stuff to stand up to the winds. But she needed ammunition.

John could give her that.

And he could give her the key she needed to unravel many mysteries if she'd only pay attention and listen.

Ears to hear, he thought to himself. She's got 'em, just doesn't know how to use 'em.

"Little John! Bring Grandpa the telephone!" he called into the cavernous house. His son, Barrett, was out as usual, meeting with a client or playing handball or something unnecessary to the world. Little John attended day care and studied violin

302

under the watchful eye of a housekeeper named Mrs. Hewitt. As an unexpected kindness, Barrett had given Hewitt the week off during his father's visit. Only a hired nurse interrupted his precious hours with Little John.

"Here you are, Mr. Thundercloud," the nurse called as she and the boy delivered a silver cordless phone. "I'll leave John here for a moment while I prepare your morning medications."

The old Indian smiled, a rare event for him these days. He'd smiled often when Elizabeth had been alive.

"Are you happy, Grandpa?" the boy asked, wiping pancake syrup from his small, cupid's mouth. "Your invisible legs hurt today?"

Thundercloud was about to answer, when something on the television screen jerked him to attention, and his old eyes narrowed into slits. "Quiet now, Little John," he said softly, taking the boy's hand. "Listen."

"...performing miracles all around the Chicago area," the redhead told the two Ken-doll males. "I didn't believe it until I saw it with my own eyes. Jared Buchanan is his name, and he claims he can even raise the dead."

Jared Buchanan?

Here it comes, Thundercloud thought, his hands shaking so fiercely he dropped the boy's small fingers. *Signs and wonders.* Somewhere this false prophet's followers were beginning to muster, and their numbers would grow, and their leader would lie.

And many would believe the lie.

And then the beginning of the end would come.

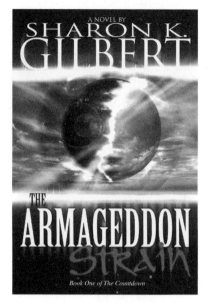

The Armageddon Strain
Sharon K. Gilbert

A plague has been unleashed that could lead to the end of the world. After her father's sudden death, Dr. Maggie Taylor begins a journey that will determine the fate of the world. As an avian flu epidemic grips the country, a mysterious package arrives in Taylor's office—a computer with an encoded message of doom.

Maggie is in the midst of a vast conspiracy—a key player in the fight against a demonic plot to bring on Armageddon. Who can she trust? Maggie must learn how her father's untimely death is linked to the deaths of nearly two dozen other scientists and the truth behind a doomsday weapon known only as the BioStrain chip.

Will she discover the truth in time?

ISBN: 0-88368-810-7 • Trade • 304 pages

www.whitakerhouse.com

www.deepercalling.com